THE NON-MAGICAL

DECLAN MOORE

WINTERTHORN
BOOK ONE

NATHAN TAYLOR

THE WINTERTHORN SAGA

THE NON-MAGICAL DECLAN MOORE

Copyright © 2023 by Nathan Taylor

ISBN (digital): 978-0-6457595-1-8

ISBN (paperback): 978-0-6457595-0-1

Cover designed by MiblArt

Edited by Falcon Faerie Fiction

Magpie Drive Press

 Formatted with Vellum

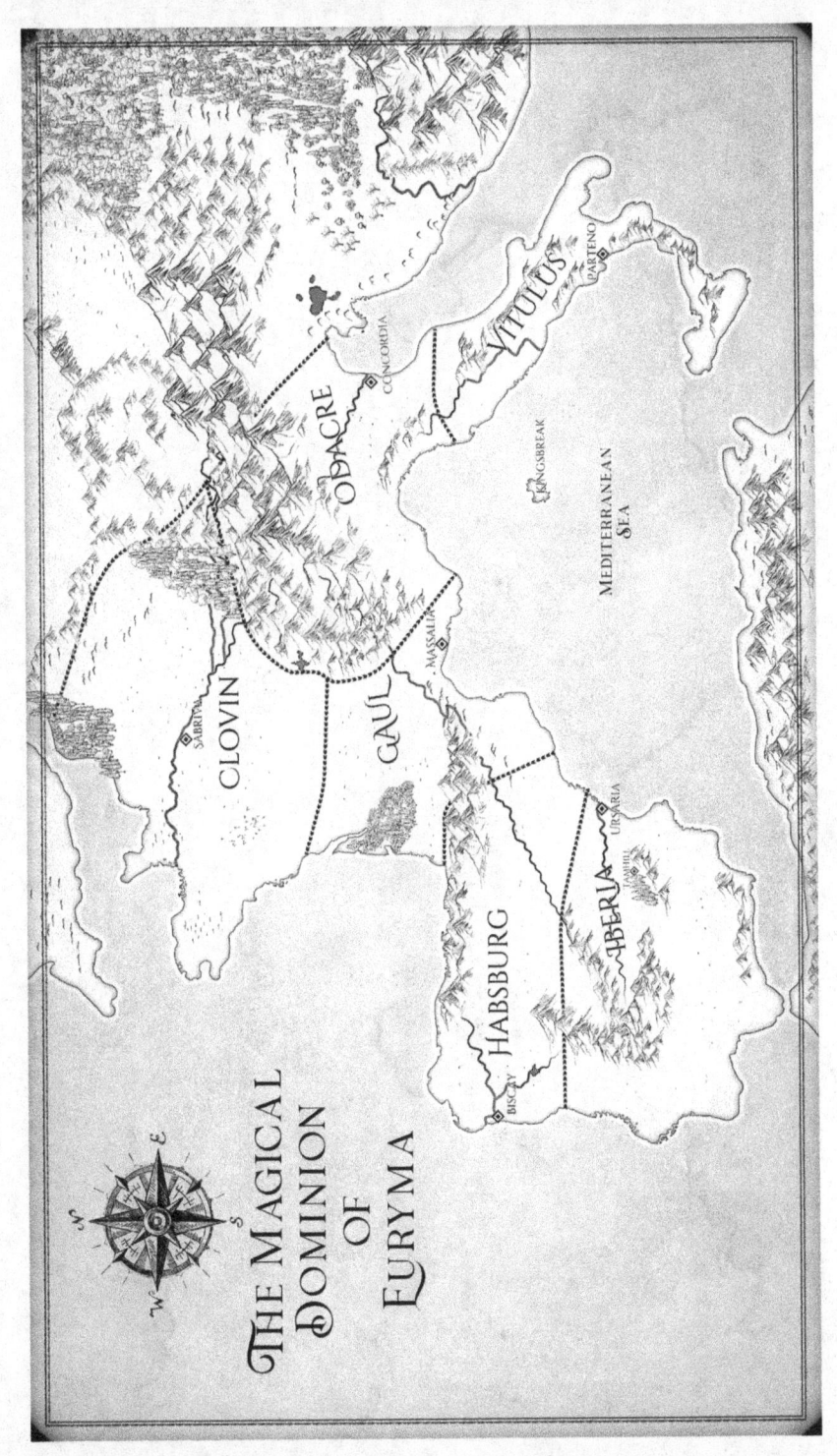

For Rebekah, Jensen, Naomi and Jacey-Mae

THE NON-MAGICAL

DECLAN MOORE

WINTERTHORN
BOOK ONE

NATHAN TAYLOR

CHAPTER 1
DECLAN

DECLAN NEVER EXPECTED that his headmaster would be the one to destroy him.

Yet here they were. The room sat in stunned silence. Seventeen-year-old brains struggled to interpret what they had just heard. Declan Moore, their celebrated classmate, the great-great-grandson of famed war hero Arman Moore, had exactly zero magical Potential.

Declan had spent his whole life spinning an elaborate web of lies to cover his shameful truth. And now Headmaster Leed had announced it to the entire senior cohort. Three rows back in the windowless homeroom, Declan sat frozen, mouth agape, while molten dread burned a hole inside him.

"Master Moore," Headmaster Leed repeated, shuffling through his clipboard, unaware of the utter ruin his words left in their wake. "Please join the other LAMP students in classroom eighty-eight."

Declan hated that acronym. LAMP. Lacking All Magical Potential. The headmaster's words were like a wasp sting

1

on his soul, and those words gave life to a chorus of whispers.

"Declan's a LAMP?"

"He can't do magic?"

"But, he's a Moore?"

"No way! A Moore with no Potential?"

Headmaster Leed looked up from his notes. "I'm afraid I've misplaced my list of delegates. Please remain seated while I organize a replacement." His stern gaze fell onto a raven-haired girl in the front row. "No nonsense while the room is unattended."

He left through a glass door at the front of the room. As soon as it closed, the raven-haired girl spoke. "I knew he was a fraud."

The words made Declan's spine go rigid. Spoken with such venom, they could only come from Lyle Arthur. Her soft voice filled the room like a noxious gas. "This explains everything." She turned to face him. "I wondered why you never came on college tours, or why you never mentioned your Potential. Everyone thought it was because you didn't want us to feel small compared to the *great Declan Moore*." She laughed; her petite features twisted in a cruel mask. "You've been leveraging your famous surname for popularity points this whole time, haven't you?"

Declan's face burned. He dropped his gaze to the floorboards, tears pressed against the backs of his eyes.

"Oh, and now he's blushing." Lyle's voice rose. "Sweet boy," she said, "you shouldn't be embarrassed. We need LAMPs to sweep our streets, fold our clothes, make our coffee."

Pockets of students chuckled at the remark, then cut short as the headmaster reappeared at the door. Declan clenched his fist. He wanted to throw something at her. He wanted to throw something at the headmaster. He wanted to —

Ace followed Headmaster Leed into the room. At that moment, Declan would have wagered his family name that every student had the same thought. *Does Ace know his best friend is a fraud?*

"Take a seat, Master Marley," Headmaster Leed said. Ace slipped into the chair beside Declan, but Declan didn't dare look at him. The headmaster tapped on a clipboard. "We were discussing today's change of schedule. Students with Potential will meet with college delegates in the main hall. All others will be supervised by..." he checked his notes. "Mr. Hern in classroom eighty-eight."

"That's you, Dex," Lyle said in a carrying whisper. Declan kept his eyes firmly on the floor.

Headmaster Leed ignored her, or perhaps didn't hear. He scanned the room and his expression transformed into one of stern authority. "You will have the morning to resolve any queries you have regarding Mag-Ed and the enrollment process. College applications are due tonight. It would be foolish to leave school today without a clear idea of which college you think best suits your Potential." His ancient eyebrows drew together. "This goes without saying, but I will say it. You are representing Arman Moore's Preparatory School. I expect you will represent it well. Dismissed."

The senior cohort stood up. Ace nudged Declan's elbow. "What's up?"

"Oh, don't talk to him," Lyle said. She'd appeared at Ace's side before Declan could open his mouth. "He's off to eighty-eight with the other LAMPs, aren't you?" She looked from Declan's hunched form to Ace's perplexed expression and cackled with glee. "Oh, you didn't know?" she grinned.

"Seems the famous Declan Moore has some explaining to do."

"Hey, Lyle," Ace said.

She raised an eyebrow.

"Go away." Ace's deadpan voice carried only the smallest hint of annoyance. It was enough. Everyone knew Ace's Potential. He was scores more powerful than Lyle, even without college instruction. She winked and joined the mass of students leaving the room.

Declan tried to control his breathing. The entire room rippled, folded, seemed to turn. He was going to be sick.

"They found out, did they?" Ace whispered.

Declan blinked, then swallowed. He waited until he was certain words, and not vomit, would leave his mouth. He looked up. "You knew?"

Ace nodded. "It wasn't hard to put it together."

"Why didn't you say something?"

"Master Moore," interrupted Headmaster Leed. "You are supposed to be in room eighty-eight. Master Marley, you should be in the main hall. Kindly save the gossip for the schoolyard and go to your appropriate destinations."

"Of course, sir." Ace rolled his eyes so that only Declan could see, then dropped his voice. "Survive the morning, Dex. I'll see you at lunch." He slung his bag over his shoulder and rushed out of the room, leaving Declan alone with the ancient headmaster.

"Is there a problem, Master Moore?"

Yes. And you bloody well caused it, Declan thought. "No, sir." He rose slowly on unsteady legs. "No problem at all."

"You're late, Moore."

The crease in Mr. Hern's forehead appeared deep enough to hide loose change. It seemed it did not impress him to be babysitting the handful of LAMP students whose non-magical parents could afford Arman Moore's Preparatory School.

"Sorry, sir," Declan said from the doorway. The students stared at him in blatant confusion.

"Well?" Mr. Hern said. "Are you waiting for a red carpet?"

Declan blinked. "I'm sorry?"

"Find a book." Mr. Hern gestured to the bookcase running alongside the room's windows. "Then find somewhere to read it." A hand went up to their left. Mr. Hern sighed. "What is it, Gibbons?"

"Giddons, sir," said the girl. Her lip quivered. "That's…. That's Declan Moore. He should be in the main—"

"He's right where he needs to be. No more questions needed." Mr. Hern raised an eyebrow at Declan. "Come on now. Just because your surname is on the gate doesn't mean you can ignore instructions. Get a book. Get a seat."

A tense silence filled room eighty-eight. Declan refused to look at anybody. He grabbed the first book he passed and collapsed into a chair at the back of the room. The other LAMPs stole glances at him, no doubt second guessing everything they knew about his famous lineage. He could imagine them rehearsing how they would tell their parents. By dinner time everybody in Tamhill would know the Moore family secret.

Mr. Hern cleared his throat. "Save the chit-chat, boys and girls, you should be reading." He leaned back in his seat as a slender, dark-haired woman appeared at the entrance. She knocked on the open door and Mr. Hern straightened at once. "Uh, hello, Mrs. Winter. To what do I owe the pleasure?"

Mrs. Winter smiled. "I've been sent to relieve you."

"Already?" Mr. Hern glanced at some papers on the desk. "The timetable says I'm here until—"

"Headmaster's request," Mrs. Winter said. Her gentle voice held little room for argument.

"Oh... Not to worry then." Mr. Hern seemed uncertain if this was a good or bad thing. "Uh, yes, very well. Thank you." He left the room awkwardly.

Mrs. Winter roamed the room. Declan liked her. She was an excellent teacher, stern but fair. He wondered if *she* knew his secret. A pang of embarrassment followed the thought and a fresh wave of heat prickled his neck. As Mrs. Winter grew closer, Declan opened his book, *An Encyclopedia of Euryma's History,* and pretended to read. She passed without a word. From the corner of his eye, Declan watched her circle to the front of the room and sit.

They read in silence. The morning's disaster played over and over in Declan's head. For thirty minutes he sat, book in hand, mind busy, simmering on one thing. Revenge.

Lyle Arthur. The bad blood between the Moores and Arthurs went back generations. Now she had everything she needed to destroy him. Declan flipped pages absently, ruminating on what he could do to pay her back. More than once, he thought Mrs. Winter was watching him. Yet every time he looked up, her attention was elsewhere.

You're being paranoid. Declan turned a page to a gruesome visage; soldiers repelled by enormous cauldrons of hot liquid. The artist had spared no details illustrating their injuries. The image sparked a dark idea. Senior students had free rein over the coffee cart in the dining hall. Declan considered the soldiers' disfigured faces. Lyle's voice echoed in his mind. *We need LAMPs to make our coffee.* A searing cup of coffee on Lyle's delicate face would serve her right. It wasn't revenge, but it was a start.

"Good morning, Declan." Declan nearly jumped out of his skin. Mrs. Winter stood at his side. He hadn't noticed her arrival.

"H-Hi Mrs. Winter," he stammered. "How, um, are you?"

"I am well," she said. "Thank you for asking." She glanced over his shoulder at the image on the page. "Ah, the first battle on the Sabrivan Plains. A pivotal moment in Euryma's history."

"Uh, yeah," Declan said. He hadn't read a single word all morning. "Very interesting."

"Indeed." Mrs. Winter's powder-blue eyes twinkled; she was not shy about her love of history. "Interesting that this happened before the Magical Awakening. None of those soldiers had an inkling of magical Potential when they agreed to defend their homes and families, yet they went to their deaths bravely. Marching with swords and spears against an army wielding power they could not comprehend," Mrs. Winter paused, gaze fixed on the open page. "It would seem that the quality of a person's character has nothing to do with his or her magical ability."

Declan didn't know what to say. He looked at the page and shrugged. "Seems more like stupidity than bravery."

Mrs. Winter laughed. "Some say courage and foolishness are two sides of the same coin. It's not until you've flipped it and the dust has settled that you see which was which." She nodded to the page. "These men sparked the flame that formed Euryma, so we call it bravery. Had they died in vain, we may have called them fools." Her lips twisted in a sour expression.

"You disagree?" Declan asked.

"I do," Mrs. Winter said. "I think it's simpler than that. Courage is acting foolishly to help others. Stupidity is acting foolishly to help yourself." Her eyes met Declan's and his heart skipped a beat. For a moment, he wondered if she could see inside his head. "I hope you're smart enough to understand the difference, Declan."

For the second time in as many minutes, he did not know how to respond. Mrs. Winter smiled sadly, then continued on without another glance. Declan thought on her words, shook his head, and returned to planning his revenge. When the bell rang for break, he put *An Encyclopedia of Euryma's History* back on the shelf. He could have sworn Mrs. Winter watched him from the desk, but when he turned to leave, she was deep in conversation with another student. Declan ignored them both as he headed to the dining hall for morning tea.

And coffee.

CHAPTER 2
DECLAN

THE COFFEE CART WAITED, unattended, in the corner of the dining hall. Muted sunlight streamed through the narrow windows along the ceiling's edge while a queue of students meandered around two long tables in the room's center. Declan filled a disposable cup from a black kettle, ignoring the whispers and glances from seated students on either side of the room. Heat radiated from the corrugated cardboard; it would burn his hand if he held it too long. Declan stared at the clear water. Three small bubbles formed at the cup's base. *You're being an idiot.*

He chewed his bottom lip for a long moment. Even the famous Moore name wouldn't save him if he deliberately threw hot water on a student's face in a room full of witnesses. *Don't make a bad day worse.* It sounded like something Ace would say. With a sigh, Declan put the cup down and turned to find himself face to face with Lyle Arthur. A small group of seniors stood a step behind her. Lyle's eyes darted from Declan to the abandoned cup. "Getting started on your LAMP duties so soon?"

"Drop it, Lyle," Declan muttered. He tried to push past her, but big Joel Mercado stepped up to block him.

"You're not done yet," Lyle said. The entire dining hall stopped to listen. "Where's my coffee, LAMP?"

Hands shaking, Declan turned back around. An irrational hatred bubbled inside him; it would be so easy to splash her with scalding water. He took a deep breath. Then another. When he was in control, he reached for the instant coffee.

"I haven't got all day," Lyle said. Her voice carried over the dining hall. The whole school watched in silence.

Declan ignored her. When the coffee was ready, he gestured to the cart. "There you go, Lyle," he said. "Now leave me be."

"Hand it to me." Satisfaction laced Lyle's melodic voice. "Hand me my coffee."

"No."

Joel Mercado cracked his ham-sized knuckles. "I won't ask again," Lyle said.

Declan didn't trust himself. He couldn't be certain, but the likelihood of him scarring her face, and his life, increased infinitely the moment he picked up that cup. He wanted to do it, to burn the smug smile off her fragile face.

"If only the Moore's of old could see you now. Cornered. Useless. Shaking like a little mouse." Lyle held his gaze. Her emerald eyes sparkled with delight. "Now hand me my coffee."

Mrs. Winter entered the hall. Beside her, Ace carried a stack of papers and a lopsided grin which faded as his gaze followed the shared attention of the dining hall. Ace started towards him, but Mrs. Winter barred his way with her arm. Her powder blue eyes met Declan's and her voice echoed in his head. *Stupidity is acting foolishly to help yourself. I hope you know the difference.*

Declan's chest swelled. He released a big breath and held the coffee to Lyle. "Here you are."

Lyle accepted it, then let the cup fall from her hands. Scalding liquid poured down Declan's arm, splashing the front of his pants. He leapt back in pain and knocked the kettle over. It splashed the backs of his legs. The dining hall roared with laughter. Lyle's face split in a broad, unkind smile. "Whoopsies."

She walked away, cackling, as Declan dabbed himself with napkins. Ace arrived by his side, with Mrs. Winter not far behind. "Are you okay?" He handed Declan a roll of paper towels.

"Yeah, I'm..." Pain radiated down his left leg as he straightened. The coffee had burnt his upper thigh. Declan hunched forward, wishing he could vanish from that moment and be anywhere else in the world. He blinked back tears. "She did that on purpose." He looked at Mrs. Winter. "She let it fall on me."

Mrs. Winter pursed her lips. "I'll look into it, Declan." Her eyes darted to his legs. "First, let's get you to the first-aid bay. I will deal with Miss Arthur later."

———

The first-aid bay had a large blue curtain that could be pulled around the bed for privacy. Declan sat on one side, pants down to his knee with a clear gel slathered over angry red skin. Ace sat on the other side, tapping his pen against paper.

"What are you doing?" Declan asked.

"College applications," Ace replied. "They handed them out this morning. Due at midnight tonight."

Declan nodded. A wave of jealousy washed over him. He took a moment to compose himself. "Tonight? Wow! Plenty of notice on that."

Ace laughed. "They called it an initiation. The turn-around is just as fast."

"What do you mean?"

"Three days and we'll receive offers. We'll know by the end of the week."

"Wow." Declan attempted to straighten his left leg. The burn protested with an intense flash of pain. "How do they do it so fast?"

"Blood," Ace said. "You blot a thumbprint of blood onto the bottom of the application. Apparently, that tells them everything they need about your Potential."

Or lack thereof, Declan thought. He leaned back against the thin mattress, unsure of what to say. Ace's scratching pen filled the silence. For a long while, it was the only sound in the room. When it stopped, a pause stretched out on either side of the curtain.

"One delegate said that you have no business enrolling in Mag-Ed if you can't function under tight deadlines. I think a lot of us thought it would be easier than that... You may have dodged a bullet."

He's trying to make me feel better. Declan tested his leg again. It still hurt to move, but not as much. The clear gel was doing something. He leaned forward. "How long have you known I couldn't do magic?"

Before Ace could answer, the door clicked open. "Declan Moore?" asked the nurse's monotonous voice.

"Yes," Declan answered.

"Your mother is here to collect you. Do you need help… getting organized?"

Declan assumed that was code for 'getting your pants on'. He was glad that the curtains blocked his warming cheeks. "No. No thank you, I'll be okay."

"Very well. Mrs. Moore is waiting at the Administration Office. Mr. Marley—could I ask you to run to the senior homeroom and collect Declan's bag?"

"Sure thing," Ace said. "I'll meet you at the office, Dex."

Declan listened to his footsteps disappear down the hall. Inside the first-aid bay, the nurse rummaged loudly through some cabinets. A moment later, a yellow tube with a red lid slid under the curtain. "That's BurnGel for you, Mr. Moore. Apply as much as you need until the pain settles."

"Thanks," Declan replied.

"I'll get out of your way so you can get organized."

The door closed. Declan began the arduous task of getting his pants over his burnt legs, which came with plenty of delicate movements and muttered curses. When he slid the curtain back, he was surprised to see a loose sheet on the floor. He leaned down to pick it up.

Magical Education Applicant Form 470B: King's College.

Declan's eyebrows climbed into his chestnut curls. King's College was the most prestigious school in the entire Dominion. *Ace must have left it.* Declan folded the sheet, slid it into his back pocket, then hobbled to the door.

Walking hurt. Walking faster hurt worse. By the time he reached the administration block, Ace was nowhere to be seen. Instead, his mother waited in dirty gardening overalls with his backpack and a sympathetic smile.

"Oh, Declan," she said. "What have you done to yourself?"

A thin spread of clouds did little to hide the glittering night sky. Moonlight shone through them, casting a perfect circle that glimmered with shades of blue and violet. A cool breeze played along the crowns of the oak trees lining the street. Otherwise, all was still.

Declan sat on a bench opposite a bright red post-box. A folded sheet in his hands. His legs still hurt, but liberal amounts of BurnGel had transformed searing pain into a dull ache. He bit his lip and unfolded the paper.

Magical Education Applicant Form 470B: King's College.

He hadn't had time to return it to Ace. Instead, his untidy handwriting filled the page. Every section completed in blue ink, save for an empty box with instructions in small letters. *Blood print here, ensure to keep sample inside the border.* Declan sighed, leaned back and resumed his staring match with the post-box.

What will this accomplish?

The box loomed ahead of him. The gatekeeper of a future he desperately wanted. A future he would never have. *Why not? Why can't I learn magic? Maybe the tests were faulty. Maybe I do have Potential?*

Declan looked down Milworth Drive. All the lights were off at his house; his parents went to bed hours ago. He turned back to the post-box. Lyle's words crept—uninvited —into his mind. *If only the Moore's of old could see you now.*

As if in a trance, he withdrew a small penknife from his jacket pocket. Declan pushed down on the point, felt a prick of pain, and a sphere of blood formed at the end of his index finger. Carefully, he pressed it inside the empty box, leaving a bloody circle.

He folded the sheet and slipped it into an envelope. On

the back, in his shakiest handwriting, were five words. *Attention: Enrollments, Kings College, Kingsbreak.* Declan crossed the road and dropped it into the post-box before he had time to second guess himself.

It's done. He thought.

A moment later. *What have I done?*

Somewhere in the distance, a clock chimed midnight.

CHAPTER 3
DECLAN

THE NEXT MORNING, Declan's legs were fine. The BurnGel worked like magic; he half suspected the nurse had imbued it with some sort of spellwork. Now, he carried a new pain, a mix of guilt and embarrassment. *I applied to Mag-Ed.* He couldn't imagine how they would react when the response arrived in the mail. *I applied to King's College.*

Declan's miraculous recovery meant he had school. As expected, word of his normalcy spread like wildfire. To Declan, the walk to Iberian history felt like walking a plank. He stood at the classroom door for far too long, took a deep breath, and entered.

Mr. Cogwell's stern gaze met him at the door. "You are late."

"Sorry, sir." There was no point arguing with Mr. Cogwell. Around the room, students looked at him with a collection of amusement and pity. Ace waved him to an empty seat in the second row of desks. Declan avoided everyone's eyes. He sat down, retrieved his notebook from his bag, then looked up at the board. His mouth went dry. *Oh no.*

Mr. Cogwell cleared his throat. "Today we will cover the Rainy Rebellion, a major event in the founding of this school." Heat crept up Declan's cheeks. "Four hundred and six years ago, William Fendragon inherited the throne of Euryma. Who can tell me what the social climate was at the time?"

Ace's hand leapt into the air. "King William was a polarizing figure across the Dominion. His idea of democracy divided Euryma's traditionalists."

"Well said Marley. When King William dissolved the Monarchy, he nearly destroyed the Dominion." Mr. Cogwell tapped the board. "A conflict that peaked with what history remembers as the Rainy Rebellion."

To his horror, a small groan escaped Declan's lips.

Mr. Cogwell raised a crooked eyebrow. "First you arrive late and now you're making stupid noises." He shook his head. "I would expect you to have more respect than this. It is your greatest great-grandfather who led the decisive battle against this rebellion, and here you scoff like an entitled brat." He pointed to the door. "Either sit quietly or get out of my classroom. I have no time for seniors who act like toddlers."

Declan shrunk into his chair. He lowered his eyes, listened to the greatness of his bloodline, and wished he had never been born.

"I'm home," Declan said to nobody. The kitchen was empty. Out the window, his mother knelt by a glorious circular garden. Gold and royal purple blooms exploded in a tall spiral. Behind her, his father shaped a miniature bay-laurel into a sphere. The hedge trimmer's roar filled the backyard.

Declan shook his head. They could have done it all in a moment of magic- if they wanted to.

He grabbed an apple from the bowl on his way outside. "I'm home!" he called again. The hedge trimmer died and his mother looked up. "Hey Dex. How was school?"

Declan shrugged. "Good, good. Nothing exciting." The lie tasted bitter on his lips. He took a bite of the apple; it wasn't much better.

"Well, if excitement is what you want, I've got news for you." Declan's father waved a wide arc. The hedge trimmer floated into the garden shed. "I spoke to your headmaster today. The school is looking for an apprentice grounds-man." He looked from his wife to his son. "How would you feel about taking up a job working the gardens?" His moustache bristled with delight.

"A groundsman?" Declan suppressed a shudder. *Do they really think so little of me?*

"A groundsman." His father beamed. "It's a dream job for someone in your position. You'd be tending some of the nicest gardens in Tamhill *and* getting *paid* for it!" He pulled Declan into a one-armed hug.

Someone in your position. Those delicate, well-intentioned words cut deeper than he cared to admit. His magical parents would never understand.

Declan's mother clapped her hands together. "That's fantastic. Do they have a starting date? How many hours?" Her eyes danced between father and son; a smear of mud marked her cheek. "This is so exciting! Your first proper job!"

"Hey! I've worked!" Declan gestured to an oval-shaped garden bed. "I dug out that section of lawn for you."

His father nodded. "And that's the best part of the yard.

You're a natural. And I thought to celebrate we could go out to dinner."

Declan swallowed. His parents looked so proud. So proud their boy would spend his life working in dirt. He shrugged out of his father's hug and turned to face them both. "That sounds great, but not tonight."

His mother's face fell a fraction. "Why not?"

"I, uh, I already told Ace I was going to come over and help him study."

"That's not like Ace to need help." His father frowned faintly.

"We're covering the Rainy Rebellion in history." Declan shrugged. "I offered to give him the inside scoop to make his essay pop. I was actually going to head over now."

His mother nodded. "You're a good person, Dex."

"Raised by the best." Declan leaned down and kissed her mud-free cheek. "Why don't you two go out? Have a night together. We can talk about jobs later."

"Not a bad idea." His father's face lit up once more. "Fancy a date at the garden center, Miranda? We could pick up some more rhododendrons?"

Declan's mother laughed. "Maybe *you* should take that job." She smiled at Declan. "Be safe Declan, have fun with Ace."

"We love you," his father added.

Declan nodded and left them in the garden.

Declan sat on a hard bed cramped into an attic bedroom. Dust hung from corner cobwebs; the room smelled of mildew. "How many did you end up applying for?"

"Forty-nine out of fifty." He frowned through a curtain

of dark hair. "I still can't believe I missed King's. I could have sworn I got a form from the delegate."

Guilt pricked Declan's neck. He inspected the back of his hands for a long moment while Ace copied notes from a textbook. He wanted to tell him. He wanted to tell Ace so badly. But he couldn't. Better to leave things as they were. "You never told me how long you knew I was a LAMP."

Ace's pen paused.

Declan looked up from his hands. "What gave it away?"

"You never spoke about Potential." Ace met his gaze, then shrugged. "You're not shy about good news. If your Potential matched your reputation, you would say so, but whenever it came up in conversation, you would steer the subject elsewhere."

Declan turned to hide his flushed cheeks. "You picked up on that, huh?"

"You did it well." Ace went back to copying notes. "I just have a knack for noticing what others don't."

"So, how long have you known?" Declan asked again.

"A while. Probably a week after we first met."

"Four years?" Declan stared in shock. "And you didn't think to ask?"

Ace shrugged. "It wouldn't change anything."

"I..." Declan's cheeks burned as he struggled to find the words. "I figured you wouldn't want to be friends with a..."

"Friends with a LAMP?" Ace rolled his eyes. "Potential has no impact on character, Dex. We're friends because we look out for each other. Not because of what we can or can't do with magic."

The words cut in a way Declan didn't dare say. Ace had known he was a powerless nobody for years and had stuck with him, and Declan had betrayed his chance to apply for the best college in Mag-Ed. *I should tell him I applied.*

20

But Declan couldn't. He just sat there, looking everywhere in the room but at his friend.

"Are you going to take the groundsman job?" Ace asked.

"How did you know about that?"

"Leed spoke to your dad on the phone while I was trying to get a late application to King's."

Declan leaned back. "Did you?"

Ace shook his head. "I had until midnight and I missed it. I can apply to transfer after a year at a different college. Don't think I can't see you changing the subject. What are you going to do?"

"No idea," Declan said. "Dad was so excited when he told me... But..."

"I get it." Ace smiled sadly. "I'm not sure they realize you don't feel the way about gardening that they do."

"I don't think they realize nobody in the entire Dominion feels the way about gardening that they do."

Ace laughed. The room fell silent except for the pen's gentle scratch. The knot in Declan's stomach tightened with every passing minute. He stayed as long as he could bear, then said goodnight and slipped down the attic ladder.

He passed the living room on the way to the front door. Ace's parents sat shouting at their television; it was all they ever did. Declan shook his head. They were LAMPs like him, but that was no excuse for their useless parenting.

CHAPTER 4
DECLAN

THE NEXT MORNING, Declan peeked out through his cupboard's wooden slats, feeling closer to seven than seventeen. That didn't matter. He held his breath as footsteps approached the door.

"Good morning, sunshine," his mother called. "Are you up?"

Declan remained silent. He had no intention of going to school. Not today. Today he was staying home to burn the college rejection letter coming his way. The door clicked open. He retreated behind a wall of school blazers. Through the slats, his mother's brown curls bobbed from side to side. After a long pause, she turned away. "Angus," she called. "Is Declan down there?"

"Not here," his father boomed from downstairs.

"Try the bathroom."

"I just came out," his father called. "Did you lose him?"

His mother didn't answer. She stepped into the room. Declan hoped she was reading his message. His mother sighed. "He's left a note on the pillow," she called. "He left something at Ace's house. Did you hear him leave?"

"I didn't."

Declan tried to catch a glance of his mother's face. Instead, he nudged a blazer off its hanger. Two more fell when he tried to catch it. Quick as a whip, the cupboard door snapped open. Declan's mind went blank. His mother's face turned stern.

She held up the note he had left on his pillow. "Odd place for a morning walk."

"I- uh- I don't feel well." Declan cringed at his own excuse. *Really?*

She raised an eyebrow. "Do you think I'm stupid?"

"What?"

"I know what today is, Declan. I know what you're trying to do."

"I'm serious," Declan said. "It's not what it looks like—"

"Yes, because sick people naturally leave fake notes and hide in cupboards."

"—but it's just terrible timing. I feel awful!"

It was exactly what it looked like. Miranda Moore maneuvered around the bed. "Today is not a big deal. It's Offers Day. Kids who get into college will be more excited than usual. That's all." She led him out of the cupboard, stood on her toes and kissed his mop of dark brown hair. "Treat it like a normal day."

Thoughts evaded him. "But... I don't feel well..."

"You're fine," she said. "Plus, you're too old to be crying sick." She opened the curtains. Morning sunlight invaded the teenage cavern. "Downstairs. Five minutes or you're making your own breakfast."

She left without another word. Declan scowled after her. *I don't feel well? You idiot.* He glanced at the pen on his desk. Applying for Mag-Ed seemed like such a good idea at the time. Now, just the thought of his parents finding out set his ears aflame. A heavier set of footsteps climbed the stairs. His father appeared, frowning over his bushy moustache. "What's the matter, Dex?"

"Do I have to go to school today?"

"It's Friday. On Friday you go to school."

"I really don't want to."

"Because it's Offers Day?"

"No," Declan lied.

His father sat on the bed and motioned for Declan to join him. "Magic is a human quality, like being intelligent or having a good sense of humor or being kind. Some people are magical with grass for brains. Some people are magical, but incredibly boring." He squeezed Declan's leg. "You aren't magical. But you are intelligent, you have a great sense of humor, you are kind."

"That's easy for you to say," Declan said. "You've got all that plus magic."

"I'll quote you regarding my sense of humor. Can I have that in writing?"

"Dad."

"Declan." His father's face turned serious. "You are the only one in this family who has ever put stock in being able to do magic. Your mother and I do not care. You're a good person. We love you. Let that be enough." He stood up. "Now come have breakfast."

Declan nodded. Begrudgingly, he followed his father to the kitchen. His mother smiled; all sins apparently forgiven. Her hands moved like a puppeteer, jerking back and forth in a staccato of loose fingertips. A procession of sausages and eggs assembled above a cast iron pan, then marched through the air. The delicious display settled neatly onto three plates while a jiggling sphere of orange juice slipped into three glasses.

Declan barely noticed. *Okay. You've screwed up Plan A. Time for Plan B.* He pushed his breakfast around the plate as his mother settled across from him. "What are you two up to today?

"Work," his father said. "Though I don't know why. Still no materials. Suppliers haven't answered calls in weeks. They might as well have dropped off the face of the planet." He sipped his juice. "Yes, just work."

Declan frowned. If he couldn't burn the rejection letter when it arrived, he'd have to wait until after school. He glanced at his mother. "How about you?"

"The rose patch," she said, brushing a dark curl to the side. "If I don't weed it soon, it will be too late to replant the straggly ones."

Declan chewed on his lip. "Sounds like a quiet day..." His parents eyed him suspiciously. Declan continued. "I was thinking maybe you might go shopping for me."

His mother's eyes narrowed. "Shopping?"

"Offers Day got me thinking, you know, about my future..." He shrugged, a picture of innocence. "I thought maybe you could pick me out some groundsman's clothes, steel-toe boots."

A slow smile spread across his father's face. "Am I dreaming?" He asked. "Is this really happening?"

"You're going to take the job?" Wide eyes betrayed his mother's level voice.

"Like you said, Ace will most likely be heading off to college next year. I'm going to need some money if I ever want to visit him." Declan shrugged. "A job's a job, right?" They were the same talking points his parents had parroted when he got home last night. Declan held his breath. His parents exchanged glances.

"Got your father's looks, your mother's mind, and a

green thumb from both." His father nodded. "I'm proud of you."

"That sounds brilliant." His mother beamed at him. "I'm so glad you've come around."

"It just made sense." Declan fought to keep his voice casual. "What time do you think you'll be back?"

"Depends," his mother said. "Do you want me to go to Ursaria to get you proper tools?"

"Buy nice or buy twice, right?"

She chuckled and checked the clock above the door. "If I head to the city this morning, I should be back late this afternoon. Angus, can you organize dinner on your way home?"

His father helped himself to a huge forkful of eggs. "I'd cook a five-course banquet to get this boy ready for his future."

Declan grinned. Relief washed over him. He skewered a chunk of sausage. A weight lifted off his chest. *Plenty of time to burn the mail. Declan, you're a genius!*

Declan waited a little way off the gathering students. His lack of Potential appeared to be old news—today was Offers Day. He ignored their excitement, instead opting to stare at his mailbox halfway down Milworth Drive. His parents would be away until evening, by which time his offer would be a pile of ash. Despite this, Declan couldn't shake a growing sense of anxiety, as if something terrible waited on the other side of the day.

"Hey Dex," said a smooth voice. Mason Harris lived on the other side of the block. He had short hair, broad shoulders and looked out of place without a girl on his arm.

"Morning, Mason. How's it going?"

"Good, good... Big day today, hey?"

"Not for me."

Mason's smile slipped. "Ah, right..."

"No harm." Declan shrugged. "How about you? Nervous?"

"Not really. I put a couple in. I'll be okay."

Declan didn't press. Kirsten Zillmere walked past and took Mason's attention with her. They sat in silence until Ace arrived.

"Morning lads," he said, beaming.

"You're happy," Mason noted.

"It's Offers Day," Ace said, avoiding Declan's eye.

Their pale blue bus lumbered to a halt. The doors hissed open, they climbed aboard. Declan sat behind Ace and Mason. The bus was chaos, the noise inside a steady roar until old Mrs. Betten screeched at them to settle down.

Mason and Ace discussed their potential offers, their promising futures. Declan tuned them out and pressed his head against the cool bus window. Outside, Tamhill's streets rushed by. Handsome old houses gave way to lush acreage. Large mansions sprawled amongst the hills, enclosed in shimmering iridescent domes- security enchantments. As a child, Declan thought they were gigantic soapy bubbles. Now they were another reminder of what he'd never have.

"I'd love to learn more about Imbusion," Ace said.

"Imbusion?" Mason raised an eyebrow.

"Making normal objects magical," Ace said. "There's an enormous market for it up north."

"You'd go north?" Mason wrinkled his nose. "My old man says they're different up there."

"Different isn't bad," Ace said. "Euryma's a big place. I

can't imagine anything worse than being stuck in Tamhill forever."

Embarrassment pricked Declan's neck. The streets he would never escape rushed past. Jealousy bubbled inside him. His palms itched, Ace smiled, Mason laughed, too loud. The bus was too loud. It pressed on him.

Declan shut his eyes. Counted his breaths. *Ten. Nine. Eight.* For years, he had controlled his envy. *Seven. Six. Five.* Today would not be the day he slipped. *Four. Three. Two. One.* The pressure melted. Declan opened his eyes.

As they drove south, the green fields faded to a steady rise of sloping lawns. The bus slowed. The ornate metal gate decorated with initials *A. M* swung outward and they rumbled towards Arman Moore's Preparatory School.

Half an hour later, Declan pressed into the main hall. Big, bright, crowded. Polished floors reflected fluorescent ceiling lights. The school's armadillo emblem rippled on a banner hanging from the rafters. Excited chatter reverberated through the hall until Headmaster Leed approached the lectern. The room fell silent.

"Good morning seniors," he began. Headmaster Leed's lined face shone with pride. "Today is a very special day. A day that marks the first step of your journey into a bright future."

Declan scanned the crowd. *Why am I even here?* He had been at Arman Moore's Preparatory School for ten years. Walking these halls was his birthright, but he didn't belong. He never had.

"With your acceptance into Magical Education, you will

finally test the Potential tested within you so many years ago."

LAMP enrollments weren't unheard of. Often the result of overbearing parents who could not accept their child's shortcomings, or those—like him—who were part of the right family. Most LAMPs didn't last long at Arman Moore's. He was the unexceptional exception. Declan leaned back while his peers sat on the edge of their seats.

"Your first test starts this morning. A test of self-control." The headmaster pursed his lips. "By Law you must receive your offers before ten o'clock this morning. However, Arman Moore's Preparatory School will not tolerate the tearing of envelopes, nor the chaos of elation. We expect nothing less than honorable, respectful patience."

Two days ago, Declan was Arman Moore's royalty. Now, he was an afterthought, a shriveled branch on an ancient and powerful tree. Proof that, given enough time, even the mightiest bloodlines can dwindle to nothing.

"Regardless of which college accepts you, leave today knowing that you are alumni of Arman Moore's Preparatory School. You are a product of excellence. Because of this, you will continue to be excellent."

Declan thought about his application. *Maybe King's College won't even send a response. Maybe they threw my application in the trash.* He wouldn't count on it. If his parents found out what he had done—

Declan jumped, startled by the sudden applause. Headmaster Leed had finished his flowery address; he now watched the crowd with a satisfied smile. Excited voices replaced clapping hands until homeroom teachers instructed them to move. Declan fell alongside Ace amidst a wave of students. "What did he say?" Declan asked as they exited the auditorium.

"Weren't you listening?"

"Why bother?"

"C'mon Dex, this is our future!"

"Your future," Declan said.

Ace looked at him sideways. "Sorry. We're headed back to homerooms. Leed said we would receive a response for each application we submitted. We are to show our *exemplary self-control* until the last bell of the day. Only then can we open our offers and find out if we got in to Mag-Ed. No envelopes to be opened during school hours."

Declan stopped in his tracks. "A response to each application submitted? Even if it's a rejection?"

"That's what he said."

A cocoon of nerves formed in his stomach. "And they're handing them out now?"

"Right now, in our homerooms. Mrs. Winter will have ours."

Declan's face went pale. He had assumed King's College would send their response to his home address. *This is so much worse. You'll never live this down.* The cocoon hatched into butterflies.

Everyone, Ace included, was about to learn that he, the LAMP, the black sheep of his bloodline, the unremarkable Declan Moore, had legitimately applied to the most prestigious Mag-Ed College in Euryma.

Suddenly, Declan's bright idea seemed incredibly dim.

CHAPTER 5

DECLAN

DECLAN'S HEAD swam as he entered the homeroom. The creamy floorboards, large windows, bookshelves and bag racks seemed to sway from side to side. At one end, soft couches surrounded low tables. At the other, eager students filled empty chairs. He searched for an excuse to escape.

"Surprise, surprise," said Lyle from behind. "I didn't think you'd bother coming today."

Declan looked at her blankly. She would crucify him for applying. The walls were closing in.

"What's wrong?" Lyle raised an eyebrow. "Too stupid to speak?"

"Ignore her," Ace muttered as he led Declan to a seat.

Declan tried to nod; he had forgotten how.

Ace must have sensed his discomfort. "Are you okay?"

No. Declan opened his mouth. Another door swung open. Mrs. Winter entered the room, arms piled high with an enormous mound of yellow envelopes.

"Well, this is exciting!" she said, beaming at them. She set the envelopes on her desk, then scanned the homeroom. "Before I pass these out, I want to reiterate what Head-

31

master Leed said this morning about *self-control*. We are required to deliver your offers this morning, but remember, there is still a day of learning ahead of you. Respect that. Do not open your envelopes until you arrive home."

The students groaned.

Mrs. Winter rolled her eyes. "If not opening an envelope is the worst thing that happens to you today, you are living a charmed life." She placed her hand on the pile. "When I call your name, come collect your offers. If you think there is a mistake, see me at break." Mrs. Winter paused. Her lips twisted in disgust. "Mr. Harris, get your lips off Miss Zillmere. This is homeroom, not a back alley."

The class erupted into laughter, but it stopped the moment Mrs. Winter picked up the first few envelopes. "Lyle Arthur."

Lyle strolled to the front of the room. Mrs. Winter handed her a small stack without comment. As Lyle preened back to her seat, Declan wondered how she concealed so much spite beneath such delicate features. She caught his eye and smirked. He glanced at the floor.

Mrs. Winter continued calling students up to collect their futures. Declan's neck prickled. Sweat dotted his palms. The room shrunk with every name.

"Horace Marley."

There was a moment of confusion. Then Ace stood up. The homeroom murmured in collective realization. Nobody ever called Ace by his full name. Mrs. Winter hoisted a stack of envelopes into eager arms. "An impressive response, Ace. You should be proud."

Declan tugged his damp collar. *I'm next.* Ace sat back down with his mountain of offers. Mrs. Winter picked up the next envelope, expression unchanged. *This is it. I'll never live this down.* Declan braced himself.

"Anita Mulstrom."

Tiny Anita stood to collect her single offer. Declan blinked. Sweet relief embraced him. He grinned at Ace, who struggled to keep his envelopes from tumbling over, then laughed like he'd cheated death. *Of course, I didn't get a response. I'm a LAMP. They wouldn't have even considered me.*

When Kirsten Zillmere collected the final two envelopes. Mrs. Winter clapped her hands. "And that's that. I wish you all the best of luck when you open them... *this afternoon.*"

Ace glanced at his precarious pile. "I need a bigger bag."

"You need another bag." Declan laughed. "That haul is enormous!" He shook his head and relaxed. It was over. He'd escaped unscathed.

Someone knocked on the side door. A head of shaggy, red hair popped into the room. "This one got mixed up, Ma'am," said the red hair's owner, holding up an envelope. "Application Responses for Declan Moore."

Mrs. Winter stared at the boy. Declan's stomach vanished. "Excuse me?" she asked.

Stunned silence smothered the homeroom.

"Hah!" Lyle called into the awkward abyss. "The LAMP's trying to get into Mag-Ed!"

Heat engulfed Declan from head to toe. The red-haired student hesitated, crossed the room, and placed the envelope on Mrs. Winter's desk. She stared at it; lips pursed. Everyone waited. "Declan Moore," she said at last. "I believe this belongs to you."

Declan dragged himself off his chair. The walk to the front of the room felt like an eternity. His heart strobed in his chest.

Mrs. Winter studied him as if he were some strange animal. She said nothing, but offered the parchment envelope. Declan took it, refused to meet her eyes, turned, and walked towards his seat.

"You dirty rat LAMP." Lyle hissed. "Keep your filthy trash blood out of Mag-Ed."

"Excuse me, Miss Arthur?"

"Nothing, Ma'am."

"Don't *nothing* me, Lyle." Mrs. Winter's voice was glacial. "I heard something."

"Maybe you're just getting old, Ma'am."

Mrs. Winter clapped her hands together. Magic dragged Lyle through the air to the front of the room. Shocked gasps punctured tense silence. "What did you say, Miss Arthur?"

Lyle's confident demeanor shattered. "I called him a rat LAMP," she squeaked. "I told him to keep his trash blood out of—"

"Samantha!" boomed Headmaster Leed from the far entrance. "What on earth are you doing? Release her!"

Lyle dropped to the ground and scurried back to her seat. Mrs. Winter drew herself up. "I will not excuse discrimination in this room, Headmaster," she said in a level tone.

Headmaster Leed's eyes darted from Mrs. Winter to the seated students. His creased cheeks contorted, Declan waited for him to explode, to fire Mrs. Winter on the spot. Instead, he waved to the students. "Seniors, you are dismissed. Please put your offers in your bags. Lyle Arthur." His voice dropped an octave. "Kindly remain."

The homeroom emptied quickly. Students stuffed envelopes into bags as they went. Ace struggled to keep his enormous collection together.

"Quickly, thanks Mr. Marley."

Declan grabbed an armful of his envelopes and led Ace out. Lyle watched him pass, green eyes alight with hatred.

Something unseen slammed the door behind them. Declan looked sideways at Ace, who continued cramming offers into his threadbare backpack. "I... I should've told you I applied."

Ace looked him in the eye. "You should have." His attention darted to the envelope in Declan's hand. "Where did you apply?" His tone of voice betrayed the innocence of the question.

Declan frowned apologetically. "King's College."

"Dex..." Ace shook his head. "Damn it, Dex. That was my application, wasn't it?"

"I'm sorry," Declan said. "I... I don't know, I..."

"You didn't want to be left behind," Ace said.

Declan nodded, embarrassed.

"And you didn't care how that would affect my future?"

"I'm sorry," Declan repeated.

Ace nodded. His lips were paper thin. "Yeah. You said that."

"Ace."

"I'll take those offers," Ace said, nodding to the pile of his envelopes Declan had picked up in the homeroom.

Declan had no response. He handed Ace the pile, and his friend turned on his heel. His footsteps echoed down the hall, leaving Declan alone with his offer.

Declan walked in silence. He mulled over Ace's words until he entered a cobblestone quad. A gleaming statue stood amidst a bubbling fountain, Arman Moore, an imposing bearded figure in flowing bronze robes with a hand outstretched to the sky. Jets of water arced from his greatest-great-grandfather's palm into the shallow pool. A silver armadillo perched on his shoulder.

The entire area was a beehive of anticipation, not the ordinary exhilaration of Offers Day, something else. Darting glances, inaudible whispers. The quad leaned towards him.

"Looks like you're a minor celebrity," Mason observed. Declan hadn't noticed him appear at his side.

"Well... It is Offers Day."

Mason laughed. "So modest, Dex. People don't care about their offers. They're talking about *the LAMP who dared*." He chuckled at his own joke. For a split-second, Declan wanted to wipe the smug smile from his lips. "What did the letter say?" Mason asked, a little louder.

"I haven't opened it." There were no rules against applying to a Mag-Ed without Potential, but he didn't dare push his luck. "It's staying sealed until after school."

"Fair call," Mason replied. "A bunch of us are gathering at Bluebells this afternoon to open envelopes." He nodded to a group of students gawking at them. "What do you say, Dex?"

Declan considered the envelope packed away in his bag. *Well, I guess I don't have to rush home anymore.* He knew they didn't actually care. He had gone from legend to novelty in forty-eight hours. "Sure. Bluebells it is."

Mason returned to the curious onlookers. Declan wandered to a lone figure seated by the western entry. "I'm sorry Ace. I'm an idiot. I was thinking only about myself, about how useless I am, and that's being a sucky friend."

Ace stared straight ahead. "You're not useless," he said.

"I shouldn't have done it. It was such a stupid thing to do."

"Are you kidding me, Dex? I thought that was great."

"What?" Declan blinked. "How?"

Ace shrugged. "Magical Education divides people. Selective colleges that only care about magic? It's nonsense. It creates morons like Lyle who believe witches and wizards are better than LAMPs."

"But they are. They have magic."

"Does that make them less of a person?" Ace turned to face him. "If that's true, the world *needs* a change."

Declan considered it. "I'm not trying to change the world—"

"I know you're not. I know you sent it in because you're insecure as hell. That doesn't change the fact that, deliberately or not, a LAMP just demanded to be seen as equal."

Declan shrugged. "They're going to reject me, you know?"

"They will," Ace said. "But once word gets out that you applied, it won't be long until others try as well. A single snowflake can start an avalanche."

"I'm really sorry."

Ace didn't respond. The murmur of a hundred conversations seemed to melt away as he ran a hand through his hair. "I know," Ace said at last. "But that was King's College. *King's College.* I'm trying to be rational about it, but that's a real sucker punch, Dex. I wish you'd asked me for any other application." His gaze darted past Declan's shoulder. "Brace yourself."

Lyle entered the quad, Headmaster Leed and Mrs. Winter on either side of her. She walked towards them with a cracked smile and stopped a step too close. "I'm so sorry for what I said to you," she practically shouted in his face.

Declan held her scorching green eyes. "Thanks Lyle," he said. "I appreciate your apology."

With a snort of derision, Lyle turned back to the entrance. Headmaster Leed left. Lyle spared a glare for Declan before she stormed away, but Mrs. Winter lingered a little longer, watching intently, holding a small stack of envelopes.

Declan's attention wandered to the statue in the middle of the quad. Arman Moore. The legend who led two linchpin battles where the small city of Tamhill now stood. The school was built in his honor. Every Moore since had enjoyed the privilege of eating in his shadow. Declan noted the sculpture's stern expression and wondered what his greatest-great-grandfather would think of his current predicament.

By the time the last bell rang, Declan was ready to sink back into obscurity.

"You're still coming to Bluebells, right?" Mason asked as they climbed onto the bus.

"I guess..." Declan trailed off at old Mrs. Betten's deep scowl. *Even the bus driver knows.* Ace walked past without a word, ignored the empty seat by Declan and continued to the back of the bus.

Mason plonked down by Declan's side instead. "We're getting off at Central and going straight there."

Declan bit his lip. "Alright, sure. Give me a minute." He pulled out his phone. Mason looked away as if embarrassed he'd let his amusement slip. Witches and wizards used looptap to communicate over any distance with just their hands. Compared to that, LAMP gadgets like phones were a laughable novelty. Most sensible witches and wizards would not be caught dead using a cellular phone. Declan's parents happily flaunted the social taboo to maintain contact with their son. Declan typed a quick message. *Going out with friends. C U at dinner.*

By the time Declan had slid his phone into his bag, Mason was chatting to a pair of girls in front of them, trying to impress both and failing on all counts. Declan busied himself watching the world pass by. The security enchantments surrounding the large manors in the distance were gone. The houses looked eerie without their soapbox covers. After a few fruitless minutes, Mason finished flirting and turned to him. "Not long now. How are you feeling?"

Declan held his bag on his lap to hide his shaking hands. "You know it's going to be a rejection."

"Maybe," Mason said. "But who knows? This has never happened before."

With an ear-piercing screech, the bus jerked to a stop. It hurled Declan into the chair where his backpack endured the impact. Mason wasn't so lucky. His forehead collided with the hard plastic, leaving a large red splotch above his right eye. All around them, students shouted in shock, pain, or both.

"El burro morons!" Mrs. Betten screeched louder than the tires and waved a finger at the jet-black van stopped in the middle of the road. She had stopped just in time. The thick, acrid smell of burnt rubber filled Declan's nostrils.

A man with a red beard leaned out the window and gestured some sort of apology. Mrs. Betten gestured back something quite distant from an apology and maneuvered the bus around the van. The bus reached cruising speed around at the same time Declan's heart stopped racing. As the adrenaline faded, he turned to Mason. "Are you okay?"

The first hints of a spectacular purple and yellow bruise were forming over his eye. Mason nodded, though his dazed expression did not fade. They sat in silence until the bus pulled in to Central Tamhill. Declan kept a close eye on Mason as they climbed off the bus until something buzzed in his backpack. Declan retrieved his phone. His stomach dropped. There were six missed calls, a low battery warning and a message from his father—*We need to talk. Call asap.*

Declan froze on the pavement.

"What's wrong?" Ace asked. Declan hadn't noticed him standing behind him.

"The school must have looptapped home. I need to call my dad." A coldness slithered down his spine. Ace waited, unmoving. "You go ahead, I'll catch up." Declan turned to the small crowd walking up the street. "And keep an eye on Mason. He hit his head pretty hard—he might have a concussion."

Ace nodded and followed the rest of the seniors. Declan leaned against a vacant storefront. He took a deep breath as a second bus stopped at the lights. *Maybe I should catch that one home.* He dialed his father, then braced for the worst.

No answer.

He tried once more. The second bus hissed to a stop right in front of him. The call rang out again. He tried his mother; it rang out too. "Weird," he muttered.

"It is, isn't it?" said a voice dripping with resentment.

Declan looked up. Lyle stepped off the second bus, four friends close behind. Declan's heart skipped a beat. There was a contradiction in her burning eyes and frozen smile that made his skin crawl.

"Uh, hey Lyle." Declan gulped. A lemon-sized lump back flipped in his throat. "Sorry—"

"Oh, no need," she said. "No need to apologize. We can settle it right now."

Declan's legs were warm jelly. Lyle's four companions blocked his exit. Joel Mercado flashed his teeth.

"Listen, Lyle—"

"No funny jokes? You're so funny, after all. Applying to learn magic with the all the Potential of a matchbox—clearly hilarious."

Declan looked for a gap, for some sort of escape.

Lyle seemed to enjoy his discomfort. "Look at this trapped little mouse," she said to her followers. They laughed. "I don't like mice. But they can be useful to practice with."

She twisted her hands in a slow, deliberate pattern. Declan's feet lifted from the ground. His jaw snapped shut, his arms locked to his sides. Lyle clenched her hands around an invisible leash and walked him into the alleyway off the street. Declan floated, helpless, beside her. As soon as they were off the street, Lyle relaxed her grip and pushed.

Declan slammed against the side of the building. His head made a dull thud against the cement wall. Pain bloomed from the point of impact. Lyle spread her hands. Nothing happened. She cursed, repeated the motion, and spread her hands again. Declan gasped as the air squeezed from his lungs. "Help!" he wheezed.

Lyle clasped her fingers together and cut him off. "Quiet, little mouse," she said. He couldn't breathe. She spread her hands wider. Declan stretched in all directions. Hot tears rolled down his cheeks.

"Look at this!" Joel Mercado called behind her. He held Declan's bag in one hand, his envelope in the other.

"Oh good!" A cruel smile split Lyle's face. "Considering

this rat had my offers confiscated, it's only fair I confiscate his rejection." She formed two fists that froze Declan in place. Lyle took the envelope and tore it open.

"Please..." Declan breathed.

Lyle ignored him. She ripped the other offer open, scanned the page, shrieked with laughter. Victory blazed in her emerald eyes. "Rejected!" she shouted with glee. "Rejected, rejected, rejected!" Even through his tears, Declan could see red ink stamped across the page. Lyle looked up at him. "You see?" she said sweetly. "You are nothing, Declan Moore."

Footsteps cluttered around the corner. Ace entered the alleyway. "What the hell? What are you doing? This is illegal!"

Lyle sneered at him. "Come to rescue your pet LAMP, Marley?"

"Put him down, Lyle."

"Or what?" Joel Mercado dropped the bag. The other goons turned towards Ace.

Declan tried to shout a warning. All he managed was a strained whisper. "Run!"

Ace didn't listen. In one fluid motion, he flicked his wrists, interlaced his fingers, and pushed. A white haze appeared from nowhere, blew into the alleyway on a sudden gale. Everyone, Lyle included, tumbled backwards. Her spell collapsed; Declan landed in a heap. Ace's hands moved like a blur before he clapped them together. The white mist solidified around them, leaving team Lyle frozen to the ground.

Declan staggered to his knees, his brain reeling from the whiplash of the moment. "Where... where did that come from?" he rasped.

42

Ace blushed. "No parental supervision, plenty of time to practice."

What just happened? Nothing made sense. Declan looked from Lyle to Ace. "But... like you said... illegal... how?"

"When I say plenty of time to practice, Dex, I'm talking years." Ace chewed his lip as he scanned the alleyway. "Please don't tell anyone. I don't want any trouble."

"What about them?" Declan gestured to the frozen students.

"Give them an hour. They'll be fine." Ace stooped down to collect Declan's rejected offer. "I imagine they'll be too embarrassed to say anything," he said. "Four against one. Who would believe them?"

Declan nodded, embarrassed by his helplessness. "Thanks, Ace."

"Don't mention it. *Seriously*," he added with a small smile. It faded as he looked down at the rejection. "But this changes nothing. I'm still angry at you."

There was nothing to say to that. Declan retrieved his bag. Pain shot up his shoulder. Every movement hurt. "I think I'll go home. Can you tell the others I had to go?"

Ace nodded, he held up the crumpled rejection. Red ink stood out like a bloodstain. "Yeah, no worries."

"Thanks again, Ace. You saved me." Declan stuffed the paper into his bag and limped back into the street. Ace waited with him until the bus arrived, then waved goodbye. Declan sat at the back as he shuddered down the road. For the second time that day, he pressed his head up against the window. The cool glass splashed relief against his throbbing head. He closed his eyes and tried to ignore the steady ache ballooning all over his body.

CHAPTER 6

HORACE

HORACE HAD NEVER LIKED his nickname. Despite consistently achieving the highest grades in his cohort, he didn't feel like an 'Ace'. It made him feel like a fraud. The son of welfare-dependent LAMPs that had lucked into a high Potentiality score.

How alike we are, Horace thought as he watched Declan's bus disappear around the corner. He wanted to hate his friend, but he couldn't. Declan was his polar opposite, a LAMP born into prestige, an impostor. *Just like me.* Horace banished the thought and turned in the other direction. He crossed the road to avoid the alleyway he had defiled. A red brick building lay ahead, above it, a large neon light read *Bluebell's Pizzeria*. At night, it blazed electric blue.

Mason looked up as he entered. Torn yellow envelopes littered the surrounding tables. "There you are. Where's Dex?"

A dozen other students glanced up from their offers. Kirsten sat on Mason's lap, smudged makeup bled down her cheeks, a crumpled sheet in her hands. "Yeah, where's the LAMP?" she asked.

Horace tried to mask his irritation. "He needed to take off. Family emergency."

Mason raised an eyebrow, then winced; his forehead had turned a deep purple. "Everything okay?"

"Not sure. He was getting off the phone when I arrived, then left in a hurry."

"He's probably in trouble." Kirsten gave a great sniff. "I guess I'll be in the same boat once my parents find out..." she trailed off. Mason put a hand on her shoulder.

Horace dropped his bag onto an empty chair in the corner. Fluorescent panels lit a room decorated with plastic plants and antique newspaper prints. A group of seniors crowded the buffet. Horace sat in silence. Soon, he'd never see them again. *Good riddance*. Horace turned his attention to his backpack. Thirty-two applications, a ticket to a new life. *None of them King's though*. He ignored that thought and got to work.

Jensen's College—Accepted. The Naomi Center for Magical Learning—Accepted. South Jacey College of Magical Education—Accepted. Horace couldn't believe his luck. He continued to tear into the pile, a crowd gathered around him. Fifteen minutes later, his fingers were raw.

Mason let out a low whistle. "Thirty out of thirty."

"Thirty-two actually." A weight lifted off him. Horace was so sure he would fail. Certain each college would look into his childhood—into his parents. *I'm in the clear*.

Kirsten Zilmere stood at the front of the group—shoulders slumped. "And I couldn't even get into one."

"Looks like Ace has enough for all of us," Mason grinned. "You could probably even get the LAMP into Mag-Ed."

Horace blinked. "Excuse me?"

"I'm..." Mason's smirk dissolved. "I'm just kidding. Good-natured joke, okay?"

Horace straightened his pile of acceptance letters and slid them into his bag. "He has a name."

"Dex wouldn't care—"

"—I care."

"Why?" Mason couldn't hide the exasperation in his voice. "I mean, Declan's a nice guy, but he's not one of us. Not anymore."

Horace squeezed his eyes shut. An envelope crumpled in his fist. He spoke in a measured tone. "What did you say?"

Mason's eyes darted around the room. His easy swagger replaced by discomfort. "Forget about it. No harm—"

"I want to hear it. C'mon Mason."

"Nothing, noth—"

"WHAT DID YOU SAY?"

Bluebell's Pizzeria froze. Horace was on his feet. He did not remember standing. All eyes were on him, even the servers hopping from table to table. Threads of magic glittered around the room like transparent spaghetti. Waiting for Horace to take hold and weave, Horace ached to grab them, put them to work, put Mason in his place.

Mason's face burned. "I just said that he's different. He's not going to Mag-Ed, he's going to finish school at Arman Moore's, do a regular LAMP job. That's all. Really."

Horace zipped up his bag, gathered his torn envelopes, dropped them in the bin. Everyone watched, nobody spoke. Horace looked Mason in the eye. "You're not better than him."

"I never said I—"

"If you think being born with the Potential to do magic

somehow puts you above anybody else in Euryma, or in the world, you're an idiot. People are people, blood and power be damned."

"Ace, I'm—"

"And if I had any say in the matter, I'd burn the entire system to the ground."

The crowd waited for Mason to respond, but he didn't. The room remained still.

"That's pretty dark, Ace," Kirsten said.

Horace didn't answer. Instead, he left. He fumed the whole bus trip home. When he arrived, his parents were in the living room, illuminated by the light of the television.

"That you Horace?" his Pa called.

Horace popped his head into the room. "Hi Pa. Sorry, I was out doing school stuff."

"Do I look like I care? Take the trash out, truck comes in the morning."

"Kitchen's dirty too," his Ma added.

Horace nodded, but neither noticed- the flashing box held their gaze. In the kitchen, a week's worth of dishes waited in the sink, accommodating a parade of tiny flies. With a flick of his finger, Horace drew the heat from the light bulb and incinerated the insects. He scraped the plates into the overflowing bin, then carried the bin out the back door. His parents were arguing when he returned.

"I don't care if he's the boss. He can't talk to you like that!"

"It didn't mean anything, Jeb. He flirts with everyone."

"Reckons cause he's magical he can do whatever he wants? Wizard filth."

"It meant nothing. Just leave it."

Horace picked up his backpack, took a deep breath,

walked into the lounge room. "Hey, Ma, Pa, I've got some news."

His parents looked up, looked irritated. "Well?" His Pa picked absently at his teeth. "What is it?"

"Well, I... I thought I'd tell you I got accepted into the Magical Education Colleges I applied for."

"And?"

"I just thought..."

His Ma smiled gently, but father shook his head. "You want us to be proud of you? Proud of your fancy scholarship school? Bunch of kids who think they're too good for us. Don't you end up like those uptight mageholes."

Horace held the sigh in. *Of course, they don't care.* "Yes, Pa. I know."

But Jebediah Marley was no longer listening. The commercials were over, and with it, his brief stint of fatherly attention. Horace climbed the stairs, backpack full of offers that somehow felt heavier than before.

CHAPTER 7
DECLAN

DECLAN WOKE with a start to a poke in the shoulder. The elderly bus driver stepped back, clutching her chest. "Oh, thank heavens," she said, shaking her head. "I thought you was dead!"

"Uh, sorry..." Declan blinked a few times, eyes adjusting to the dim light. The bus was empty. Outside, the last vestige of sunlight peeked over the hills. "Where am I?"

"Bus depot on West. Where're you s'posed to be?"

"Milworth Drive." Declan sat up and groaned. He felt like a steamroller had gone over him, twice.

The bus driver scratched her short nose. Her face had a pug-like quality. "That's not far from here. There's a walking track up the hill, cut through there. You'll reach Milworth before too long." Declan reached for his phone; a flair of pain bit his shoulder. The bus driver frowned. "Y'had a rough day?"

"You have no idea." Declan tried his phone, but it was dead. He dropped it back into the bag. "Thanks, for, uh, waking me up".

"Thanks for being awake," she said. "Boss would'a killed me if you was dead. You walk safe, okay?"

Declan climbed gingerly off the bus. The large parking depot smelled like gravel. A line of flickering lights illuminated the way out. Declan breathed in the cool evening air as he hobbled out past the chain-link fence. Half way up the hill, he found a dirt trail leading into the trees. It was wide and flat, worn in by weekend wanderers. Insects chirped from its depths. Declan shuffled down into the darkness.

The night pressed tight against him; it forced Declan to rely on the crunch of the dirt to guide each weary step. After a short walk that felt like forever, orange streetlamps shone below. Declan attempted to jog the last leg of the walk, eager to escape the dark, but managed only a hurried stagger. By the time he stepped onto the well-lit road, he was gasping for air.

Milworth Drive was part of Tamhill's old neighborhood. It was popular among witches, wizards and anyone looking to boost their reputation. Large, handsome houses—fronted by well-manicured lawns—lined the street. Declan limped along the footpath leading home. As he did, an unwelcome sense prickled his neck. Something was wrong.

Declan glanced behind him. Nobody followed. There was nothing. He paused. *Nothing?* Declan turned again. It was early evening. People should be returning from work, or out for an evening stroll. Tonight, there was nothing. *The entire street is empty.*

Declan limped a little faster. *It's your imagination*, he told himself. *Just get home.* He rounded a bend and his house came into view. Declan froze.

A car-size hole was missing from the right side of his house. A pile of splintered rubble spread over the lawn.

Declan's heart went into overdrive. Adrenaline drowned his aches and pains and he sprinted towards his home.

"What's this then?" a rough voice called from the front of the house. Declan froze halfway up the mound of rubble. With nowhere to go, he flattened himself against splintered walls, broken brick and shredded insulation material that stunk like dirty socks.

"What do you mean?" said a second voice.

"All these bodies." The first voice did not sound pleased. "How many did you waste on these two?"

"Nine. They were ready for us."

"She will not be happy with this. Let's pack 'em up. Hey. Stop that! No magic, remember?"

Declan lay motionless against the cold brick, not daring to move. He listened to the men grunt and groan as they 'packed up'. The adrenaline wore off, pain crept back into his body.

"Alright," a voice said. "Move the casts."

A violent cramp ignited in Declan's leg. He bit his lip, desperate to remain silent, and straightened his knee. The rubble beneath him shifted. It set off an avalanche of crumbled brick and shattered boards.

Declan half jumped—half fell down—the pile. He landed with a crack, tried to stand, and failed. Something in his ankle had snapped. An intense wave of pain ran up his leg. He wanted to vomit.

Two figures rounded the house, hands at the ready. One was tall with a thick red beard, the other was a smooth faced teenager. He looked as young as Declan, with short blond hair. They wore black regimental coats embroidered with an anvil and hammer. Declan cowered as they walked towards him.

"What are you doing, lad?" asked the man with the red beard. He looked strangely familiar.

Declan shuffled back. Blood dribbled down his lip. "Who-who are you?"

"Never you mind that," the man said. "Why are you at this house?"

"This is my house!"

"Your house?" The bearded man looked at his companion. "Check him, Ward."

The blond boy, Ward, flicked his wrist and pulled Declan from the ground. His shattered ankle hung limply in the air. Ward removed something short and silver from his coat. Without warning, he forced it into Declan's side. A white-hot flash of pain filled his abdomen. A moment later, it was gone.

"Well?" asked the bearded man.

"Patience, Raul," Ward replied. "Test results take time."

"We don't have time. You've got a van of bodies here. We need to get gone."

"What are you suggesting? Fierise him and be done with it?"

Raul shook his head. "Her conditions are absolute-witches and wizards only."

Ward held the silver rod to his eye. "Do you have any magical Potential?"

What type of question is that?

"We will know if you lie," Raul said.

Declan thought of the letter scrunched in his bag, the word 'rejected' stamped in red. "No."

A soft click and a small strip of paper jutted loose of the silver tool. Ward held it to the streetlight and nodded. "He's not a liar, not a wizard either."

"That's that then." Raul held his eye. "Not a word of this, right lad?"

The spell vanished. Declan landed on the ground; his ankle ignited in agony. He teetered and fell to the grass. The black-clad men walked away. A misshapen pair of pillars leaned against their van. A black van. The van that had blocked their bus earlier. *That's where I know him from!* Declan hobbled after them. "Wait! What have you done to my house? Where are my parents?"

Raul turned around. His eyes flashed. "Your parents cost me nine good men tonight, lad. I'm half inclined to take it out on *you*. Count yourself lucky that *our* orders include keeping LAMPs like yourself alive. But don't push me, or I may forget those *orders* long enough to do somethin' unprofessional." He bent down beside Ward and heaved. Together, they shifted one heavy pillar into their black van.

"What did my parents do to you?" Declan shouted.

Raul paused, turned, then replied. "Magic." He bent down and lifted the second pillar. They stepped momentarily into the streetlight. Declan gasped. It wasn't a pillar at all. It was his mother, frozen, an iron sculpture, cold and lifeless. The men loaded it into the van.

A train of emotion hit him. Declan tried to speak, tried to think, tried to move. He was drowning—beset by a waterfall of questions—with no way to swim upwards. In the absence of thought, rage welled up inside him. Declan stumbled to his feet and staggered towards the van. He didn't care that he was injured, that they were wizards. It didn't matter. Ward raised an eyebrow as he approached.

Raul rolled his eyes. "Take care of it."

Declan's insides vanished as something pulled him backwards. He arced across the yard, thrown like a rag doll that crashed through his upstairs window.

As Declan tumbled onto the carpet, the van screeched into the night. Warm, wet blood streamed down his neck and arms. He tried to stand, to get up. The room swirled into a dreary haze and gently faded from view.

CHAPTER 8

DECLAN

DECLAN STOOD IN HIS BEDROOM. It seemed much larger than he remembered. The walls were baby blue, a single bed in the corner, a tall set of drawers covered in dragon toys by the window. His hands were small and pudgy. A dinosaur bandage stuck to his wrist; he had chosen it himself from a wide variety of options. *It's for the ouchie.* The man gave both the bandage and the ouchie to him after and during his test, other than that he was fine.

His parents stood in the doorway. His mother's eyes were swollen. She must have been crying. *Was it something I did?*

His father kissed her on the forehead and entered the room. "Come, sit down here buddy," his voice was gentle. He lowered himself onto the bed, it squeaked beneath his weight.

Declan climbed up beside him and looked out the door. His mother was gone. "Daddy, why is mumma sad?"

His father smiled, a soft, sad smile. "Your mother just got some unexpected news, that's all."

Declan wondered if the news had been about him.

"Son, you know that your mother and I love you, right?"

He nodded.

"And nothing in the world could ever change that. We will always love you."

Declan nodded again. Confused, but certain his father was about to fix everything.

His father continued. "Well, remember today we went and saw the man?"

"The one with the funny bandages?"

"Yes," he said. "And do you remember the spec-tromonoscope?"

"What's a specomoonscope?" Declan asked.

His father smiled. "The big silver thing."

"Oh." Declan looked at his arm. "The one that made my ouchie?"

"Yes, that's the one. But it was a little ouchie, wasn't it?"

Declan grinned at his bandage. He loved dinosaurs.

"Well," his father went on. "They did that to see... to see if... if you could do what we can do. With the colorful lights and moving toys."

Declan looked up at his father. The corners of his eyes glistened, but his smile remained.

"You mean if I can do the magic?" Declan asked.

"Yes," his father replied. "But the test said... It said..." he breathed out a long breath. "Well, that you won't be able to do magic." He paused, watching Declan's face intently. "But we love you Declan. Your mother and I love you more than anything in the universe. We might not always like what you do—"

"Like when I poured the milk on the floor?"

His father laughed. A sad laugh. "Yes, like when you pour milk on the floor. But no matter what you do or what you are, we will always, always, *always* love you."

Declan nodded slowly, still confused. Of course he couldn't do the magic- *that's what mumma and daddy are for.*

His father hugged him. Declan felt air being squeezed out of his little chest. "Can I play with my dinosaurs?"

But his father didn't let him go. The hug became tighter and tighter until Declan could barely breathe.

"Daddy, stop. It hurts."

His father didn't respond. The squeezing sensation grew even tighter.

"Dad! Stop!"

Intense pain woke him. Declan gasped for air, disoriented and sore. So sore. He was still in his room, but it wasn't the same. The baby blue walls and dragon toys were gone. Broken glass lay scattered around him. Thin cuts covered him from head to toe. Blood soaked his clothes. He tried to push himself up, but crumpled like a sheet of paper. Everything hurt. Declan dragged himself through the glass up onto the bed. Red and blue flashes alternated through the window.

Reality flooded back- the disaster of Offers Day, Horace finding out, Lyle catching him off guard, stumbling home to find a hole in his house and his parents... gone. Declan squeezed his eyes shut, wishing it was a bad dream. His parents' expressions—cast in iron—scarred his memory. They were gone. Taken by men in black coats. *I have to find them.*

"Is anybody there?" a voice called from below. Declan wheezed an inaudible reply. His lungs burned, his attempts at calling for help were faint whimpers. A blinding beam of light landed on Declan. A man in uniform lowered his flashlight and stepped back into the hall. "There's someone in here!" he called. "He's in bad shape. Bring up medical."

Declan urgently wanted to tell the policeman to go, to

find the black van, and save his parents. But he was so weak. It was a fight to remain conscious as a team of four in matching blue overalls lifted him onto a stretcher.

"What happened here?" said one of the medical-team.

"I don't know," said another. "The whole block is a ghost town. What happened here?

An icy breeze washed over him. Declan turned his head. They were downstairs. The hole in the wall looked even worse from the inside. Shattered furniture, books spilled across the floor, broken glass everywhere. It looked as if a tornado had passed through the living room.

"Maybe this one knows," yet another voice said. "I doubt he'll be talking much until we reach the hospital."

Outside, the yard was a mess of cars and lights. Squad cars had torn muddy tracks through the immaculate front lawn. Flashing lights illuminated dozens of police officers. They swarmed the house like an ant nest—taking photos and scribbling in notebooks.

"Ward," Declan croaked. The person leading the medical-team, a man with short brown hair, looked down at him.

"You've been through a lot, champ. Just hang tight. We'll take you to the emergency ward."

Declan shook his head, but the man's attention had shifted. They were loading him into the back of an ambulance when another police car pulled into the drive, siren off, lights flashing purple and green.

Two men climbed out. They wore police uniforms, except unlike the LAMP police in their navy blue, these officers wore maroon.

"Who invited them?" whispered one of the medical-team. The maroon officers spoke to their non-magical counterparts. One of the policemen pointed towards them. The two men strode toward them.

"Magical Law Enforcement Agency," one said. Both flashed golden badges. Both looked cut by the same bureaucratic cookie cutter. "My name is Officer Glenn Shaw, and this is my partner Officer Wilfred. We need this young man for urgent questioning."

The man with the short brown hair scoffed. "Questioning? He's barely alive. If you take him in now, he probably won't survive the trip."

Both officers fixed him with a serious gaze.

Officer Shaw grit his teeth. "Sir, you do not understand the gravity of the situation."

"Look at him," the man replied. "Does he look like he's in any condition to answer questions?"

Officer Shaw looked down at Declan. The journey through a second-story window was not pleasant. Cuts of varying sizes covered every inch of him. His torn clothes were blood-soaked, his ankle twisted at an awkward angle. "We'll take care of him," he said.

"Not in this condition."

"Need I remind you that obstructing an MLEA investigation is a punishable offense?" Officer Wilfred's eyes were daggers.

"And need I remind you," the man returned. "That the Patient's Wellbeing Act trumps your investigative powers."

Officer Shaw bared his teeth. "Are you going to stop me?"

"If you have a problem, take it up with your superior," Officer Wilfred said coldly. "But we are taking him now."

The medical personnel looked at the man with the short brown hair. He glared at the officers, but stepped back. "I guess he's all yours," he said. "I will be writing a detailed report of this exchange, and I will be filing it with your office."

"Sounds great. I'm sure the Commissioner will study it." Wilfred smirked at Shaw. Both officers rotated their hands in unison. The stretcher rose a little higher. The medical-team exchanged concerned looks as the pair led him towards their car.

"Stretcher won't fit in a squad car," Wilfred observed. "How are we getting him in?"

The medical team watched them from across the yard. "Probably in a way that will not set those do-gooders off," Shaw replied. "Just make it look gentle."

They lowered the stretcher onto the grass. Declan groaned under his own gravity. The flashing lights made his eyes ache. "Who are you?" he managed.

"Save your strength, Mr. Moore. We need to get you into this car."

Shaw opened the door; his gaze swept the scene. Amid the sea of red and blue lights, the medical-team hadn't moved. "Too much attention, Wilfred. Care to remedy that?"

"Copy that." Wilfred stepped behind the car where no one could see him. A moment later, Declan's house began to shake.

"It's coming down!" someone shouted. The front door burst open. Chaos erupted as officers cleared the area. The tall, handsome house swayed. Bricks cracked. Wood splintered. Tiles wriggled loose and shattered on the ground. Then the house was gone, replaced by a cloud of dust that got smaller and smaller as the squad car drove away.

Something wet pooled against the faux leather. It was too dark to tell if it was sweat or blood. Whatever it was, it created a slippery surface. With no seatbelt, Declan slid with every turn. Conversation bounced back and forth between the driver and the front-seat passenger. Declan tried to concentrate, to understand what they were saying. He couldn't tell who was who, but with enough concentration, their words made sense.

"So, this is him, huh?"

"That's the kid she's looking for."

"Someone said he applied for King's College."

"Dirty LAMP's applying to Mag-Ed. What next? They'll be asking to join the force."

"No way. Johannasberg would never go for that."

"Johannasberg wouldn't, but he won't be the High Mage forever."

A moment's pause followed, until, "So, if he's a plain old LAMP, why does *she* want him?"

"That's not our job to know."

The finality of his tone cut the conversation short. They drove on in silence. Declan's hazy mind tried to make sense of their words. Who *was she? What did she want with me?* He thought of his parents, now little more than scrap metal. *What have I done?* Tears mixed with blood running down his cheeks.

"Did you see that?"

"See what?"

The passenger seat squeaked as Officer Shaw turned back. "I thought... Looked like something came over the top of the roof..."

"I didn't see anything. Probably a bird or something."

"Yeah, must've been. We're here. Just up ahead. Pull over up there, on the right, before the hydrant."

The car slowed to a stop, and the doors opened. Declan listened intently; his heart drummed in his chest. The officers were speaking to someone, but it was too quiet to understand. Declan tried to shift his weight to look up. Pain shot down his shoulders and back. He grit his teeth and pushed through it until his head was high enough to peek out the window.

Two officers in maroon stood side by side, backs turned. In front of them, a third figure, face hidden from view. Declan tried to assess his options, but thinking didn't work. His head felt packed full of sponges and plugged into a hose. One officer shifted and the third man came into view. He was young, blond, with a black coat. Ward.

The officers turned, and Declan dropped back out of view. A flare of pain erupted at the base of his skull, but he ignored it. He could hear footsteps outside. The door swung open. Declan lurched out and emptied his stomach across the road. The officer holding him took no notice. He clenched his hand; Declan floated like a battered helium balloon towards the edge of an overpass bordered by tall trees.

Ward smiled as he approached. "Well, look who it is. Looks like you've had a rough day."

Declan's insides churned. Ward eyed the officer that held him in place. "Enough of that now. Let him down."

The officer nodded, and Declan descended. Once he reached the ground, it took all of his focus and strength to stay upright; his ruined ankle trembled, ready to give at a moment's notice. At last, Declan found the strength to speak. "Why?"

Ward adjusted the cuffs of his jacket. He looked at the officers and then back at Declan. "Why? Because you lied to me. Because Haberdeen wants you. Because I still haven't forgiven your parents for destroying nine of my brothers. Pick a reason."

Declan's head spun. "What do you mean, I lied? Who is Haberdeen?"

The officers exchanged uncomfortable glances; Ward bared his teeth. "She is Haberdeen. Remember that name, because your insignificant life isn't worthy of hearing it repeated." He paused. "And as for your lie, I don't know how you outfoxed me, but we know the truth. Don't fear, you'll be with your parents soon."

The men in maroon watched with interest as Ward's pale fists moved quickly in an angular pattern that grew and grew until he was using the entire length of his arms to create a rippling silver square. Declan stood rooted to the spot. Not by any magical force, but through the sheer terror of what was happening. Ward rotated palm over palm until the square ascended immediately above Declan's head.

It was at this moment that the squad car inexplicably rolled past them and into a rusted hydrant valve. A pillar of water burst through the cracked pipe and straight into Ward. The surge knocked him aside like a leaf in a river. The shimmering silver square vanished.

A large crack grew, shooting more water into the street. Both MLEA officers dove to escape the torrential bar of liquid. Water shot off the squad car door and high into the air with a deafening roar. It filled the area with a fine spray. Amidst the chaos, someone pulled Declan out of the mist and into the trees.

With a flash and a crack, the water imploded, collapsing in on itself as it was forced back into the pipes. Ward stormed out of the haze, hands a blur. The hydrant burned white, then welded itself closed. The officers gathered themselves from the ground.

"WHERE IS HE?" Ward roared.

The men in maroon said nothing. They busied themselves searching the area directly behind them. Declan looked around groggily. A girl crouched beside him, concentrating on the clearing ahead of them.

"Mage Ward! Listen!" one of the policemen called.

A faint sound of falling branches echoed through the forest opposite them.

"What are you waiting for?" Ward growled. "Follow them!"

The officers dashed into the trees and chased the sounds into the night. Declan watched through the leaves as Ward marched after them. At the edge of the road, he stopped, turned and looked straight in his direction. Declan's heart froze. The world froze. A long moment passed. Ward turned back and followed the officers into the darkness.

CHAPTER 9
DECLAN

DECLAN DIDN'T BREATHE until Ward and the officers were gone.

"Well, that was fun," said a melodic voice to his right.

Declan winced as he turned to the girl who had saved him. She was petite yet athletic, with a mess of short brown curls; her skin was dark and her eyes bright blue.

"Hello there," she said. "Feeling alright?"

A guttural moan was the best he could muster.

The girl rummaged through a tan satchel. "Here, drink this." She offered him a cylindrical vial.

Declan frowned at it. It was small, only as long as his thumb, with pale purple liquid inside.

"There's a release on the side."

Sure enough, on the side of the vial was a small bronze button. He pushed it in and the cap popped open. A sweet smell wafted into the night air. Declan looked at the strange bottle and then back at her. She met his gaze freely.

"If I wanted to hurt you, I wouldn't have bothered saving you."

Declan nodded slowly. Not sure if it made sense because every inch of him hurt.

"Now drink."

Declan downed the vial in one gulp. He shivered when the thick syrup touched his lips. A tingling sensation followed by a gentle heat. It rolled down his tongue, down his throat and the warmth followed- it tasted vaguely of watermelon and washed his aches and pains away.

"Feeling better?" the girl smiled.

Declan flexed his hand. First left, then right. No pain at all. He looked up at her. "What was that?"

"Sanarmelon juice, well, a concentrated version. Potent, isn't it?"

"It's amazing." Declan inspected the backs of his hands; the cuts and bruises were gone. "I feel... well... over-whelmed," he admitted, "but overall... fine." He wiggled his fingers and touched his cheeks. The swelling was gone. As far as he could tell, he was as good as new.

The girl laughed; it sounded like the soft chimes of bells. "Good to hear. I'm Ava, by the way." She extended a hand. "It's a pleasure to meet you."

Declan took it. "I'm Declan—"

"Yes, I know."

She watched him closely. He was unsure of what to say. Without warning, his parents' iron cast faces flashed into his mind. Declan's cheeks burned. Dots of sweat prickled the top of his head. His heart raced. His breathing couldn't keep up. "What-What's happening to me? Who are you? Where are my parents?"

Ava's smile faltered. She scanned the surrounding forest, her eyes glimmered like sapphires in the moonlight. "I'm sure you have lots of questions, Declan, and I'm happy to talk- but not here," she said. "Those smoks are gone, but there's no way of knowing who else could be listening in the dark."

Declan remained on the ground. Somewhere in his mind, he knew this was a panic attack. Physical pain had been the only distraction keeping him above an ocean of despair. Now it was gone. His thoughts spiraled out of control. *My parents are gone. Forever. I'll never see them again. I should've been there. I should have warned them. I should have stopped them. I should've-*

"It wasn't your fault, Declan."

Declan ignored her. Tears rolled down his cheeks. He tried to control his breathing, but it seemed to make things worse.

"Declan, it wasn't—"

"I shouldn't have sent that stupid letter! I should have gone straight home!"

Ava knelt down so that her eyes were level with his. She put a feather-soft hand on his shoulder. "What would you have done?"

"Something!" Declan gasped for air between words. "I. Would've. Helped. I. Could've. Saved. Them."

"No, Declan, you would've gotten yourself killed. Look at what they did to you just for arriving late? Imagine what they would've done had you tried to stand in their way?"

Declan buried his head in his hands. He could see his parents' smiling faces at breakfast, then their frozen iron casts. *I'm sorry. I'm so sorry.* He lay on the ground and the strength ran out of him. He shivered and sobbed in the dirt.

Ava surveyed the area. "Declan. You need to get a handle on yourself. Save the breakdown for later." She nudged his leg with her shoe. "C'mon. We need to get moving."

Declan didn't move.

Ava crouched beside him. "Your parents aren't gone. But we will be if we stay here." She stood up, slung the satchel over her shoulder and extended a hand towards him. "Come with me."

She pulled him up with surprising strength and led him through the trees. Gleaming stars peppered the sky above, insects chirped and whistled all around them. They walked without talking; Declan tried to think of something, anything, to take his mind off the past twelve hours. "Who are you?" he asked at last.

"Who is anyone?" she replied in a whisper. "Can *you* sum yourself up in one sentence? Who are you?" She glanced back at him.

The question caught Declan off guard. They walked in silence for a little while. *Who are you?* He considered it. "I'm the full stop of a famous magical bloodline. Thousands of years of magical power and the sum result is a no-good nothing LAMP. How's that?"

"Well—for starters—that was two sentences." She stopped and grinned. "But a decent attempt. I suppose it's only fair I try." She fell silent; Declan followed, content to leave her to think. Dead leaves crunched beneath their feet until they reached the edge of a hill. The lights of Tamhill shone below them. Ava turned to him. "I'm the only hope for a family driven mad by a misplaced sense of responsibility." She glanced down the slope. "You ready?"

Declan opened his mouth, but Ava leaped off the hill; half jogging, half sliding down the leafy descent. Declan followed at a much slower pace. When he reached the bottom, Ava was already waiting at a bus stop. Declan joined her. "What's a smok?"

"Sorry?"

"You said it before, about Ward and the MLEA. You called them smok."

Ava smirked. "Slip of the tongue, pardon my language."

A pair of headlights appeared around the bend and Ava hailed the bus. She looked back at Declan and her eyes lit up. She stooped past him to pick something off the ground. "Finders keepers," she said, holding a crumpled five-dollar note.

The bus doors swung open, and they climbed aboard. A heavy-set woman with tight black hair perched in the driver's seat. "Where're ya headin' loves?"

"Two for Main Street, thank you," Ava said.

The woman punched in some numbers and two slips of paper printed out.

"That'll be five dollars."

Ava grinned at Declan and handed the bus driver the crumpled bill. She took both tickets and led him to two seats towards the back. The vehicle jostled to life and the bus stop disappeared into the darkness. "So, a family driven mad..." he let the words hang. Ava hit him with a sharp glance. Declan took the hint. "Okay, next subject, how did you find me?"

Ava looked toward the front where the driver spoke loudly into a headset. There was nobody else on the bus. She sighed. "My employer knew of your application. Finding your home address was easy enough, but by the time I got there, they were bringing you out on a stretcher. I waited down the road and hitched a ride on the MLEA cruiser."

Declan raised an eyebrow. "You... hitched a ride?"

Ava batted her eyelashes. "What? You've never surfed on a car before?"

"You say that like it's completely normal." Declan

considered her words. "What do you mean by my application? I saw the response. King's College rejected me."

Ava's eyebrows climbed into her curls. "You don't know?"

"Don't know what?"

Ava extracted a crumpled sheet from her satchel.

Declan saw the bold red writing and recognized his application response. "How did you get that?"

"Do you always leave your backpack strewn across the grass outside your house?"

The bus shuddered to a halt. "Main Street," the bus driver called. "Your stop, loves."

Ava shoved the paper back into her bag. "C'mon, I'll show you inside."

Central Tamhill. It was the same stop from his run-in with Lyle earlier. Declan shuddered at the sight of the alleyway. "Where are you taking me?"

Ava spun around. "I'm not taking you anywhere. We're going together, because I saved your butt and you want to talk." She paused and waited for a response. When none came, she smiled. "Now c'mon, let's go get a hot chocolate and I'll tell you a story," she patted her satchel and the letter inside. Declan frowned, then followed.

A thought popped into his head as he hurried to catch up. *What is so special about being rejected?*

———————

The bright neon lights of Bluebell's Pizzeria cast soft shadows down the street. Ava continued past it without a second glance, up the footpath until they came to a narrow street alive with small coffee houses. Partway down, she stopped at a brown brick building. Declan frowned at the vinyl sticker on the glass storefront. "The Coffeetorium?"

"Best place in town for a late-night pick-me-up, and the only one in town that sells scratch-n-win tickets."

Declan didn't understand why that mattered. "I'm not much of a coffee drinker."

Ava winked. "Me neither."

A bell chimed as they entered. The clock behind the empty counter showed it was just past midnight. A handful of people, none within a generation of them, waited in a loose line. Their dark jumpsuits identified the customers as citysweeps—LAMPs responsible for keeping the streets spotless while everyone else slept. Mustard yellow booths filled the space. Eclectic paintings of colorful mugs decorated the brick walls.

The bell on the door announced a new arrival. Declan turned as an older woman queued behind them. Her silver hair was fixed in an elaborate braid over her shoulder. Declan smiled. She smiled right back.

A middle-aged man worked the counter without enthusiasm. "What would you like tonight?"

"Two hot chocolates, please," Ava said.

The man punched the register. "That'll be eleven dollars."

Ava turned to Declan expectantly. Declan raised both eyebrows. "I don't have any money."

The man frowned. "Eleven dollars."

"Ooh, look at this." Ava disappeared below the counter. She emerged triumphantly with a dollar in her hand.

"And the other ten?" the man behind the counter said.

"I changed my mind. One scratch-n-win, please."

The cashier rolled his eyes and ripped a ticket from a

roll behind the counter. Ava handed over the dollar and started scratching.

"Next please," the man said.

"Hold on," Ava interrupted, she thrust the ticket towards him. "I'll take those two hot chocolates after all."

Declan and the cashier looked down at the same time. The ticket was a winner. Eleven dollars exactly. *Impossible*, Declan thought.

"Your lucky day," the man said flatly. He accepted the ticket and rung it up. "Here's your number."

Ava accepted the plastic '7' on a stand, then led Declan to a booth in front of the lone bathroom door at the back. When seated, Declan fixed her with a knowing stare. "How did you do that?"

"Do what?"

"Find that dollar, win that money..." Declan thought back. "You did it at the bus stop as well."

Ava didn't reply. The woman with the silver braid took a booth two rows behind them. She opened up a magazine and read in silence. After a long moment, Ava shrugged. "I got lucky, I guess."

"*Lucky* would be doing it once... You found the perfect amount of money on the ground for us to ride the bus. Now you've won a scratch-offs for our hot chocolates," Declan thought back further. "And those branches falling leading those—"

"Shhhh." Ava's eyes were on the woman behind him.

He dropped his voice to a whisper. "Leading those officers away, that was you too!" He glanced back. The woman continued to read her magazine, but now her fingers moved in a distinct pattern, tapping on her palm. He recognized it immediately. "She's using Looptap," he murmured.

"Stop looking back," Ava said in a low voice.

Declan straightened; the hair stood on the back of his neck. He did not know who the woman was communicating with, but after everything that had happened today, he had no desire to wait and find out. Ava remained silent until their hot chocolates arrived. They tasted exactly how Declan expected they would. Cheap. "Eleven dollars is overpriced," he muttered. "I thought you said this place was good?"

Ava smirked. "Good for avoiding unwanted attention."

"Is it though?" Declan longed to turn back, but feared it would be too obvious. He settled for rolling his eyes in the woman's direction.

"You're being paranoid," Ava whispered, though she appeared unconvinced. They sipped in silence until the woman stood up and left. Once she was gone, Ava fixed him with a stern look. "You're right."

"Excuse me?"

"The branches, the bus, the scratchy. That was all me. How do *you* think I did it?"

Declan bit his lip. "You're a witch, right?"

"Nope."

"Then..." Declan didn't want to sound foolish, but it was the only other explanation. "You're a Luck."

Her eyes narrowed. "And if I am?"

The severity of her tone caught him off-guard. "That would mean... Lucks are real." He frowned. "I'd heard stories, but you can't trust stories? Can you? I mean, you can trust some." Declan was speaking too fast. He tried to slow down. "What's it like? To be able to make anything happen?"

"Ease up on the questions." Her smile softened the atmosphere. "It's not quite like that. I can only control the likelihood of actual events. If it *can* happen, I can make it so.

73

Someone *had* lost a dollar in this café. That's why I could find it, but I can't magically create money."

"So, you can't conjure stuff out of thin air?"

"Nope. I can only work with what's around me. Tip the scales of probability- the less likely something is, the harder it is to make it happen."

Declan frowned. "Harder how?"

Ava sipped her hot chocolate. "Finding money is pretty easy. People lose money everywhere. Causing a freak mechanical fault to loosen a handbrake, then have a car miraculously crash into a high-pressure pipe? Well, that was pretty exhausting."

Declan's mouth fell open. "That was you?"

Ava nodded.

"Awesome." He dropped his voice. "Who are they? The man in the black coat, who is that?"

Ava took another sip from her mug. "He's a blackcoat."

"A what?"

"Well, I call them blackcoats, others say ironpalms. If you ask them, they'll call themselves Fatesmiths."

"Fatesmiths?" Declan frowned. "Sounds like a bad rock band."

Ava giggled and shook her head. "Like a blacksmith, but instead of shaping metal, they believe they're shaping the fate of the world. They showed up in Euryma earlier this year, a bunch of teenagers at first, but now adults are joining the fray too. They're anti-magic."

"Anti-magic? I've never heard of it."

"*Anti-magic* isn't a thing, it's an attitude, they just don't like it. Have you ever heard of Remnant Magic?"

The term was familiar. Declan thought back to Magical Theory lessons at Arman Moore's and nodded. "Yeah... Something about a theory that magic leaves traces, right?

When those traces build up, they create Remnant Magic-poltergeists that knock books from shelves or flicker lights."

"Exactly. Blackcoats believe that Remnant Magic does much more than that. They're convinced it's accruing in huge amounts and wiping places off the map. In their minds, the witches and wizards of Euryma have been using too much magic for too long. They must be fierised to protect the rest of the world."

"Fierised?" Declan asked.

"Encased in iron."

"Iron?" Declan frowned. "But iron is a magical insulator. The LAMPolice line their uniforms with it. How are the blackcoats doing magic that uses iron?"

Ava swallowed the last of her hot chocolate. "That's what's making them so hard to combat."

A glimmer of hope sparked in Declan's mind. "Encased in iron? You mean... those people turned to iron aren't dead? Just trapped?"

Ava nodded. "Trapped in stasis, perfectly safe."

"My parents are alive?"

"They are."

The spark burned brighter. "How do you know all this?"

Ava shrugged. "It's my business to know these things."

"So, what do they want with me? I'm not magical."

Ava dropped her satchel on the table, reached in and handed him the crumpled sheet of paper, the word 'REJECTED' clearly visible. "I think it's about time you read this a little more carefully." Her bright blue eyes twinkled.

Declan unfolded the letter; suddenly aware his hands were trembling. "Dear Master Moore," he read in a whisper. "Based on your application submission and magical potential, we are afraid we must reject your request to attend King's College." He looked up at Ava. She gestured for him to continue. "King's College is a prestigious school of excellence. Ordinarily, we make a point of accepting only the most powerful witches and wizards. In your case, we believe your magical potential is far too potent to be safely controlled. It is for this reason that we must regretfully decline your application to attend King's College."

Declan paused. His head felt light, like it was filling with hot air. He reread the last sentence. It didn't make sense. He tried again, slowly this time; *we believe your magical potential is far too potent to be safely controlled.* "What... what does this mean?"

Ava opened her mouth when the door snapped against the window like a mousetrap. Her eyes widened.

The woman with the gray braid stood at the entrance, six men behind her, each wearing a black coat embroidered with an anvil and hammer. One of the blackcoats leaned close and whispered something to the woman; she nodded and pointed directly at Declan.

CHAPTER 10
DECLAN

THE BLACKCOATS MOVED INTO ACTION. They pushed past the woman to surround them, their hands a blur of motion. Loud cracks exploded from the ceiling, light fixtures shattered on the floor, a waitress tripped on a chair leg and hurled a wave of coffee in their direction. Ava pulled Declan through the chaos to the back of the room.

"Don't let them get away!"

Footsteps thundered behind. Declan and Ava dived into the bathroom. The door swung shut, and the lock clicked closed. A heavy set of beams fell from the ceiling, barricading the entry. Loud bangs echoed from the other side. "Are you doing that?" Declan asked through the dust.

Ava ignored him. "Look here," she said. Decades of leaking water had pooled in the room's corner, leaving the pine floor swollen and weak. Ava kicked at the boards; bit by bit, they broke away.

The assault on the bathroom door paused, then an ear-shattering crash rocked the room. The wall crumbled like pastry. Fragments of drywall created a fine haze in the air. Three silhouettes climbed through the rubble. Their hands waved wildly and Declan's whole body grew heavy. Gravity seemed to go into overdrive, dragging the dust down and clearing the air. The extra weight pulled Ava's leg down with such force that the corner of the bathroom collapsed. Shouts of confusion followed as they disappeared from sight.

"This way!" Ava shouted. They crawled through foul smelling slime and came out onto the main street.

Ava sat on the footpath, rummaging through her satchel while Declan brushed the mud from his hands. Blackcoats piled into the alley behind them. "We've gotta go!" he said urgently.

"Just wait!" Ava pulled a vial from her bag, popped the cap and threw it back. Declan watched in amazement as her leg twisted itself back into place. "Apparently busting floors is bad for your knee." She reached out and Declan pulled her up.

The blackcoats spotted them as a passing car lost control. It mounted the curb right where they stood. Most of them were fast enough to take cover, but one was not so lucky. He screamed, pressed between the car and storefront. Ava and Declan raced down the road while the blackcoats climbed over the vehicle. Tires squealed. People shouted. A line of fire hydrants burst like cannons, their powerful columns of water shrouding the street in mist. Declan wanted to run faster, but he couldn't. Ava was slowing down.

Flashing purple and green lights appeared ahead. The Magical Law Enforcement Agency. Declan wasn't sure if the officers from earlier were turncoats, or if the agency itself was compromised. He didn't want to find out. "Quick, down here!" He grabbed Ava's arm and pulled her into a narrow walkway. She followed willingly and collapsed onto a concrete staircase. The air stunk of rotten fruit, but she didn't complain. Four sets of purple and green lights screamed at the entrance. Declan sat beside her. "That was fantastic."

Ava offered him a tired smile; she leaned her head back against the brick wall.

Declan's sweat-soaked curls dangled in his eyes. He wiped them aside with his forearm. "You need some more of your sonarmelon juice."

She chuckled. "Sanarmelon, not sonar. I'm afraid that was the last of it."

Declan looked her up and down. "You're exhausted. Do you know anyone who can help?"

Ava shook her head. "Not on short notice."

Declan looked down the walkway. "I could call my friend Ace. Do you have a phone?"

Ava raised an eyebrow. "Declan. You're wrapped up in something big right now. If you call your friends, you'll drag him into the same mess."

"He might be our only hope. You can hardly walk and I'm as useful as a bag of rice."

"Rice has plenty of uses," Ava said quietly, the corner of her lips twitched.

"Quit joking around." Frustration sharpened Declan's voice. "Ace is strong. I saw him do some stuff today. He can help."

"I'm not saying he can't help. I'm saying, if the black-coats see him, if they find out his name or who he is, his chance of living an ordinary life is gone. Are you willing to do that to a friend?"

Declan thought about the King's College application. He shook his head. *You've done enough damage to Ace's future today.* "No, I can't do that to him."

Two silhouettes appeared at the walkway's entrance. Ava froze. Declan followed suit. The figures lingered for somewhere between a minute and an hour, then moved on. A long moment later, Ava exhaled a long breath. "Give me a couple of minutes to catch my—"

A dreadful screech of steel on brick interrupted her. It echoed down from the opposite end of the walkway. A long minute passed; Declan waited for blackcoats to appear either side of them, but they never did. "So, what now?" he whispered.

Ava's eyes went wide. A rippling metallic square surged towards them. She leapt into Declan's chest and knocked him backwards. The square dissolved into oblivion. Declan staggered upright; two silhouettes stormed down from the walkway's entrance. Fifty feet and closing. "We need to go," he said.

"I can't." A note of panic rang in Ava's voice. "My leg."

Declan gasped. Ava's leg, previously smooth and dark, now shone in the moonlight. A hard, cold bar of iron. He grabbed her arms and pulled her up.

"Can you walk?"

Ava tried to take a step and stumbled. Footsteps echoed off the alley walls. "And my Luck, it's gone. The iron, it's blocking it off."

A surge of adrenaline filled Declan with unexpected strength. "C'mon, here." He bent down and slung her over his shoulders.

"Declan."

"Shhh!" Declan turned and carried her deeper into the alley.

"They're on the move," someone called behind them. Declan ran faster. The darkness swallowed them up. He dashed around a bend and saw streetlights ahead. A large metal dumpster blocked most of the path. Declan squeezed past it, then paused.

"What are you doing?" Ava said. "We need to keep going."

"They're after me, not you." Declan held her eyes. "You saved me before. I'm just returning the favor."

"Declan!"

He opened the lid of the dumpster and eased her in. Declan ignored her cries of protest. "Just stay quiet. I'll come back for you." He dropped the lid and sprinted towards the exit. Two men appeared as he came into the street- more blackcoats waiting for him. Declan threw himself at the nearest one, knocking him backwards, and shot across the road like a cracking whip. He ducked between trees and parked cars. Shouts followed him, shouts and bursts of magical projectiles that burned like flares. Declan kept low and didn't stop. He rounded corners, doubled back unpredictably, ducked through walkways and alleys until he was sure he was alone.

Exhausted, he climbed a fire-escape ladder to an empty roof. There, hidden behind an empty billboard, he lay down to catch his breath. The adrenaline dissolved. A full-moon sailed over thin clouds, goose pimples formed on his arms and legs. *I'll just have a quick break, then go back for Ava.*

Five minutes later, he was asleep.

CHAPTER II
AVA

FALLING free of Declan's arms, Ava braced herself for a rough landing that never came. Instead, there was a blinding flash of orange light and she landed with a splash in a pool of freezing water.

The shock of it wrenched the air out of her. Gasping, she reached out for something, anything, as her iron leg dragged her down. Ava kicked frantically with her good leg, but the weight was too much. She hit the bottom with a stifled thud.

Panic set in. Ava searched the murky water for possibilities she could sway with her Luck. But there were none. Her Luck was gone.

Ava's lungs burned. She mustered the last of her strength and pushed. She rose less than a foot off the ground before being dragged back down. Her body screamed for oxygen. Her vision shrank to a small tunnel. *This is how I die.* The clarity of the thought was unsettling. *After how far I've traveled, how much I've sacrificed, I'm going to drown in a dumpster with a metal leg.* A muffled roar grew around her, like the ocean itself was being sucked down a giant plughole.

———

"This is it?"

Ava's eyes snapped open. She lay on a hard floor, sprawled out in a shallow puddle like a wet cat. Two men spoke behind her. Neither realized she had regained consciousness.

"She's the only one who came through."

"And the boy?"

"It was only her."

The air seemed tense. As far as Ava could tell, she was in a small room, barely larger than a cellar. A man was pacing; his footsteps echoed in the space.

"Have you heard from Mage Ward?"

"He's on his way. He expected the boy."

"But the boy isn't here. What's so special about him, anyway?" The man's voice rose and fell as he walked back and forth.

"I don't have the foggiest. But the things they were offering for his capture... This was my chance, my shot at making a name for myself. I was *sure* they would hide in that bin. It was perfect."

A loud clang above silenced the conversation. A grind of steel on steel and light poured into the room. Ava was right. It was a concrete box—the size of a wine cellar. A ladder slid into place and a blond boy climbed down. Ava recognized him from the overpass- she'd blasted him with water. She closed her eyes as he stepped onto the stone floor.

"Report." The boy's voice has a nasal quality; still, it carried authority.

"The trap worked, Mage Ward, but not as expected. The boy escaped, but we have captured his accomplice."

Ava kept her eyes closed as they approached. With no warning, Ward dragged her upright. Ava's fierised leg burned as if the blood had pooled around it. Each jolting movement was fire. She forced herself calm and did her best to fake a slow return to reality. She looked at the pair of blackcoats by the ladder. One was bald with a goatee and the other graying on the sides. The only exit was through the hole in the ceiling or the large rectangular drains in the floor. "Where... Where am I?"

"Where is the boy?" Ward asked.

Ava's mind raced as she searched for an escape. *The drains probably just lead into more water.* She glanced at the ceiling. *The hole in the roof is too far up.* Ward stared daggers at her and Ava realized her only move was to play the compliant prisoner. "The boy... The one with the curly hair?"

Ward nodded. "The very same. Where is he?"

Ava pursed her lips. "I don't know, but I can help you find him. For the right price."

Ward raised an eyebrow. "A price? Girl, you are in no position to bargain."

Ava shrugged. "The boy has my bag. I was chasing him when your goons," she spared a glance for the men behind them, "fierised my leg. I had to crawl into a dumpster to escape." She gauged Ward as she spoke; his expression was unreadable. "I have imbued items in my bag. Items tuned to me. I can sense them a mile away. Take me to Tamhill and I'll be able to walk you straight to him."

Ward nodded slowly. "And what's in it for you?"

"I can't track my bag with an iron leg. You'll need to undo this spell."

Ward shook his head. "No. That won't do."

"You want the boy, don't you?" Ava said. "Why not?"

Ward's lips pressed together in a thin, joyless smile. "Because I'm not about to free the Luck that has spent the past three weeks getting in my way." Ava felt the blood drain from her face. *He knows.* Ward's eyes narrowed. "Did you really think it would be that easy?"

Ava tried to think of another lie, but she was stuck. "What do you want with him?"

"The same thing you do."

Ward let her go and she dropped to her knees. Ava barely had time to look up before Ward's foot caught her face. Blood filled her mouth.

"Do not test me," Ward said. "Where is he?"

Ava spat blood on the concrete; it swirled in the shallow puddles, blooming like a scarlet flower. "Go die in a pit."

Ward's boot caught her in the stomach. It knocked her onto her back. Ward stepped forward, stomped and kicked her, pausing only to ask the same question. Ava ignored him. Retreated deep into her consciousness and waited for the beating to stop.

When it did, the pain was extraordinary, like being crushed in a rockfall. Ward spoke to the blackcoats, but the ringing in Ava's ears was deafening. She concentrated on their lips long enough to pick out the end of the conversation.

"Why not fierise her?"

"Oh, I will. When she's no longer of use."

CHAPTER 12
DECLAN

A soft cooing sound woke Declan up. The air smelled fresh; dawn's dim fingers spread over the rooftops of inner Tamhill. He rolled to his side and the curious pigeon hopped back. It cocked its head to the side, ruffled its feathers, and took flight. Declan forced himself to sit up. A sheet of mist draped over the streets; a lone citysweep swept the footpath below.

Dawn fog-soaked Declan's torn school uniform. He shivered and drew his knees against his chest. As he did, his foot touched Ava's satchel, which lay open on the ground. In a landslide of memory, the previous night returned to him. His stomach sank. Declan had no idea where Ava was, just that he had dropped her in a metal bin in a dark alley. Which metal bin in which dark alley, he did not know.

Declan picked up Ava's bag, hoping to find something that might help. Instead, he found a pile of curious belongings. Some familiar- a length of endless rope, a box of dormant fireflies and a handful of empty sanarmelon vials. Others he had never seen before- a ruby ball covered in metal studs, a long spike that looked like an icicle but was warm to the touch, and a jade coin bearing a beaked dragon on one side and a bearded man on the other. Finally, he found something that might help, a phone with a flip-top case.

He flicked it open and a yellow screen blinked to life. Declan dialed his father's number, then stopped. An image of his iron parents pushed to the forefront of his mind. Declan suddenly felt sick. He took a deep breath, another. *They're gone. They can't help you. You must help them.* Declan chewed on his lower lip and tried Ace's home number. Ava's voice spoke abruptly in his head. *Are you willing to do that to a friend?*

Declan stopped again. *This is different now.* He told himself. *The Fatesmiths are gone, the MLEA too. Ace will just be helping me search for Ava.* He finished dialing. The phone rang. Nobody answered. He tried again. Still nothing. The sun climbed the horizon. Ace would be awake. He *was* the early bird. Declan tried once more. This time, a groggy voice answered.

"Who's this?"

"Ace! It's Declan."

"Dex... Why on earth are you calling me at five thirty-six?"

"Listen, my house..." he cut off. *The less he knows, the better.* "My parents found out about my application for King's College. They booted me out. Told me to come back when I'd grown some sense."

"What?" Ace said. "Your parents kicked you out?"

"I'm stranded in the middle of town with no money. Can you come get me?"

"That's not like your parents."

"Can you come get me? Please? I have nobody else to call."

After a long moment, Ace sighed. "Where are you?"

"Main Street bus stop."

"Okay, I'll be there within the hour."

He hung up before Declan could say thanks. Declan slid the phone back into Ava's satchel. He was atop the theater, which meant Main Street was a ten-minute walk east. He descended the fire-escape into the parking lot behind the building. A stray cat looked up from a bin, then returned to its breakfast. Declan tried to retrace his steps from the previous night and failed. It was a messy jumble of fear and adrenaline.

The fog began lifting beneath the morning sun. Declan's shirt and shorts were wet and cold. *I should've asked Ace to grab me some dry clothes.* The morning air was light, the exact opposite of a brick wall, which was how Declan's head felt now that he was moving. Too much had happened in too little time. The rejection letter proved the most confusing- *too strong to be safely controlled. What does that mean? Have my parents lied to me for eleven years?* The questions built up, stacking like stones, each one perched more precarious than the last. He needed some dry clothes and a rest. And Ava- he needed Ava. She was the only person he knew with answers. Declan fought a pang of guilt for dropping her in that dumpster. *It was the only way. I couldn't have kept running with her. They would've caught us both.*

Tamhill Central was busy. Morning buses stopped every four minutes, witches and wizards climbed off in fine suits with shining shoes and manicured nails. Hands controlled magic, so witches and wizards went to great lengths to keep them in immaculate condition. When the bus emptied, citysweeps climbed on—their gray overalls were filthy from the night's work.

Cautious to stay out of sight, Declan slunk into an alleyway to wait. It was the same alley Lyle had pinned him against the wall. That moment seemed like a different lifetime. A bird's nest of dark hair climbed off the bus.

"Ace, over here!" Declan called.

Ace had clearly jumped straight out of bed; he carried a plastic bag and an air of concern. His eyes swept the spot where he had frozen Lyle and her cronies to the ground. Not a trace of the incident remained—the citysweeps had seen to that. "Funny seeing you here," he said. "You look dreadful. What happened?"

Declan shrugged, Ava's warnings in his head. "Just a rough night."

"I can't believe your parents would kick you out."

"Me neither." A red rash of guilt crept up his neck. "They told me I'd disgraced the family name. Dad was so angry. They've probably cooled off now... But I can't face them." Declan felt awful lying about his parents, his loving parents encased in iron.

Ace nodded. "I'm sorry, Dex. That sounds more like something my parents would do than yours. Are you okay?"

"Yeah." Declan struggled to keep the lie afloat. "I thought I'd lie low for the day. Can you make an excuse for me at school?"

"I would. But it's Saturday." Horace raised an eyebrow. "Are you sure you're alright?"

Declan nodded quickly. "Yeah, I'm fine, just tired. Rough night. That's all."

"I thought as much." Horace tossed him the plastic bag. "I thought you might need them."

Declan looked inside to find dry clothes. "Ah, Ace. You read my mind."

Horace nodded. "You could always stay at my place."

Declan stripped off his shirt and pulled the new one over his head. "After everything that happened yesterday, I didn't think I could. I shouldn't have applied. I'm sorry." He pulled the shirt down and caught sight of two figures ahead of them. His stomach plummeted. Horace followed his gaze. "Who are they?"

Two blackcoats walked towards them, eyes fixed on Declan. "Not good," Declan said. There was nothing else he could say; he turned to run. Two more blackcoats approached from behind. "Uh, Ace, we need to go." Declan backed further into the dead-end alley.

Three men and a woman surrounded them. The woman jabbed a long fingernail at Horace. "We don't need you. Go. Speak to nobody."

"Not a bad idea, Ace," Declan whispered.

"What is this?" Horace asked.

One man spat on the ground. "Doesn't concern you. You heard Jelika. Get lost."

Horace looked from the blackcoats to Declan. "You really need to stay out of this alley," he said.

He whipped his hands up and down in one fluid blow. The ground rippled like water and became a surging wave of concrete. The blackcoats spun their own hands in intricate circles, new waves emerged. Concrete collided and burst into the air. Pillars of stone sprouted from beneath them. Declan stepped back as a crude prison jolted up around them. Ace spun around, arms outstretched, and the pillars snapped like twigs. Ace caught them in the air and sent them flying at one of the blackcoats. The wizard's movements were too slow. The stone caught his chest and threw him backwards, out of the alley, into traffic. A horn belted as a car swerved to miss him.

The three remaining Fatesmiths advanced on Ace,

hands moving in unison to create a miniature tornado. It whipped stone from the ground into a spinning sandpaper vortex. Ace needed both hands to hold it back. The black-coats doubled their efforts as the tornado inched closer. Ace strained, then let go.

He sidestepped the maelstrom, captured it himself, and threw it like a slingshot into the three figures. The woman dove out of harm's way, but it caught the two men in its depths. Their cries of pain echoed off the walls. The woman staggered upright into a surge of white mist. It was the same spell Ace had used on Lyle. It lifted her high against the building and pinned her against the wall. Ace completed the intricate weave. It solidified and left her trapped in a cocoon of ice.

Ace spun in readiness as a battered blackcoat stumbled to his feet—a patchwork of bruises marred his face. He backed away, then ran out of the alley. Ace lowered his hands. Declan knelt by the man on the ground. The tornado had shredded his coat and left him covered in cuts. He was breathing, but badly injured.

"Sheesh Ace. I knew you were good, but those were adults."

Ace looked up from the ice on the wall. His face darkened. "Who are they?"

"It's probably best you don't know," Declan said, but he knew they were past that.

"Considering what just happened, I'd like to know."

Declan sighed. "Let's get out of this alley first. There could be more on the way."

Ace nodded, they left quickly. Curious glances followed them, but only glances, nothing more. Magical duels, while rare, were not unheard of. Citysweeps would repair any damage done overnight. They crossed the street, and Ace frowned at Declan. "What is going on?"

They walked in silence. Declan tried to think of where to begin.

"Dex?"

"It's complicated." *Damn right it is, and if I tell him now, that's it.*

"That's not good enough," Ace replied.

Declan sighed and stepped into a narrow gap between storefronts. Ace stopped too, but remained in plain sight.

"Listen. You could walk away right now." Declan paused. Ace said something in reply, but he didn't hear it. Behind him, down the road, a bulky garbage truck was emptying a dumpster into its depths. Hydraulic forks held the bin high in the air. *Oh no.*

"Declan?" Ace said. "Are you even listening?"

The truck backed into the street and lumbered forward. It reversed into a gap between buildings and gathered another dumpster in its clutches. The contents fell out with a crash. "Ava," Declan whispered.

"What? Ava? Who is Ava?"

Declan walked towards the truck. It lumbered slowly away from them.

"Who is Ava?" Ace said, louder.

The dumpster was in a narrow path. A walkway.

"Declan?"

It went straight through a block, around a bend.

"DECLAN!" Horace's eyes were wide, his hands clenched tight. He looked angry. He sounded angry.

"Ace, I promise I'll explain when I can. Right now, I have a friend with a busted leg hiding in a dumpster." He pointed at the truck down the road. "I need to find her before *that* does. Once that's done, I'll tell you everything."

Ace looked at the truck. Another steel bin held high above its tray. He turned back to Declan, face tight. "Okay, Dex, but I swear... If you lie to me again, I'll let them take you away."

Declan nodded absently. *Take you away...* Horace's words had sparked a memory. *Take-away. Yes! The take-away shop near the bank. The walkway down from there.* He smiled at Horace. "Follow me."

A painful cramp forced Declan to slow to a brisk walk. Ace stamped behind like a frustrated toddler. *Can't blame him,* Declan thought.

The large and stately First Bank of Euryma came into view. Beside it was a take-away shop with dirty tables and dirtier windows. A narrow walkway divided the buildings. "Down here," Declan said. He turned to Ace; his heart skipped a beat.

The gray-haired woman from the Coffeetorium stood at a newspaper booth outside the bank. It seemed she had not noticed them. Declan rushed into the alley and gestured for Ace to do the same. A large silver dumpster waited ahead.

"Odd place for a bin." Ace turned to look back. "How would a truck even get in here?"

It *was* a tight fit. Even on its side, the dumpster left little room to squeeze by. Declan approached it. His hands trembled. He took a deep breath, then opened the lid.

Empty.

Disappointment ballooned in his chest. "She's gone."

Ace looked back towards the alley entrance. He knelt down, studied the brick carefully, brushing his fingertips across their smooth surface. Declan leaned against the wall and slid to the ground. *She saved me. Protected me. I repaid her by throwing her in a bin, to be dumped in a truck.*

"Something's not right." Ace gestured toward the street. "No truck is fitting in here, and that bin is *heavy*. If it was being dragged to the road and back, it should leave a mark." He frowned. "Plus, there's the entire issue of why it's even here. Who puts a dumpster in the middle of a walkway?"

Declan stooped to pick up a metal bottle cap and tossed it in the bin. It dropped straight through the dumpster's metal base with a flash of orange light. Hot embarrassment crept up his neck. "It was a trap."

"Some kind of portal?" Ace crouched to inspect the bottom of the dumpster.

Declan joined him. It looked entirely normal, right down to the symmetrical welded swirls on the bin's base. A sickening sense of guilt replaced his disappointment. "Where do you think it goes?" he asked.

"That's none of your concern," a familiar voice said behind. "Though I am pleased that you were stupid enough to return."

Ward stood in the center of the walkway. His black military coat neatly pressed, silver buttons shining like a razor's edge. His lips curved in a humorless smile.

"Dex?" Ace asked.

"He's the one who started it all." Declan gulped. "I wasn't kicked out of home. My parents were taken—by him."

Ward watched them the way a bird would a fat, juicy caterpillar.

Ace raised his arms in a cross, then brought them down. A layer of air compressed in front of them. With a mighty push it surged forwards, shredding the edges off the bricks either side of the passage. Ward drew a large circular portal with one arm, the other he raised high, his fingers dancing. Red bricks lifted from the path below. Ace's wall of wind swirled around Ward's portal like water down a drain; tiny shards of stone circled around into nothingness. The moment it cleared, Ward lobbed a pillar of brick into the air. The bricks reconfigured into an open-faced cube, a prison arcing towards them.

Declan rushed to slide by the dumpster. Ward stretched his hand. The metal box expanded and blocked the walkway. Ace worked furiously, hands a blur as he pulled jagged slots of stone from the wall of the bank into a makeshift shield above them. An almighty crack rang down the alley as brick met stone, pulverizing both to dust. Ace rolled one hand over the other. The dust formed a solid sphere of brick and rock that rolled in Ward's direction. It grew in size as more particles rushed into its center.

Ward waited until the last moment and, with two upturned hands, raised the ground. The massive ball rolled up the crude ramp, stopped, then rolled back. Ace hurried to unravel the boulder; dust swept behind it like the tail of a comet. Declan could see beads of sweat forming along his hairline. Ward looked untroubled.

"He's too strong! We've got to go!" Declan shouted. A wind picked up, a powerful gust screamed through the alley and swept them to their feet. Declan struggled to breathe as dust clouded the alley. Ace whirled his arms in a wild frenzy; the haze solidified into four solid beams.

Ward clapped slowly. He looked completely at ease. "You've got talent, I'll give you that."

"You have no idea," Ace growled. In one sweeping motion, he conjured a thick mist that burst forward. With an elaborate flourish, Ward snatched the mist from the air, collected it into a translucent globule, and threw it straight back. The orb of mist caught Ace's chest and carried him back into the enlarged dumpster.

Ward flicked his wrists. The mass solidified. Horace strained to get free, the veins in his neck pulsed with effort. Ward shook his head. "Seems I caught you on the wrong side," he looked at Declan. "So much for friends."

Declan looked on helplessly. A rippling silver square took shape at Ward's side. Ace continued to struggle, his eyes wide and frightened.

"Don't," Declan croaked. "Leave him, you don't want him, you want me." Ward ignored him.

The panel grew larger as it floated across the walkway. Ace thrashed wildly right until the square went straight through him. Then he froze. His face paled and hardened into an iron sculpture—a portrait of fear adhered to a swollen steel bin.

Ward glared at Declan. "Your turn."

Tears stung Declan's eyes. Hatred bubbled inside him. *Horace. My parents. Ava.* "What did you do with Ava?" He said it more forcefully than he intended to.

Ward's smile didn't reach his eyes. "I had hoped that you would ask."

His left hand rotated around something invisible, and a figure appeared behind him. Ava, covered in torn clothes and bruises. Her dark curls were untidy, her face disheveled. Her iron leg gleamed in the morning sun.

"This piece of work has been quite a thorn in my side, Declan Moore," Ward said. "She's been watching the whole time, and it's been a pleasure for her to witness this. To witness all her hard work coming to naught." Ward turned and spat on her. Declan flinched.

Ward continued his monologue, but Declan heard none

of it. Ava's sapphire eyes held his. Declan couldn't read minds, but he didn't have to. The message in those blue flames was crystal clear. *Get ready.*

"And now, this mess of a day is—"

Ava drove an elbow into Ward's side. He hunched forward, and she spun, lifting her solid iron leg so it smashed into Ward's face. The crunch was Declan's cue. He dashed to Ava's side, but she pushed him off. "Get out of here!"

Blood poured from Ward's face. He staggered upright and summoned another shimmering square. Ava shoved Declan back, then threw herself at Ward. She grabbed his waist and dragged them both into Ward's spell. Ava went straight through it, her iron figure clunked against the brick. For Ward, the square only passed through the lower portion of his body. He hit the ground with a heavy clank, both legs, left wrist, right arm and lower torso transformed into unforgiving metal.

Ward looked up at him with rabid intensity. "I'll murder you!"

Declan ran.

Down one alley and into another. Across a road. Through a walkway. He ran. He ran from Ward, from Ace, from Ava, from his cowardice. Tears mixed with sweat until he couldn't run any longer.

Ducking into an empty car park, he collapsed on a pile of wooden pallets. His legs burned, the deep burn that promises company for the coming days. His heart drummed in his ears. Between beats, he could hear laughter.

"Would you look at that," somebody said. The sun had risen atop the buildings of Tamhill and Declan squinted at the people approaching. "Well, well, well. If it isn't the non-magical Declan Moore." Lyle loomed over him, blocking out the sun. "Lost, are you?" she asked. "No Ace here to save you this time?"

An image of Ace's iron figure made Declan feel ill.

"Where's the quip, LAMP?"

Tears formed at the corners of Declan's eyes; laughter rang out around him.

"Aw, the poor baby is crying," Lyle said.

Declan looked up at her, expressionless. "Do what you want," he muttered. "I'm all done."

Lyle raised an eyebrow. She looked him up and down, her eyes lingered on the brown satchel hanging over his chest. "Well, you heard the LAMP," she said to the group. "Let's take him somewhere private and give him what he deserves."

Magic enveloped him, creating a sense of weightlessness that carried him through the parking lot. There was no way to tell who dragged him through the air, but Declan didn't care. His only solace was the hope that whatever came next might dull his sense of worthlessness.

Declan just hoped Lyle and her crew were up to the job.

CHAPTER 13

DECLAN

SALTY TEARS STUNG BLISTERED EYES. Raw wrist. Bruised body. Declan was numb to all of it.

Lyle and her friends had smuggled him into the forest outside Tamhill. For three days he was their pin-cushion. Three days of teenagers learning spells at his expense. Declan's bruised face resembled a kaleidoscope of blues and purples intermingled with greens and yellows. It should have hurt, and sometimes it did, but the pain never lasted long. The emptiness inside him swallowed it up.

Joel Mercado stood below him, a large tome at his feet. He looked from the book to the roof where Declan hovered. Slowly, he traced circles on his palm with his thumb. Declan began to spin, faster and faster, the cabin interior a blur. Nausea gripped him and he sprayed the room with pale bile.

The spinning sensation vanished. Declan dropped to the floorboards with a smack. Lyle shrieked with laughter as he lay in a crumpled mess. "Mop time!" she sang out.

The weight of Declan's body vanished. It had become a familiar sensation. The room inverted as he spun upside down and landed headfirst into a bucket, then up again. Declan coughed and spluttered; the water burned in the back of his nostrils. Lyle flicked her wrist and he swished back and forth—his long curly hair a makeshift mop for the vomit-covered floor.

"Smooth," someone called.

"Practice makes perfect." Lyle's voice was thick with satisfaction.

Declan, the human mop, hung limply in the air. It was beyond humiliating, but at least they weren't dropping him on his head anymore. *Mom. Dad. Ace. Ava.* Their faces came out of nowhere. Declan ignored them, focused on his torn, scabbed wrists instead, but it wasn't enough. *Mom. Dad. Horace. Ava.* He focused on his head, throbbing with a dull ache, on the burning bile in the back of his throat.

Flashing lights filled the room. The names wouldn't go away. Declan squeezed his eyes closed. Willing his mind to picture anything but the cold, iron figures of his friends and family.

The smell of sawdust tickled his nose. Sunlight warmed his skin. Unfamiliar sounds rang around him. A cacophony of bangs, whoomps, clatters and crashes.

Panicked shouts everywhere, muffled as if he were underwater. *Maybe I am underwater. The human mop once more. Mom. Dad. Ace. Ava. I'm sorry. I'm sorry. I'm sorry.*

"You don't need to apologize, just stand up."

Declan lay on his back in what remained of the cabin. Large sections of the walls were missing. A splintered hole took up most of the roof. Tiny specks of sawdust floated all around them. A familiar face with a familiar gray braid looked down through the haze.

"You!" he growled.

The woman frowned at him. "Yes, me. Come along, young man. Get up."

Declan refused to budge. *She's working with the Fate-smiths.* "What did you do with the others?"

"Who? Those adolescents using you for practice?"

"Are they dead?"

A combination of irritation and amusement crossed the woman's face. "They're fine. Physically, at least..." she trailed off. "Come on, hop up, we need to go."

"I'm not going anywhere with you. I've seen what you people do!"

The woman raised an eyebrow at this comment, then shook her head. "You don't have the faintest idea what you're talking about. *My* people are the ones who want to keep you in one piece." She turned back to the spot where the door should have been. A faint sound of sirens carried into the room. "Now stop being a fool. Get. Up."

Declan frowned. "You're not one of them?"

"Of course not." She reached a hand out to him. "Now come on. We're running out of time."

Declan let the woman pull him to his feet. He stumbled forward. Three days of being a piñata had turned his legs into syrup. The woman caught his shoulders and held him steady. "Are you okay?"

"I'm fine." Declan took a tentative step, followed by another. The sirens grew louder.

"Time to go." The woman grabbed his elbow and pulled him outside.

"Wait!" Declan pulled loose and ran back inside.

"What are you doing?" the woman called behind him. "We have to leave!"

Declan scanned the ruined room's remains. A thin

brown strap hung over the leg of an upturned chair. "Got it!" He pulled Ava's satchel free of the rubble.

The woman stared daggers at him.

They ran beneath the tree line as three MLEA cars came into view. The cars skidded to a halt, their purple and green lights flashing. Officers in maroon shouted for them to stop. Declan slowed enough for the gray-haired woman to keep pace. Car doors slammed shut as officers followed them into the forest.

"This way," the woman shouted. She angled towards a downhill slope. A section of wood exploded from a tree to Declan's left. The thick trunk groaned as it fell. Rows of smaller pines crunched beneath it. Spells came in volleys. Splintered branches filled the air. The old woman ducked and vaulted through the falling forest. Declan followed close behind.

"We're not going to make it!" he called after her. A row of trees ahead toppled into a crude wall.

"Down here." The woman wriggled through the carpet of leaves and pine needles. Declan followed. Even flat on his stomach, there was barely enough clearance to slide underneath. He slithered like a snake, following the sound of rustling leaves. When he came out on the other side, the woman waited on a fallen log. Leaves and woodchips made an untidy mess of her perfect braid. Her index finger danced on her palm as she tapped a message to another witch or wizard.

"Who are you looptapping?" Declan asked.

"Help," she said without stopping. "Though I fear we're out of time." She finished her message, then looked up. "We need to get to the bus stop on the other side of the reserve."

They were in a triangular nook made by three collapsed trees. A rich, earthy aroma filled Declan's nostrils. Upset birds squawked—unimpressed—from above as footsteps crunched towards them. The woman pressed a finger to her lips.

"Where did they go?" asked a gruff voice.

"Through there?" said a second.

"Impossible, we made a wall!"

"Look," an unfamiliar voice called from the other side of the tree. "Marks in the leaves. They went under here."

"Quick! Move this tree out of the way."

Declan looked at the woman. "We're trapped," she breathed. "Was it worth it?" She nodded to the bag slung across his shoulders.

Declan tossed it to her. "You tell me."

The tree behind them groaned like a waking giant. The woman opened the satchel, her lips parted. She pulled out a ruby ball covered in metal studs. "Where did you get this?"

Declan shook his head. "It's not mine. It's my friend's bag."

"The Luck?" she whispered.

"How did you know?"

Behind them, someone cursed. "It's too heavy!"

"Then cut it into smaller pieces!"

The woman held the ball up. "These are very, very rare. It is also our only chance out of this mess. Will your friend mind if we use it?"

Declan shrugged. "Do we have a choice?"

"No," the woman said. "When they move the trees, take a good mental picture of your surroundings. When I throw this." she shook the ball, "put your hands in your pockets, close your eyes and *run*."

Declan managed a nod. Butterflies filled his stomach.

With a crack like a bull-whip, the wall of trees separated into parts. Each section launched high into the depths of the forest, landing with distance crashes. Six MLEA officers blocked their path. One stepped forward.

"You are both—"

He stopped abruptly as the woman with the gray braid tossed him onto the red orb. It glowed like a hot ember. He caught it automatically, looked down, and gasped. The metal studs shot out of the ball and around the wrists of each officer.

Declan could only guess what happened next. Eyes squeezed shut, he ran, hands in pockets, through the only clear path he had seen. A shrill whistle shrieked behind him, followed by a piercing light. Even with his eyes closed, it was too bright to handle. Declan raised his hands to cover his face. He could see every bone, vein, and capillary inside them. Then silence. The light faded. His foot caught something hard, and he stumbled forward into a pair of arms.

"You can open your eyes now," the woman said. She had caught his chest.

"What was that?"

"It was an orb of disintegration. Hopefully, they remembered to close their eyes too. If not... well... probably best not to ask too many questions. Come on."

Declan shook his head. "No. Not yet."

"Declan, we need to move. This reserve will be crawling with officers and ironhands in no time."

"Not until you tell me what is going on. Who are you? How did you find me? How do you know my name?"

The woman exhaled a long breath. "I am Mary-Lou Nivin." She looked at him expectantly.

Declan drew a blank. "Is that supposed to mean something to me?"

Mary-Lou fixed him with an icy stare. "I guess not. I

thought you might. I am—after all—the King's College Applications Officer."

Declan blinked. "You're the one who rejected me?"

She nodded.

"Because I'm too powerful?"

She nodded again.

Declan shook his head. "You're wrong. I'm a LAMP. I submitted that application as a joke. I don't have a magical bone in my body."

Shouts rang out from the depths of the forest. Mary-Lou's mouth creased in concern. "If you really believe that, then by all means, stay here- let the ironhands deal with you. But I need to get to that bus stop, away from this forest." She lifted her long skirt and started down the hill, her feet crunching on the dead leaves. A few steps in and she turned back to him. "So, are you coming or not?"

CHAPTER 14
HABERDEEN

A WOMAN STOOD by an upstairs window. Her hair was loose, long, red—like faded brickwork. Her face was pale and drawn, marked by a thin scar that ran from the corner of her lips to the edge of her cheek. The woman had gone by many names in her life. Now, as the founder and leader of the Fatesmiths, she called herself Haberdeen.

Haberdeen admired central Tamhill from her hotel window. Afternoon light bathed a busy road in a golden glow. In the distance, forested hills encircled the city. As her eyes scanned the landscape, a stray memory flashed through her mind. A recollection of those same hills a thousand years earlier, before Tamhill, before Euryma. Back then, this land was Hispania. Haberdeen forced the memory down and turned to the room's only other occupant. A bearded man seated on a couch. "Tell me about the Iberian campaign, Mage Raul."

"If Sabriva's records are accurate, we have fierised about half," Raul spoke with a western accent, typical of the British Isles.

"Half?" Haberdeen raised an eyebrow.

"Half the witches and wizards. All remainin' executive officers in the MLEA have pledged allegiance to our cause in return for their freedom."

"How many resisted?"

"Not too many," Raul said. "A few misguided patriots early on. Things have improved since then."

"Media coverage?"

"None. We're dealing with anyone reporting disappearances fast enough. MLEA are doing their part to keep the LAMPs in the dark."

Haberdeen sighed. "So, why am I here?"

They both knew the answer. It was his failure that had brought her to Iberia. He had found the boy, only to let him escape. Haberdeen sighed. *Nobody said saving the world would be easy.* She reached for the bone-white dagger hanging off her belt, then stopped herself. "You had him. You could have stopped the end before it began—"

Raul scratched his beard. "With respect, your boy Ward—"

"*Mage* Ward has earned my forgiveness," Haberdeen said coldly. "*You* have not."

A splash of color appeared in Raul's cheeks. "I got his parents. That's somethin'. At least he won't be able to—." A knock on the door cut him short.

"I hope that's good news." Haberdeen settled into the leather lounge. "For *your* sake."

Raul opened the door, exchanged some soft words through a slight gap, then turned back to her. "It's Ophelia. She has a girl who was there in the forest when the boy escaped."

"Send her in."

Haberdeen looped her left-pointer around a strand of magic and looptapped a message. *Information coming your way. Be ready.* She let the thread loose. The door opened and Raul led a dark-haired girl with stunning green eyes into the room. Haberdeen forced a smile. "Hello there, darling. What is your name?"

"Hello," the girl stammered. Her hands twisted at her side. "I'm Lyle. Lyle Arthur."

"A pretty name for a pretty girl. Lovely to meet you, Lyle Arthur." Haberdeen nodded at Raul to close the door. Lyle looked back as it clicked shut. "Do you have something to tell me?"

Lyle nodded; her hands fiddled at her waist. "Well, I made the report to the MLEA about a madwoman who attacked my friends. We were in my father's log cabin. They told me you could help."

Haberdeen nodded. "I hope so. Go ahead, tell me everything."

"So, we were up the forest..." Lyle looked from Raul to Haberdeen, her voice dropped to a whisper, "practicing some magic, just basic spells, when out of nowhere, an old lady burst in and started tearing the place apart."

"How awful. Did the lady say anything?"

"No, we cleared out fast, but we had this kid with us. He's a LAMP. I think she wanted to take him. His name is Declan Moore."

Declan. The name jolted in Haberdeen's chest. She masked her surprise. "This boy, Declan, is he a friend of yours?"

A dark sneer flashed across Lyle's face. "Oh, no. Definitely not. He actually snuck up to the cabin. We don't like him. So, we told him to go home. He tripped. Fell over. Looked pretty nasty, really." Lyle's words were coming faster, her voice a touch higher. "But he's a bit of a liar, sometimes makes things up. He's a LAMP, so he's pretty jealous of us using magic, and we didn't want him to go to the MLEA with any lies."

"I see," Haberdeen pursed her lips. "That is understandable. How sensible of you to report it before he could get you into any trouble."

Lyle smiled. She looked like a smug house cat.

"So, you're learning magic?" Haberdeen asked.

"As much as I can. I know a lot of things. I'm getting quite powerful."

"Are you now?" Haberdeen considered the girl for a long moment, then patted the seat beside her. "Come dear, sit. I want to show you something." Lyle glanced nervously at the couch, but didn't refuse. Haberdeen drew a dagger from her cloak. It was matte white from hilt to point and covered in an intricate pattern of concentric circles. "Do you know what this is?"

Lyle peered closely at the dagger. "A knife?"

Haberdeen faked a laugh. "Very good, very clever. Yes, this is a knife, technically it's a khanjali. This one comes from the lands north of Euryma and is very special."

Lyle eyed the knife. "There's nothing special north of Euryma, LAMPs and barbarians."

"You would be surprised," Haberdeen said. "Not only is it special, it is powerful."

"Powerful?" Lyle frowned. "How? There's no magic in the north?"

"Well, this particular khanjali is called Winterthorn, and it is imbued with the power to draw memories from blood."

Lyle leaned closer to the dagger. "What does that—"

A flurry of motion cut her off.

Lyle gasped as the knife plunged into her chest. The

handle burned emerald, a green glow that ran down the hilt, into the blade and out of Lyle's eyes.

"You see, I know things too," Haberdeen whispered, "I know Declan Moore is no mere LAMP." She gripped the handle, knuckles white as its hilt. "And I *know* when someone is lying to me." Haberdeen's jaw tightened as seventeen years of memories flowed into her mind. Any remorse she felt for the girl vanished as she witnessed a life of spite and cruelty. From her most recent memories, she could see the boy, Declan Moore. Lyle *had* treated him like a dog. She pulled the knife free, and the girl dropped to the floor, her pale skin quartz white, drained of blood and life.

Haberdeen closed her eyes and focused on the memories. *Declan Moore.* Lyle must have hated him; every recollection was tainted with intense dislike. He looked... normal. Young, dark curly hair. Just another seventeen-year-old, albeit one that could destroy the world. *Unless you get to him first.*

Raul stepped over Lyle's body. "What do you see?"

"An unremarkable teenager." She raised her left-pointer and looptapped Lyle's memories, then glanced at her body on the floor. "The girl's knowledge may prove fruitful. If it does, I will overlook your failure."

Raul nodded. "Declan Moore. Can you see where he went?"

"Not yet. But it's only a matter of time." Haberdeen focused on the last memory Lyle had of the boy, torturing him in a cabin when a gray-haired woman knocked down the door. A phantom tap on the palm of her hand caught her attention. *En route, wait for the address.*

Raul frowned. "Forgive my ignorance, Madam..."

"It's King's College again. It would appear our ducks are lining up in rows." Haberdeen sat back in her chair. "You're familiar with the phrase 'killing two birds with one stone', Mage Raul?"

Raul nodded.

"Well, I plan on killing six." Haberdeen gestured to Lyle Arthur's body. "Now get rid of that and wait for instructions."

Nobody said saving the world would be easy.

CHAPTER 15

DECLAN

A BARRAGE of squad cars screamed past as they climbed onto a half-empty bus. Declan couldn't believe they'd escaped so easily. It wasn't until he caught sight of his reflection that it all made sense. He stared at the thick moustache his reflection sported. Mary-Lou snorted when he tried to stroke it. All Declan felt was his smooth upper lip.

"Sorry to manipulate your appearance without asking," she whispered. "Frankly, you looked like you belonged in a morgue. The last thing we need right now is attention."

Declan nodded. A question weighed on his mind. "If you're not a blackcoat, why did you lead a group of them into the coffee shop?"

Mary-Lou looked at him sideways. "Not now."

An acorn of anger formed in Declan's chest. He slid across his seat, then spoke in a low voice. "If you can't give me answers, I am getting off this bus."

Brakes hissed as the bus reached a red light. Mary-Lou chewed on her lower lip as if wrestling with a tough decision. Finally, she sighed. "After the last few days, I guess you have earned some answers." She leaned close, her voice dropped to a whisper. "I didn't lead those Fatesmiths to you. They had already found you. I tried to give you some warning."

The story did not match his experience. Declan didn't like it. "But you pointed, you pointed straight at me."

"Dear boy, I pointed behind you—to the exit. Your friend saw, that's where she took you. I also managed to reinforce the washroom door. I bought you the time you needed to escape."

Declan stared out the window. The light turned green; the bus continued on. "Where are we going?"

"Somewhere safe."

Declan gritted his teeth. He wanted to scream at the woman, to tell her his parents were gone, his best friend taken. Something sharp pricked his hands- his fists were clenched so tight his fingernails had broken the skin on his palms. Declan took a deep breath. He tried to make his voice as calm as possible. Still, it trembled. "Where are you taking me?"

"I'm not taking you anywhere," Mary-Lou said. "We are going to a friend's residence. There we will wait for Laurefen."

"Laurefen?"

Mary-Lou raised her eyebrows. "Laurefen Ember is the *Dean* of King's College. He will meet us there and we will travel together to the college campus on Kingsbreak."

Declan blinked. "I'm going to King's College?"

"Well, of course, dear. We wouldn't just leave you here to fend for yourself against those ironhands."

Declan didn't know what to say, or who to trust. The searing anger inside him faded to a bubbling frustration. He leaned back against the chair and closed his eyes; his parents' iron faces stared back at him. Ace's terrified expression. Ava's body—twisted and frozen mid fall.

Mary-Lou tapped him on the shoulder as the bus shuddered to a halt. "We're here."

Declan blinked awake, slung Ava's satchel across his shoulder, and groggily followed Mary-Lou off the bus.

They were in the suburbs. The sun hung in a cloudy hammock. The afternoon breeze pushed dry leaves along a tidy footpath leading to a brown brick house. Mary-Lou rapped on the enormous door.

The door opened, as if of its own volition, revealing a polished wooden hallway. Mary-Lou winked at him and walked inside.

"Welcome back," called a dark-skinned man from the end of the hall. He wore dress pants and a pastel-blue collared shirt. He gestured them into a large sitting room where leather couches encircled a black coffee table.

"A pleasure to be back." Mary-Lou stepped aside and gestured Declan forward. "Dreyfus Poole, this is Declan Moore."

"Ah, so this is the boy who broke your gauge." Dreyfus eyed Declan's mustache, amusement twinkled in his eyes. "I didn't expect him to be so well-seasoned."

Mary-Lou waved her hand; Declan felt no different, but the change in Dreyfus's expression made it clear that his disguise was gone. "It looks like you've been through the ringer," Dreyfus said.

"I expect John can patch it up quickly." Mary-Lou scanned the room. "Where is he?"

"Unfortunately, John stepped out when you looptapped. He thought it prudent to alert Laurefen in person. MLEA reports were urgent and... worrisome."

"Worrisome, how?" Mary-Lou asked.

"A good chunk of Tamhill West Forest is destroyed." Dreyfus's eyes darted to Declan. "It seems you're quite popular, young man."

"All the better reason to return to Kingsbreak as soon as possible," Mary-Lou said. She took a long look at Declan. "Why don't you go and freshen up, Declan? There is a bathroom down that corridor. It's your third door on the left. There's a hutch in there with fresh towels."

Declan nodded. He had the feeling Mary-Lou wanted to talk to Dreyfus without him listening. He left the room and paused at the door.

"It was worth it, I presume?" Dreyfus said.

"We'll soon find out."

"Fatesmiths are everywhere, Lou. It's not safe here. I doubt there will be a free wizard in the whole city by sunset."

"They move fast," Mary-Lou said. Her shadow appeared in the doorway; Declan rushed down the hall.

The house was much larger than he expected. He wandered until he found the bathroom decorated with white and teal tiles. A creamy wooden hutch housed a stack of fluffy white towels. Declan stripped off and climbed into the shower. After four days of chaos, the hot water felt amazing. He washed his hair. It still felt dirty. He washed it again, then stood and soaked in the shower's warmth.

When he finally climbed out, a pile of clean clothes waited at the entrance. Loud voices carried down the hall. Declan dressed quickly in front of the mirror. His face remained a patchwork of bruises, but he was clean. As he approached the sitting room, the voices grew more urgent.

"I don't know how they found out, but they're coming."

"How long have we got?"

"And where is Laurefen?"

Declan entered the room. Four faces turned to him.

Mary-Lou stood at the window beside Dreyfus, across from them stood a young woman with shoulder-length brown hair and a similarly aged man with a short beard.

"Declan, this is Katie and John." Mary-Lou gestured at the two strangers. "Unfortunately, that's all the time for introductions we have."

Katie smiled as she glanced at her palm. Raised white scars crisscrossed her wrist. "Looptap from Michael," she said. Her cheeks paled as the message tapped out on her hand. She took a deep breath. "It's Haberdeen." Her voice was now a terse whisper. "Haberdeen is coming with them."

The room fell silent. A shiver ran down Declan's spine.

"How long have we got?" Dreyfus asked.

Katie looptapped the question. The answer came back almost immediately. "No time. They're on their way."

"We need to go," Mary-Lou said.

"We can't." John looked at all of them. "Laurefen. I told him you'd arrived. He's on his way too."

"If we leave now, he may walk into an ambush." Dreyfus exhaled. Nobody spoke, they just looked at each other.

"So looptap him?" Declan said. "Tell him to meet us somewhere else!"

Mary-Lou shook her head. "It's not that easy Declan. Laurefen keeps communication with some of the most powerful people in Euryma. His looptap hand changes from day to day, unfortunately today, that means none of us are connected with him."

What? Declan nodded to mask the fact he had no idea what she was talking about. Despite Ace's explanations, he had never understood the intricacies of looptap.

"I was the fool who went to Laurefen. I'll stay back to warn him," John said.

"Don't be stupid, John," Mary-Lou scoffed.

"What do you suggest?" Katie asked. John opened his mouth. She closed it with a sharp glance.

Dreyfus stepped to the window. "Lou and I can stay here. We won't beat them, but we'll hold them off," Dreyfus said. "Katie, you and John take Declan to the bus stop on Murray Street. If we're not there in ten minutes, take a bus somewhere quiet. How's your Openings coming along John? Could you get yourself to Kingsbreak?"

"I'm not sure," John said. "But I don't like it, Dreyfus. How did they find us here? And if they can find us here, why would Murray Street be any different? We should all stay and fight."

"We might have to," Katie said. The glass panels on either side of the front entrance had darkened.

Somebody knocked on the front door. Dreyfus looked at Mary-Lou. She shook her head in protest. "You're not seriously going to answer it?"

"It's a nice door. They'll break it down if I don't." Dreyfus turned to Katie. "You take Declan down to the back study. There's a hidden panel in the bookcase. Gallagher's Encyclopedia of Plants will open it."

Mary-Lou turned to John. "And you go with them. Heal Declan while you're waiting."

"Waiting for what?" John asked. "I can help! We can take them."

The knocking at the door grew louder.

"Go!" There was no arguing with Dreyfus's tone.

Katie grabbed Declan's arm and led him out. Despite being a head shorter than him, her grip was a vice. John followed them into a study enclosed by wall-sized bookshelves. They immediately started searching the spines of the books.

"Gallagher's," Katie said. "It has a red cover?"

"Maroon," John corrected.

Declan scanned the shelves. A thin maroon cover was inches from the floor. He tilted his head to read it. *The Fabled Warlock*. A loud crash echoed in the distance, books trembled, some fell to the floor. "Here it is." John pulled out a thick maroon tome and a decorative panel popped open on their right. Declan ducked inside; Katie followed. The house shook again. John pulled the panel door closed with a click.

A dim orb appeared above their heads. John frowned. "That's all you've got?"

"It's a pitch-black room, John. Aside from the static in your clothes, there's not much electricity to work with."

Declan found a switch and flicked it. An antique bulb flickered to life overhead.

John grinned. "Kid's pretty clever."

Katie closed her hands, and the orb vanished.

"Alright. Let's have a look at you." John put his hand on Declan's head. "Not too bad. Plenty of bumps, but nothing too severe."

The floorboards beneath them continue to shake. The violent crashes were getting louder. Or closer.

"Don't worry about that," John said calmly. "We're safe here. Katie's short, but she's tough, like an angry kitten." Declan looked across at Katie; her lips were pressed together, beads of sweat decorated her hairline. John placed his hand on Declan's temple. "Hold tight. This is going to feel strange."

It felt like somebody dumped his bones into an icy lake. Declan gasped. Then the pain was gone.

Katie looked him over. "Much better. Not so splodgy now." She gifted him a terse grin.

A splintering thunder shook the room; the light bulb swung to the side and smashed, bathing them in darkness. Declan held his breath. A voice slid through the gaps in the shelves and into their hideaway. A feminine voice. Smooth, like the scales of a dangerous snake. "Where is the boy?"

"I. Don't. Know. What. You're. Talking. About." Dreyfus sputtered.

"You do. I know you do because I know a lie when I hear it. I'll ask again. Where is the boy?"

"Leave him!" Mary-Lou shouted.

"Quiet now," drawled the smooth voice. A hard thud. A clatter of falling books. Declan's heart thundered in his ears.

"I have nothing to tell you," Dreyfus said. "There is no boy here. This is madness."

"Very well. Have it your way."

Mary-Lou screamed, "Dreyfus! No!"

Declan wanted to vomit. Mary-Lou sobbed on the other side of the wall. He forced himself to breathe. *Inhale. Exhale. Inhale. Exhale.* He focused on his lungs, trying to ignore the cries mere feet away. His concentration was punctured by a loud clank. Something heavy hit the ground. Declan pictured Dreyfus, tall and well-dressed, now an iron cast.

"Your turn, sweetheart."

"You might as well turn me into one of your statues," Mary-Lou replied. Her sobs turned to anger. "I won't tell you a thing."

"Perhaps you're right, my dear. Maybe there is nothing I can do... to *you*."

A tense moment passed. "What are you doing?" Mary-Lou's voice climbed an octave. "No! That can't be! That's impossible! No! Haberdeen stop!"

Declan listened in horror.

"Isn't it obvious?" Haberdeen's voice was venom. "Iron melts like any other metal. Perhaps I'll forge it into something useful, like the shovel I'll use to bury the boy when I find him."

"Don't..." Mary-Lou pleaded.

"Tell me where the boy is."

"You... You can't..."

"Last chance, darling."

No response. A series of loud thuds, fast and furious. It sounded like a whirlwind of books swirling around the room. The roar was deafening and then... nothing. "You will pay for that," Haberdeen said.

Declan strained to listen in the silence that followed. *What was she doing out there?* Behind him, something creaked. With a sound like a thunderclap, the wall behind them tore away.

Blinding sunlight gushed into their cramped hiding spot. Katie and John shielded their eyes. Declan blinked; once, twice, three times, before things finally came into focus. A tall man in a long jacket stood before them. He had wavy gray hair and a pointed beard. His hands were outstretched, holding an entire section of the house in the air above his head.

He tossed it aside and locked eyes with them. "Where is Dreyfus?"

John jumped onto the grass. Before Declan could react, Katie grabbed his shoulders and half pushed, half tossed him down. He hit the ground off-balance; John caught him by the shoulders. "You all good, kid?"

Declan was speechless. The old man nodded curtly, blue eyes ablaze. "Where is Dreyfus?"

"He's inside with Mary-Lou," Katie said.

The old man pushed past them. "Take the boy to Kingsbreak."

"But Laurefen," Katie called after him. "She's here. Haberdeen."

A crash of shattering glass broke the momentary silence. Blackcoats poured out the windows. Laurefen's hands whipped into action and a wall of soil rose up around them. He turned back to John and Katie.

"Then we are too late. John, can you make an Opening?"

John paled. "Uh, I can try."

Laurefen's protective wall shuddered. Something battered it from the other side. He dragged more soil from the surrounding yard, reinforcing the barrier with a flick of his hands. It continued to shake and fall away. "Can you make an Opening, or not?"

John took a step to the side and moved his hands. He closed his eyes and his brow creased. Up ahead, a small triangular window appeared in mid-air. The wall crumbled. They were being assaulted on all sides; the soil was falling away faster than Laurefen could conjure it.

"What is that?" Declan whispered to Katie.

"An extra-dimensional doorway. We call them Openings."

The triangle grew larger. It began to spin, then collapsed. John tried once more, but it wouldn't work. "I can't... I can't do it."

"Damn it, John." With one hand dancing to maintain the wall, Laurefen turned his other hand to the space where

John's spinning triangle had failed. This time, a larger window appeared. It spun rapidly, growing into a circle large enough to walk through. "It's ready," he said, face drawn into hard lines. "Go!"

Katie leapt forward, and Declan followed with John close behind. Laurefen came last. The spinning triangle slowed to a halt before shrinking to nothing. The last sight he caught before it vanished was Laurefen's earth wall exploding in spectacular fashion. Grains of dust settled at their feet.

"Laurefen," Katie said. "Dreyfus. Mary-Lou."

"We'll deal with it," he replied. He looked back to where the Opening had been.

Declan looked around. An ancient cedar towered over a stone courtyard. Ahead of them lay a marvelous array of exquisite stone buildings. "Where are we?" he asked in wonder.

"Do you have to ask?" A small smile broke through John's concerned scowl. "You're on the island of Kingsbreak."

Laurefen turned to face him, though he did not seem overly pleased about his presence. "Against all odds, here you are. Welcome to King's College."

CHAPTER 16
DECLAN

KING'S COLLEGE WAS EMPTY. Almost. Students were home on semester break, a skeleton staff remained to keep the college functioning. Mostly, the exquisite buildings, sweeping lawns and gentle beaches of Kingsbreak were a ghost town for Declan to explore. He roamed through ancient classrooms, arcane libraries and magical training theatres with a sense of reverence, but even the famed halls of King's College couldn't fill the emptiness inside him.

Why aren't they helping me find my parents?

He had posed the question repeatedly to John, his unofficial babysitter, and received the same infuriating answer. "Ask Laurefen."

It was easier to nail water to a wall. Laurefen left the campus just as soon as he arrived. When he was on Kingsbreak, it was often only for hours, busy hours where he had no time to talk to a grief stricken seventeen-year-old.

Three weeks after their arrival, Declan sat alone in a common room. John was away on college errands, leaving Declan with his thoughts. He sank back into the chestnut couch. The shock of his parent's disappearance had faded—

the blaze from loss now burned down to coals of sorrow. *Mom. Dad. Ava. Horace. Dreyfus. Mary-Lou.* In his mind's eye, their smiles darkened until only cold, hard iron remained. Declan pushed the image away. Forced himself to think of something else. *The rejection letter. Your magical potential is far too potent to be safely controlled.* The words were etched in his mind, but they made no sense. *I can't do magic.*

Declan buried his head in his hands. His mind wandered a painful road lined with his parents, his friends, and his unknowable potential, until somebody touched his shoulder. "Here you are," John said. "I've been looking all over!"

"Sorry," Declan said. "What's up?"

"It's Mary-Lou. She made it out." John was grinning from ear to ear.

"What?"

"Wild, right?" John said. "I have no idea how, but she wants to talk to everyone. Present company included."

Declan frowned. He didn't trust Mary-Lou, and this seemed far too convenient.

His hesitance must have shown. John offered a hand. "C'mon," he said. "Everyone's already gathered in the Village."

Out of everyone at King's, John had been the most accommodating. He organized Declan's food and clothing; even found him a vacant room. Despite being busy with his own work, John always had time to answer his questions. Declan forced a smile, then let John pull him up.

Lazy afternoon light welcomed them. Three weeks in and Declan still marveled at the stone architecture and meticulous greenery of King's College. Lush hedges bordered vibrant lawns cut by polished cobblestone paths.

John led them towards the setting sun. They passed beneath a stone archway, and the path widened to a street dotted with brick cottages.

The Village housed the permanent staff, away from the busy student blocks. According to John, the houses were nice, but full of 'old people'. A porch light illuminated a red brick home with an open door. They walked into a spacious living area where a group of adults waited. He knew Katie, Mary-Lou, John and Laurefen. In the corner of the room stood a young woman with long blond hair. She was pretty, with cream skin and gentle eyes.

"Declan!" Mary-Lou stood, beaming. Her gray hair hung loose, and a shawl covered her arms. "I'm so glad you're okay! How do you like King's College?"

Declan's smile didn't feel quite right. "It's great," he replied awkwardly. "How... How did you get here?"

"A question we are all eager to know the answer to." Laurefen stood behind a lounge chair, his thick moustache curled at the corners. "Now that we are all here, Lou, would you mind telling us what's going on?"

"Why is the boy here?" asked a gruff voice. Declan had not noticed the older man standing by the window. It was Dreyfus, but it wasn't. A harder version of the same man.

"Michael." Laurefen frowned. "That's enough."

"No, it's not," he replied. "You were right Laurefen, he shouldn't be here—"

"Michael," said Mary-Lou, but he ignored her.

"And now look. My brother's gone. Gone because you waited too long, because you didn't trust your—"

"Enough!" Laurefen's tone was final. "No amount of anger and blame will bring Dreyfus back. Do not let it consume you."

Sweat prickled against Declan's collar. He looked down at his shoes. "I'm sorry," he said. Michael remained silent.

"We are not here to assign blame or guilt," Laurefen continued. "Lou. How did you escape Haberdeen?"

Mary-Lou's eyes were on Michael, her lips a tight line. She looked from Declan to John and finally settled on Laurefen. "You saved me," she said simply. "Haberdeen had me, there was nothing I could have done. She's strong Laurefen. So strong." Mary-Lou took a deep breath. "She had me and then you tore the wall away. She threw me aside, and I went straight through the plasterboard. I heard her go after you. I was in no condition to follow. I buried myself in the rubble of the house and waited."

"But it's been three weeks!" Katie said. "Where have you been? Why didn't you contact us?"

Mary-Lou shook her head. "I couldn't. Ironhands are everywhere in Tamhill, everywhere in Iberia. Haberdeen has the MLEA in her pocket. I laid low and went slow."

"But you could have used magic?" Katie pushed.

Mary-Lou unwrapped the shawl from her hand and held it up high. Her pale skin was gone, replaced by cold iron.

"Is that...?" John whispered.

"It is. She was starting on me when Laurefen arrived, a moment longer and I'd be nothing but an iron figure."

"Does it hurt?" asked the young woman with the long, blonde hair.

"It did at first, but not anymore. But I can't do anything with magic. The iron won't let me take hold of anything."

"Three weeks though, Lou," John said. "That's a long time for a short journey, even without magic."

Mary-Lou shook her head sadly. The corners of her eyes

reflected the lamplight. "I didn't travel alone. I needed to bring Dreyfus back."

"More like what's left of him," Michael growled. He shot a venomous look at Declan and stormed out of the cottage. Katie started after him, but Laurefen raised a hand.

"Leave him be."

John glanced at Mary-Lou. "What's *left* of him? What does that mean?"

Mary-Lou's shoulders slumped. "You shouldn't have to see this... but you need to. Follow me." She led them outside. A white fence bordered a well-kept courtyard. Beside it, a puddle of solid iron lay on the grass. Katie gasped.

"I don't understand," John said, looking at Mary-Lou.

Tears rolled down her cheeks. "It's him. Haberdeen fierised him and then..."

"Melted the iron," Laurefen finished grimly.

A wave of nausea hit Declan. He searched for somewhere to empty his stomach. John put a hand to his forehead. A trickle of cold went through him and his insides settled. Declan nodded in thanks.

"Can you do anything for him, John?" Mary-Lou asked.

"I don't think so, that's... that's catastrophic damage." He crouched by the remains and tentatively put his palm against it. "No," he shook his head. "It is solid iron. Any magic I can do is useless."

Mary-Lou's head dropped.

"How though?" Katie asked. "How could she use magic on iron?"

Laurefen dropped to a knee and inspected the metal pool. "Amber, have you heard anything that would explain this?"

The young woman's long blonde hair swayed as she

shook her head. "Nothing," she said. "The Fatesmiths are made up of young people. Most are between eighteen and twenty-five. There is no record of their college or Potential. Haberdeen herself is a mystery. We have no idea where she came from or how she can do what she does."

Declan stared at the iron mass. "What is this?" he finally asked. "King's is a Mag-Ed College. Why are you concerned with this?" Declan looked at each of them. Words tumbled out of him like a landslide. "Why are a bunch of college scholars so interested in Haberdeen turning people to iron? Why are they hunting you? Why are they hunting me? When are you going to get my parents back? Why do you think I have powers when I'm clearly a LAMP? None of this makes sense!" His voice echoed in the early evening. He had not meant to be so loud.

Laurefen directed a meaningful look at Mary-Lou. She replied with a curt nod, then turned to Declan. "I will explain everything, Declan, I promise. First, though, it's time we test your Magical Potential. We need to know for sure if you are who we think you are."

Nobody said a word. Mary-Lou led them back to the living room. Declan meandered behind, wondering if this was the moment his fantasy came crashing down.

John pulled a wooden chair into the room's center. Katie left and returned with a jingling box marked 'P. G.'. She placed it before Mary-Lou, who gestured for Declan to sit down while she rummaged through the box. Sweat prickled Declan's neck as she fitted him with strange gloves. They were like medieval gauntlets with thin wires extending from the fingertips, joining into one thick cord connected to a white box. The box had a glass face with a gauge beneath it; the circle was divided into quarters, each a different color. A thin red arrow was at rest in the middle.

"Now, I'm going to guess that you had the standard Magical Potential Test done when you were six years old." Mary-Lou reached into the box and pulled out a silver instrument. It looked like a can-opener with a needle on one end. "This is a spectromonoscope. Jostle any memories?"

Declan nodded. "Yeah, I remember it hurt like a—"

"Anyway," Mary-Lou went on, "a spectromonoscope is reasonable for a quick and easy test, but they're not infallible." She put the silver tool away and flicked a switch on the base of the box. She motioned to the gauge. "This, on the other hand, is a Potentiality Gauge. Much more sensitive and much more accurate. We can run applications through here for reliable results based on a tiny blood sample."

A nervous itch blossomed on Declan's neck. The heavy gauntlets started to hum; his heartbeat quickened. Mary-Lou fiddled with some dials on the back of the box.

"Now, if you look closely at this circle here, you'll notice that it's split into four colors- gray, green, purple and red. These roughly correspond to your magical potential. Anyone who lands in the gray is Lacking All Magical Potential, a LAMP. Green means their Potential is limited. Purple is the minimum requirement for acceptance into King's College."

"And the red?" Declan asked.

"Red means danger. It is rare, but at that degree of magical Potential, you become a hazard to yourself and to those around you. Individuals with that much power are often better off learning from a private tutor who has the necessary... *infrastructure*... to mitigate the risks that come with such potential."

John laughed. "That's official talk for 'we don't want you here because you'll blow the place up'."

Declan nodded. "And, based on your rejection letter, I am in the red?"

Mary-Lou traded glances with Laurefen. "Let's just do the test, shall we?" She checked the gloves one final time. "This will feel a bit odd, like something crawling up the back of your shirt. It will go away shortly." With that, she turned a dial. The white box beeped a single note. A spider-like chill ran up his spine. Declan snapped into perfect posture. He closed his eyes and tried to shake it off. When he finally opened them, Mary-Lou's face split in a wide grin. John let out a low whistle and Katie's eyebrows had disappeared. Declan looked down. The red arrow rested squarely in the gray.

Panic and disappointment bloomed in his chest. "Doesn't that mean I'm a LAMP?"

Mary-Lou nodded. "You'd be forgiven for thinking that, as would anyone else who ran this test." Declan stared at her blankly. Mary-Lou continued. "You see, when I first ran the test, I was confused. Why would a LAMP be applying to Mag-Ed?"

Declan didn't say a word.

"So, I decided to test it again. This time, I noticed something out of the ordinary." She flipped the switch again. "This time, when I press the button, do your best to ignore the tingling sensation and watch the arrow. Closely. Ready?"

Declan nodded and watched the small red arrow intently. Mary-Lou turned the dial. Declan flinched, but kept his eyes open. The little red line rotated quickly, from the gray to the green, to purple, to red and then right around to gray. It repeated one more time around the gauge before settling on gray. Declan stared at the little red line. "What does that mean?"

Nobody answered.

"We don't know," Laurefen said at last. He had been watching silently from the corner of the room. "A normal LAMP never leaves the gray. We have never seen anything like this. Our best guess, and keep in mind the key word there is *guess,* is that you are somehow orders of magnitude stronger than the most powerful witches and wizards in existence."

Declan turned to Mary-Lou. *This must be a joke.*

"And that's why they want you," Mary-Lou said. "We don't know how they found out, but they either want to use you as a weapon, or to make sure you can't be used against them." Her eyes flickered to Laurefen. "Some of us were unsure of what to do with your results. In fact, the letter we wrote to you was not supposed to be mailed out until we had made time to discuss the matter."

"Whatever stroke of luck put that letter in your hands saved you from the tyranny of the Fatesmiths." Laurefen pressed his fingertips together and stared into Declan's eyes. His face radiated a stern authority. "Like it or not, Declan Moore, you are a part of this now. As such, I insist you remain at King's College for the safety of yourself and the entire Dominion."

CHAPTER 17
LAUREFEN

A GLITTERING tapestry of stars decorated a clear night sky, but all Laurefen could think of was the boy. Declan Moore had left for the student quarters hours ago, but his place at King's College had changed everything.

"It's not the machine," Mary-Lou said from behind the Potentiality Gauge. She snapped the back of the box shut. "His results are genuine. He's the real deal."

"Which may leave us with a real problem," Laurefen said.

"Or a real opportunity." Mary-Lou carried the white box out of the room and left Laurefen to mull over her words in silence. Michael sat in silence by the wall.

Mary-Lou returned with a steaming mug. Laurefen shook his head as she sat. "I have not given seventy years to this organization to have my legacy destroyed by a clueless teenager." He looked at Michael. "What are the latest reports?"

"Bad." Michael said flatly. He leaned back and took a drink of something sharp enough to make Laurefen's nose twitch. "We've gone from over a thousand to under two-hundred. Our Alumni are vanishing faster than we can track."

"And the ironhands?"

"Growing in numbers and influence every day. The western corner of Habsburg is completely theirs; not a free witch or wizard in sight."

"They're getting more confident, Laurefen." Mary-Lou looked worried. "Raids in Iberia and Gaul on the same night. They're spreading across Euryma and we're not doing anything to stop them."

It was the same bad news. Laurefen glanced skywards. The sparkling night offered little solace. "What *can* we do?"

"Give them the boy," Michael said. "Tell them they can have him if they leave the Dominion." He downed more of his drinks.

Mary-Lou rolled her eyes. "Perhaps that's enough liquor tonight, Michael."

Michael paused mid-sip. "You think you're so clever, Lou. Do you take us for idiots?"

"Michael, that's enough," Laurefen said.

"Clerical error. Ha!" Michael stood and lost his balance. He steadied himself and shook his head. "You sent that letter out. You went behind Laurefen's back and now look what you've done."

Mary-Lou's expression never changed. "I'm not playing this game. I understand you're hurting right now. I am sorry about Dreyfus."

"Yeah, yeah, yeah," Michael waved her off and made for the front entry. "It's on your head, Lou," he called as he left. "It's on you."

He slammed the door shut. Laurefen shook his head. "He's in a dangerous spot."

"He is." Mary-Lou nodded. "And I daresay you're the

only one of us left he respects enough to listen to. You may need to talk some sense into him sooner rather than later."

Laurefen sighed. "I hope they'll remember me for more than talking down drunkards." He turned away from the window and fell onto the couch. "Well, the boy is here. You read his application. Tell me about Declan Moore."

"Born and bred in Tamhill. No registered Magical Potential but attended Arman Moore's Preparatory School on account of being a descendant of the founder." Mary-Lou paused for a sip of her tea. "Great grades, excels in problem solving. Outstanding athlete, represented his college in sprints at all levels across the Dominion."

"If he had no registered Potential, why did he apply?"

Mary-Lou shrugged. "Probably a question for the boy. Maybe one you could ask while you train him?"

"No." Laurefen held her eyes. "Until we know more, we must assume he's a disaster waiting to happen."

"Or our answer to Haberdeen."

"Or something else entirely."

Mary-Lou raised her eyebrows. "Like what?"

"Your guess is as good as mine. Ire tides, green magic, who knows what a result like that means?"

"Ire tides?" Mary-Lou scoffed in disbelief. "Can't use Ire Tides until you learn how to manipulate. And green magic? Might as well worry about the bogeyman." She fixed him with a knowing gaze. "Be real Laurefen, you're not worried he's a monster, you're worried he's going to tarnish your precious legacy." Mary-Lou took a long sip of tea. "We've found a sword that you refuse to use."

"I would like to be sure which way the sword is facing before I wield it," Laurefen said. "Our allegiance is to the people of Euryma. He is just as likely to be their doom as he is our savior."

"There won't be anyone in Euryma if we let things continue."

Laurefen chose not to argue back. Declan Moore's application had grown from curiosity to a wedge; he had no intention of driving it deeper. He searched for a different subject. "How are our new recruits?"

Mary-Lou paused and considered it. "They're... well, they're kids. They all have their strengths. Amber is quiet, introverted. Probably not the most practical witch, but she does well with Imbusion and will be an excellent teacher, *if* we have any students left to teach." She took another sip of her tea. "Katie is... distracted. She misses her mother, but if you can distract her, well, she isn't afraid of challenging ideas. I think she'll go far in whatever direction she wants. And John..."

"John nearly created an Opening in Tamhill, quite quickly, and under immense pressure."

"I don't doubt his talent, Laurefen, he's just..." Mary-Lou seemed slow to find the words, then smirked. "Rash."

Laurefen smiled. "That's a nice way of putting it. Michael's words were 'incapable of thinking before acting'."

"He'll get there. There's nobility in his blood, in all their blood." Mary-Lou placed her empty mug down. "They're nice kids, but I'm worried. None have even attempted Approval," she paused, "Laurefen... Can we trust their blood?"

"We have to. We're short on time and shorter on people."

She sighed. "We are, but we want the right people."

"I trust the old magic; it hasn't failed us yet."

Wind rustled in the trees, the air grew cold, Laurefen closed the window. When he returned to his seat, Mary-

Lou looked troubled. "What are we going to do? With Dreyfus gone... There are only three of us."

"There are others. You heard Michael, more than two hundred good witches and wizards, good men and women."

"Good, but not suitable to lead. How will we stop this new magic?"

Laurefen took a deep breath. A soft glow bled over the hills, a promise of dawn. "I wish I could tell you. It may not be our place to stop it. We may just have to survive it."

"Will you train the boy?"

"No."

"Never?"

"I honestly don't know, Lou. For now, our focus is on helping Euryma. And surviving."

Mary-Lou nodded. "What do you need me to do?"

"Continue with your work; send word out to our people in Iberia and Gaul to be on alert. I will need Michael to go to Sabriva and liaise with the High Mage."

"Michael will need time to grieve."

"I expect so."

Mary-Lou stood to face the dawn. "Don't write the boy off so quickly, Laurefen. Haberdeen wanted him, which means she fears him. He may be the difference and he's here."

You may be right, dear woman. Laurefen kept his face passive. As the entire Dominion collapsed before their eyes, they had managed to snatch an unlikely victory from nowhere. Declan Moore was on the island of Kingsbreak. It was no guarantee, but it was something. Mary-Lou walked down the steps and Laurefen waved goodbye. *Hope remains. For now.*

CHAPTER 18
DECLAN

A FLY ZIG-ZAGGED amongst the low reeds lining the lake. For all its agility, a silky spider's web trapped it the moment it strayed too close to the water. Declan watched with interest as a pond spider emerged to collect its breakfast. The fly struggled against invisible constraints and Declan felt a pang of empathy for the insect.

The previous night haunted his thoughts. *Orders of magnitude stronger than the most powerful witches and wizards in existence.* Laurefen's words were a sledgehammer. Since hearing them, Declan had experienced euphoria, excitement, guilt, shame and everything in between. Now, in the warm morning sun by the lake, he felt trapped. Declan waved a stick through the spiderweb; the fly buzzed away. *If only it were that easy.*

"Morning kid." John strolled down the path, a paper coffee cup in his hands.

"Morning," Declan said. "Were you looking for me?"

John shook his head. "Nah, I needed to escape the drama." He nodded to the bench. "Mind if I join you?"

Declan shifted to make room. "Drama?"

"Michael and Mary-Lou, at odds again," he said. "You saw them last night."

"He must hate me," Declan said. "And I can't blame him."

John sipped his coffee. "You did nothing wrong. Neither did Mary-Lou. Haberdeen did this; Michael knows it—he's just angry. He needs to direct that rage at something."

Declan said nothing. The lake sparkled in the sun. Something had been on his mind for most of the morning, something he couldn't shake. "John..." he started, then stalled, unsure of how to continue. "How do you think the Fatesmiths found out about me?"

John gathered a pebble and skimmed it over water's surface. "I honestly don't know," John said at last. "The obvious answer is there's a traitor in our midst, but I can't imagine who it could be. The Directive has been operating out of King's College for centuries. I've only been a part of it for a few months, but every member has either done Approval or are blood relatives of those who have."

"Directive? Approval?" Declan was lost. "What are you talking about?"

John chuckled. "That's right, you're a newbie. Sorry. I forget how little you know."

Declan attempted to shrug. He hoped it looked natural.

"Okay, here's the brief version. King's College was founded a few hundred years back when magical folk agreed to rewrite Euryma's laws. One of those laws was to allow anybody with Potential to come here and learn to use magic. With me?"

"I know this," Declan said, recalling his classes at Arman Moore's. "King's College was founded by William Fendragon after he married a LAMP and dissolved the Monarchy."

"Good. Fendragon opened the college when he stepped down as King and created the Mage Council. What isn't public record is that King Fendragon was not comfortable giving up all his power. He worried about the new democracy. It was a colossal risk. He wanted safeguards in place to straighten out any dramas that came from his changes." John skimmed another rock on the lake. "So, within King's, he created an organization called Directivus, charged with keeping Euryma from going off a cliff."

"So, everyone who teaches here is part of some secret authority called the Directivus?" Declan raised an eyebrow.

"Not quite." John grinned. "For starters, it's no longer the Directivus, just the Directive. Secondly, it's only open to those the Dean nominates for Approval." A shadow crossed his face. "Or a direct blood relative of someone who has passed Approval."

"Passed?"

"Approval is a test of, well, *worthiness*, I guess. Which is why it's so hard to imagine a traitor in our midst. You can't get into the Directive without demonstrating that you are honorable beyond reproach."

Declan leaned against the stone bench and absorbed the new information. John started describing each Directive member in detail, but Declan was lost in his own thoughts. "So, let me get this straight," he said, cutting John off. "Laurefen heads a secret Dominion group called Directivus-"

"Directive," John corrected. "And it's not overseen by the Mage Council. It's a separate entity, backed by King's immense wealth, answerable only to itself."

"Okay." Declan stared at the lake. "So Laurefen is the head of the Directive, which is made up of witches and wizards who have passed a test of... worthiness?"

"That's it."

"Did anybody outside the Directive know about my application results?"

"Just us," John said.

Declan looked him in the eye. "I know who the traitor is."

John rubbed the back of his neck, a wry smile spread on his lips. "It's not Mary-Lou."

Declan's jaw dropped; he closed it quickly. "It has to be," he said. "She was the one who brought the blackcoats to me, pointed me out to them. She found me again and ran me away from the police, who were probably trying to save me. She took me to the *house* that Haberdeen found shortly after and then miraculously escaped unharmed? It has to be her!" Declan stopped to catch his breath. "And she was looptapping someone the entire time!"

John shook his head. "She didn't have a choice. Those ironhands were going to find you, regardless. By taking them to you, she could at least help out with your escape." John skimmed another stone. "The MLEA are in Haberdeen's pocket. We don't know how or why, but they answer to her. And Dreyfus's house. Well, I've got no clue how they found out, but Lou had every opportunity to hand you over—me and Katie as well." John shrugged. "It's not her."

Declan pressed his lips together and looked off into the distance. "What about Ava?"

"Who?"

"The girl who helped me escape the first time."

John's brow furrowed in concentration. Declan had told him the entire story shortly after his arrival at Kingsbreak. "You mean the Luck?"

Declan nodded.

"No Luck's here. She's not a part of the Directive *or* King's College."

"She knew about my enrollment. She wanted to get me away from the blackcoats."

"That's promising. She might be able to help us uncover the leak." John skimmed his last pebble, then sat beside him. "Do you know where she went?"

A familiar tide of guilt surged in Declan's gut. "She... she sacrificed herself so I wasn't captured. Remember? They turned her to iron."

"Oh. That's right." John put a hand on his shoulder. "I'm sorry Declan, I forgot."

They sat in silence for a little longer. The sun rose higher, grew hotter. Waterfowls left to find shade; a familiar pond spider started spinning a new web. Declan wondered if Mary-Lou was doing the same for him.

John stood up. "I've got to head back. Laurefen wants to do more testing on Dreyfus. Well, his remains, I suppose." He looked at his feet, then back at Declan. "What are your plans for today?"

"Me? Nothing. What can I do?"

"Learn magic?"

Declan snorted. "And blow up the world?"

John peered into the distance. "You'd be excused for believing the world was perfectly fine here. The grass is green, the trees are tall, the lake is full. Everything is beautiful at King's College." Declan followed his gaze over the immaculate grounds. "The future is not so certain. I'm worried that if we can't fight this new magic that Haberdeen is peddling, then we may not be able to preserve what we've got."

"What do you mean?"

"I mean that this incredible power you have, Declan,

may one day be necessary. And that day may be nearer than any of us expect."

"Power? In me?" Declan laughed. "John, I've been in half a dozen magical confrontations over the past month and every single time, bar none, I've needed someone to rescue me. My parents, my best friend, Ava, Dreyfus. People are being imprisoned; people are dying because of *me*."

"I don't think they are." John shook his head slowly. "People aren't risking themselves for you, Declan. They're risking themselves for the hope that comes with you."

"They're in for a disappointing surprise."

John considered him. "You've lived your whole life thinking you were a LAMP. A lump of coal amongst diamonds. And now, you find out that you may sparkle after all."

Declan remained silent. The spider finished its web and returned to its vantage point, watching and waiting for unsuspecting prey. Waiting for blissful ignorance. *Waiting for me.*

"I imagine you've built up some walls, kid. Those walls won't come down overnight, but they will, if you give them the chance."

When Declan looked up, John was gone.

———

A thundering knock sounded at the door. Declan rushed to answer, became tangled in his blankets, and fell to the floor. He opened the door with a red face and a sore elbow. Mary-Lou beamed at him; an emerald shawl covered her fierised hand. "Good morning, Declan."

"Morning, Mary-Lou. You look very fancy today."

"So nice that you noticed. I'm actually on my way out, important business-"

"Directive business?"

Mary-Lou squinted at him suspiciously. "Where did you hear that word?"

"John told me."

She pursed her lips. "Not his business to be telling you about that. Make sure you keep what he said to yourself."

"I live in an empty dorm. I keep everything to myself." Declan smiled to soften the words. "So, it is Directi-" Mary-Lou silenced him with a glance. "Sorry," he said. "So it is that kind of business, then? What about your hand?"

"I'll be fine. No need for magic where I'm going. Anyway, I dropped by for a couple of reasons. The first is to return this." From beneath her shawl, she produced a tan satchel.

"Ava's bag?" Declan accepted it eagerly.

"Yes, quite a few nifty tricks in there, very fashionable too. Keep it safe for your friend." Mary-Lou rummaged in her pocket. "The second reason is to tell you that Laurefen wants to meet with you today in his office. Main administration building at the front of campus, eleven o'clock. Don't be late." She handed him a slip of paper with the same details in typed letters. "And finally." Mary-Lou opened her arms, her iron hand gleamed in the morning light. "I wanted to say farewell." Before Declan could say anything, she pulled him into a hug that smelled like rose oil. His mother wore rose oil. When she let go, Declan feigned a sneeze to wipe his eyes.

"You've entered a brave new world, Master Moore, but I think there is greatness ahead of you."

"Thanks Mary-Lou. Have a, uh, good time," he said

awkwardly. Mary-Lou winked and turned down the hall. Declan stared at the slip in his hand. *What does Laurefen want with me?*

CHAPTER 19
DECLAN

JOHN HAD GIFTED Declan an impressive amount of clothes from lost property. What started as a mountain by his bed had separated into two smaller piles on the floor. One was clean clothes, the other Declan ignored. He dug through the clean pile until he found a jacket. Outside, a wall of water drenched the grounds.

A door slammed down the hall. It was Amber. She smiled when he stepped out of his room. "That came out of nowhere." She was soaked from head to toe. "The Storm-cloud Agency must be swamped to let that through."

Declan grinned. "Hold up, I'll get you something to dry off." He ducked back into his room and returned with an almost-clean towel. Amber accepted it gratefully.

"Thank you," she said.

Declan didn't know what to say. He stood awkwardly to the side while she dried her hair and tried not to smile when her hair puffed up like an enormous cotton ball.

"Is it that bad?"

"Not at all," Declan lied. "What were you doing out there?"

Amber shrugged. For a moment, she seemed as awkward as he felt. "I was seeing Mary-Lou off." She handed the towel back to Declan. "There is a washing machine down the hall."

Declan looked at the towel. "Is it that bad?"

"Not at all." Amber winked.

A silence formed and stretched between them. Declan rushed to fill it. "I've got a meeting with Laurefen today. Any idea what it could be about?"

Amber's hair wobbled comically as she shook her head. "No clue. Mary-Lou mentioned John was spilling college secrets. Maybe Laurefen wants to erase your memory."

"Oh." The blood drained from Declan's face. Amber laughed. It was the first time he'd heard her laugh.

"I'm only kidding." Amber glanced up. Rain drops drummed against the roof. "Well, that doesn't sound like it is going anywhere in a hurry. When's your meeting with Laurefen?"

"Eleven."

"You've got a bit of time. Any plans?"

"I was going to go for a walk but..."

"Not in this weather," Amber finished. She seemed to be warming to him. "I know the feeling. I was going to imbue matchsticks to strike eternal flames," she glanced out the window. "That's not happening anymore either."

Declan considered her. "You're an Imbuer?"

"I am." Amber stood slightly taller. "In fact, after break, I will be the head of the King's College Imbusion Lab."

"Sounds very fancy," Declan said. "So, you're like an expert on different magical items?"

"I try." Amber raised an eyebrow. "Why?"

"Well, Mary-Lou just returned a bag of magical stuff that my friend left for me. She said there were some cool tricks in there. We used one already," Declan paused, remembering his escape from Lyle's cabin. "I think it was called a ball of disintegration."

Amber raised both eyebrows. "An orb of disintegration?"

"Yeah, that's it. I wanted to check out the rest of it, but I also don't want to disintegrate myself."

"That would be a shame."

Declan shrugged. "Maybe we could look together?"

Amber's eyes brightened. "Sure. Let's have a look."

Declan opened his door, caught sight of the messy floor before then turned back. "Maybe we could go to the common room at the end of the hall?"

A knowing smile crossed Amber's lips. "Sure thing."

Declan collected the satchel, and they walked to the spacious wood-panel common room. Once there, he emptied it onto a table.

"Wow." Amber sat in one of the green leather chairs arranged around the room. Her eyes sparkled as she picked through the satchel's contents. "There's some cool stuff in here. Do you recognize any of it?"

Declan picked up a circular brown cord with a gilded bead on the end. He had seen something identical in his parent's seldom-used camping equipment. "This is a never-ending rope, right?"

"That's correct, you twist this," she touched the bead, "and the rope will adjust to whatever length you need. What else?"

Declan pointed to the vials. "Those were filled with a weird liquid. It was like a healing potion."

"We imbue vials like these with protective charms to keep whatever they hold fresh and unspoiled. Good for preserving magical ingredients." Amber pointed to a cylindrical spike. "What about this one?"

The spike looked to be made of frosted glass. Declan picked it up. It felt warm, as if left in the sun on a hot day. "No idea."

"Stab it into the table."

Declan raised an eyebrow. "But it'll ruin the table."

"An easy fix," Amber said. "Go ahead."

The moment the spike pierced the wood, a bubble emerged from the spike, encompassing them completely. Declan gasped. A large iridescent dome surrounded them.

"A portable shield," Amber said. "Though I've never seen one so large." She pulled the spike from the table and the dome vanished, leaving only a chipped hole in the table. "Handy in case of emergency. Again, quite rare. Your friend must be very wealthy."

The thought of Ava brought a raft of memories Declan wanted to ignore. Amber didn't seem to notice. She picked up a small yellow cube, only the size of a grape, and squeezed it. An internal mechanism clicked. When she opened her palm, the cube fell to the floor and popped, like a corn kernel, into a large plastic crate. It jerked and shuddered and continued to expand until it filled a large section of the room. When the crate stopped growing, it was tall enough for both Declan and Amber to stand inside. "Storage cube," Amber said. "Great for moving dorms." She pressed a small square on the crate's side wall; it hissed like a deflating tire until only a grape-size cube remained.

"That's amazing," Declan said.

Something had caught Amber's eye. She tilted her head. A breath of a gasp escaped her lips, then swept something into her palm. A coin. It was green stone with a crowned monarch carved into its surface. Amber held the coin as if it were a snowflake. A beaked dragon was carved on the other side. "This must be a fake," she muttered. She locked eyes with Declan. "Can I borrow this?"

"It's not mine to give away," Declan said. "But I can't see why you couldn't borrow it."

Amber studied the coin even more closely. "What exactly do you know about your friend?"

"Almost nothing. Her name is Ava. She's a Luck. That's about all." He wanted to continue going through the satchel, but the coin had Amber spellbound. She turned it back and forth, rubbed its edges, held it up to the light. Eventually, Declan's curiosity got the better of him. "Where do you think it's from?"

Amber blinked free of her trance. "What do you know about the world outside Euryma?"

Declan considered it. "Farmers. Miners. Workers. Euryma is the only magical nation in the world. Beyond that, there is nothing but LAMPs earning riches supplying us with raw materials."

"And what about Euryma's beginning?"

"The Founding?" Declan thought back to his history lessons. "Wizards came from the north. Euryma formed to fight them back. Now they're gone." He shrugged. "What does that have to do with a coin?"

"What do you think happened to the wizards when they drove into the Dangerous North?" Amber said. "Do you think they just vanished?"

"They didn't vanish, they were killed, weren't they?"

Amber shook her head. "Euryma drove its enemies north using their new magic. Those enemies decided they needed to fight fire with fire. They took our magic and twisted it; they formed their own nation built on green magic."

"Then why haven't I ever heard of a second magical nation?"

"Because *apparently* it didn't last. Green magic is volatile, dangerous. The northerners played with fire and got burned."

Declan threw his hands up in mock exasperation. "So, what does that have to do with the coin?"

Amber chuckled. "Because that's the Mage Council's official story. What if the green magic didn't destroy them? What if a second magical nation still exists? A nation to rival Euryma. A nation with witches and wizards of unimaginable power who wield despair like a sword. A nation where they wear green clothes, live in green houses and trade in green coins." Amber held the coin out to him.

Declan stared at the beaked dragon carved into the green stone. "What was the nation called?"

"Vedmark."

The rain stopped. The room suddenly became too quiet. Declan looked up at Amber. "Do you really think that's a coin from Vedmark?"

Amber shook her head. "I doubt it. Vedmark is a story for naughty children who refuse to go to sleep. My guess- someone carved this coin based on those stories. Still, I'm interested to hear Michael's take."

"Michael?"

"He collects coins. Knows all about them, too."

Declan didn't know what to say. Michael was a prickly topic. He picked up a small cardboard box. "I've seen these. They're fireflies. I got some for my birthday once. Wake them up in water and they'll put on a cool show."

"You're definitely close, but I think these are something different." Amber took the box and read the script on the back. "These are flareflies. Potent ones too—this box must have cost your friend a fortune."

"Flareflies?"

"Similar to fireflies. Same family, different species. I can see how you'd mistake them, but these... they... pop and undo magic."

"What?"

Amber giggled. "Okay, that was a terrible explanation." She opened the box and held up a dormant flarefly; it looked like a black glass jellybean. "This is a male flarefly. For the most part, it's just like your ordinary firefly, lights things up when tossed in water." She reached into the box again, then held up a blue jellybean. "This, on the other hand, is a female flarefly. When you toss her in water, she'll fly around and drive the males wild, to the point where they burst and release a pulse of energy."

"And what does that do?" Declan eyed the glass jewels.

"Anything magical caught in the pulse will be returned to normal. Imbued objects lose their power. Spells wear off."

Declan thought about Mary-Lou and her iron hand. "Would it work on fierisation?"

Amber froze. She looked at the flareflies, then at Declan. After an extended moment, a wide grin spread across her face. "Declan, you might be a genius." She dropped the beads back into the box—they clinked like a wind chime.

"But Mary-Lou has already gone."

"She'll be back for this," Amber looptapped a message on her left palm then put the box in her pocket. "I've got to go; this could be huge."

"Uh. Yeah, sure, go for it." Declan was in a daze. "Uh, okay. Well, I'll see you later."

"Sure thing. Thanks Declan!" Amber beamed. "This has been... nice..."

"Uh, my pleasure..."

Amber nodded. "I'll see you later." Her long hair bounced as she left. Declan looked down at the pile of Ava's belongings on the table and thought about what Amber had said. *Who are you, Ava?*

At eleven o'clock, Declan sat on a firm, leather lounge chair. Laurefen sat behind a desk made from carefully assembled slabs of driftwood, his long fingers interlinked as he studied Declan the way a bird might study an unfamiliar insect. Declan made a conscious effort to keep his hands from fidgeting under Laurefen's steady gaze.

"It has taken longer than I would like to meet with you, Declan, and the circumstances that have brought you to my school are... irregular." Laurefen's perfectly curled moustache twitched. "I did not ask for you to be here, and as of this moment, I am still undecided whether I want you to be here."

Declan was uncertain how to respond. The silence extended, as if Laurefen would not continue without a response. "I... I understand, sir."

Laurefen nodded. "Despite all this, your presence here is through no fault of your own. You have been thrust into circumstances beyond you and, whether I like it or not, King's College seems to be the safest place for you. For now."

"Thank you, sir."

Laurefen waved his hand in a small circle, his fingers moved in a blur too fast to see, and the ceiling began to quiver. It looked like a thin film of detergent, ready to be blown into bubbles, only with a slight yellow sheen. The shimmering film pulsed to the edges of the ceiling and down the walls, bleeding down the walls until they were encased in a shimmering cube. "Compressed air," Laurefen said in answer to Declan's confused expression. "I dislike that these measures are necessary, but this conversation is for our ears only." He pressed his fingertips together. "Declan, what do you want your legacy to be?"

The question caught Declan off guard. He tried thinking of something articulate but, at that moment, forming comprehensive thoughts was beyond him. After an awkward pause, he shrugged. "I hadn't really thought about it."

Laurefen's lips turned in distaste. "It is an important thing to think about. Our lives are fleeting moments, yet a legacy can last forever. What will Declan Moore's legacy be?"

Again, Declan had no idea what to say. "I... want to be able to do magic."

"That is not a legacy," Laurefen said. "Plenty of people can do magic. No, this is something more. How do you want to be remembered?"

"I..." Declan trailed off. Not because he didn't know what to say, but because he knew exactly what to say, but didn't dare give the words breath. He sat, silent, until that silence became unbearable. "I want to live up to my family name. To not be the failed Moore. To not be the dark secret of the family, or looked at with sympathy. I want to be remembered like my parents. A good wizard, a capable wizard."

Laurefen considered him. His bright eyes darted back

and forth, stern and searching. "You would aspire to be good rather than great?"

"I just want to be more than nothing." As he said it, he felt a weight lift from him, a weight he hadn't even realized was there. Declan glanced at Laurefen, who watched still with steady eyes. A question pulled at him, though he was unsure he wanted an answer. *You have to ask,* said a voice in his head. He took a deep breath. "Were my parents attacked because of me?"

"No, Declan. Fatesmiths have been fierising magical families for nearly eight months now. They pick a place, make a plan, and attack en masse. An unfortunate coincidence that it happened the way it did, nothing more. Your parents were not the only ones turned to iron casts on the first of November."

"How?" Declan asked. "Why aren't the police stopping them?"

"Magical Law Enforcement will not resist the Fatesmiths because they are working together."

"But, the Mage Council? They wouldn't let witches and wizards die?"

"No, but they seem perfectly content to consign them to a temporary stasis." Laurefen sighed. "There are two reasons why High Mage Johannasberg won't help us stop the Fatesmiths. The first is that he is conservative by nature. He believes magical leadership to be a necessity. The Fatesmiths under Haberdeen's leadership are pushing a more extreme version of his philosophy. They say magic should be limited *only* to leadership. Do you understand?"

Declan mulled it over. "The blackcoats have the same ideals, just dialed up a notch?"

"Exactly," Laurefen said. "While they share similar sentiments, Haberdeen wants magical usage reduced for fanciful reasons that Johannasberg does not believe, let alone endorse."

"Remnant Magic?"

Laurefen looked at him in surprise. "How do you know that?"

"Ava," Declan said. "The Luck who rescued me that night the blackcoats took my parents. She said they think Remnant Magic is destroying the world."

"Your friend is correct. Haberdeen seeks to prevent a natural disaster born of her imagination. Johannasberg can't agree with that, but he will happily allow magical usage to be reduced Dominion-wide. I fear his legacy will be one of poor choices and weak governance."

"And the other reason? You said there were two."

"Simply put. He can't stop her." Laurefen's expression soured. "Haberdeen's fierisation magic cannot be blocked or countered. It's magical iron, a paradox, because as you are aware—"

"Iron resists magic."

Laurefen nodded. "As long as Haberdeen is only abducting citizens, Johannasberg will let it slide. He'll sit in Sabriva Tower, ignore the disappearances, even redirect the media to keep things quiet."

"He doesn't want to start a fight that he knows he'll lose?"

"Precisely. To make matters worse, many MLEA officers are now working directly for the Fatesmiths, drawn to their power, perhaps seeking to learn some new tricks."

A pit formed in Declan's stomach. These people had taken his parents with seemingly no consequences. "So, who's going to stop them?"

Laurefen opened his mouth, then closed it. A shadow of

a smile crossed his lips. "It seems you have a talent, Declan, for extracting information."

"They took my parents," Declan said, bolder than he felt. "And like you said, I've been dragged into this unwillingly. I think I deserve some answers."

Laurefen leaned back in his chair. "It is a valid argument."

"Why do the Fatesmiths want me?"

Laurefen did not answer immediately. When he did, his expression was softer than Declan had seen. "Have you ever heard of an opal eagle?"

Declan shook his head.

"They are not native to Euryma. They are an exotic creature imported by traders from the Dangerous North. Enormous birds with brilliant plumage that shines all manner of colors." Laurefen looked out the window. The storm was clearing. "They are majestic creatures that can soar high into the clouds and dive as fast as any wind. However, their most prized quality is their hatchlings' habit of assimilating to its environment."

Declan frowned. "I don't understand."

The edges of Laurefen's lips twitched. "The egg of an opal eagle can be left with any flightless fowl, and the owner can be assured it will stay put. Often, people will hatch them with common chickens. These massive, beautiful birds will go their whole lives believing they are a common poultry. Despite their powerful claws and wings, they will never leave the ground. This combination of power, beauty, and subservience is very valuable."

"But what does that have to do with..." Realization swept over him. "You're saying I'm a bird that thinks it's a chicken?"

Laurefen nodded. "Glad to see there's something going

on up there," he said. "Haberdeen considers you the powerful opal eagle who still believes he's a chicken." He pursed his lips. "And she is the keeper, eager to exploit you."

A stray thought hit Declan with all the force of a cannonball. An idea that he never dared consider, a notion that had forever been so far from his grasp that he would sooner try to catch the moon than pay it any attention. He met Laurefen's intense blue eyes, butterflies crowded his stomach. "Will you train me to use magic?"

"No."

Declan's fragile hopes shattered.

"You have the potential to be powerful, beyond powerful. We do not know how that will look, or if it is even safe." He sighed. "In such circumstances, I would consider referring you to a private tutor who could safely explore your potential." Laurefen closed his eyes for a moment, as if sending Declan away would solve all his problems. "But these are not normal circumstances."

"So, you'll keep me as the chicken?" The question sounded harsher than Declan had anticipated.

"Declan, our main goal here is to keep you safe. To protect you—"

"Protect me? By the sounds of it, you can't even protect yourself!" Declan's despair transformed unexpectedly into rage. "What's stopping Haberdeen from showing up tomorrow and taking me? You said it yourself. You can't stop her."

"You are safe here." Laurefen's voice remained level. "Kingsbreak is protected by the Ancellum, a spell beyond the ability of any living soul, Haberdeen included. You are safe here. We all are."

Declan leaned back. *I can't believe you let yourself think things might be different. You'll never be a wizard.* He looked down at his hands. Small beads of sweat dotted the lines of his palms. "I'd like to go now, if that's okay."

Laurefen waved his hand. The shimmering yellow walls dissolved away. Gentle songs from birds outside trickled through the windows. "I can sympathize with your frustration, but my decision is final. This is for the best."

Declan said nothing as he left. Outside, all evidence of the morning's storm was gone. The sun shone bright and hot; the azure sea twinkled in the distance. Declan dragged his heavy legs and heavier heart back to his room with a dark voice whispering in his ear. *You'll never be a wizard.*

CHAPTER 20
MARY-LOU

"YOU NEED to see things for what they are," Mary-Lou snapped. Her visit to Sabriva had left her in a foul mood—the High Mage was insufferable. "Habsburg belongs to Haberdeen, half of Iberia too. Declan will need time to learn. If you leave it too late, he'll be useless."

"You miss the point," Laurefen said flatly. "What's the point in saving Euryma if there's none of it to be saved?"

Mary-Lou sat back and huffed. Laurefen stacked cases of flareflies on the linoleum bench, one of many that lined the Imbusion Lab. White ceramic walls looked as sterile as a hospital hallway. She'd never liked these rooms, and being in them did nothing for her mood. "Have you seen the boy lately? He's miserable. Put yourself in his shoes. Parents gone, friends gone, then holed up a thousand miles from home to hide in a student apartment."

Laurefen turned a case in his palm. It tinkled like a music box.

"Don't ignore me, Laurefen."

"So the boy is miserable. Better miserable than dead, or

an iron cast, or guilty of destroying a continent because he couldn't control his own strength."

"How long will you wait? How bad must things become?"

"Worse than they are now. Michael is tracking the latest raid as we speak. If we can find where Haberdeen's storing the witches and wizards—"

"Then what?" Mary-Lou demanded. "Where are we going to store thousands of iron statues?"

Laurefen looked up from the box. "Then we will evaluate our options and make the best choice."

"Best choice for who?"

"For everyone." Laurefen slid the box towards her and turned away from her.

Mary-Lou rolled her eyes. She loved the man like a brother, but Laurefen was as stubborn as she was, and as much as she hated to admit it, his logic was reasonable. *There's no telling what Declan Moore is capable of.* She hefted her iron hand onto the stone bench. It was cold, heavy, but otherwise painless. Laurefen filled two small metal bowls with water and placed them beside her.

"Shall we?"

Mary-Lou took a long, calming breath, tempered her hope, and nodded. "No time like the present".

Laurefen dropped a handful of black beads into one of the bowls. They landed with a plop, the water hissed and winged insects with silver bulbous tails emerged from the liquid. They circled the bowl, emanating a low buzz. When all the beads had transformed to flareflies, Laurefen took the bowl and poured the remaining water over Mary-Lou's iron hand. The flareflies followed like ants to honey. They crawled over her palm, feasting on the water.

Mary-Lou cringed. Bugs were definitely not her forte.

Laurefen plucked a sky-blue pebble from the box. "Here we go."

He dropped it into the second bowl of water. Immediately, another flarefly emerged, this one snow white with a sapphire tail. It fluttered above the bench as if finding its bearings, then shot towards Mary-Lou's hands. The black flareflies hummed angrily, as if guarding their territory.

Disgust momentarily put aside; Mary-Lou observed with fascination as the female flarefly circled her hand. The males grew louder and louder; their irate buzz became a roar, filling the room like a waterfall. With a flash like a camera, they popped. Mary-Lou looked down at her hand.

Cold, hard iron.

Disappointment swept through her. Laurefen sighed. He ran a hand through his mane of gray hair. Nothing had changed. Mary-Lou turned her wrist, then gasped. "Laurefen!"

Fleshy knuckles poked through the metal, like little pink islands in a sea of gray. Laurefen froze with his hand on his head. He stepped closer, leaned close, and inspected her wrist. "It worked?"

"It worked." Mary-Lou whispered. She could not believe it; she had worked so hard not to get her hopes up. With her other hand, she poked against the fleshy protuberances. The fierisation had been reversed. "Tell Amber she's brilliant."

Laurefen clapped his hands together. He looked happier than she had seen him in months. "We're going to need more flareflies!"

CHAPTER 21
DECLAN

OVER THE NEXT MONTH, Declan would check in with Laurefen every chance he got. Each time he would hint at the prospect of some sort of training, some sort of instruction, even a piece of advice on how to start accessing his Potential. It was pointless. The rest of the Directive came and went in a revolving door of 'College Business' and left Declan alone to wonder if tomorrow would be the day Laurefen changed his mind.

Another month passed when John let it slip that Laurefen was seeking alternative places to house him. He didn't want him on the island at all. When Declan heard that, he went to bed and didn't get up.

Days passed in a blur of meal breaks and bathroom stops. Declan let them go. He wanted nothing to do with passing time. He stayed in his bed and let it move without him. Days turned into weeks and weeks to months. Morning frosts blanketed King's lawns in sheets of crystal. Declan stayed in bed.

A gray shirt draped over a bedside lamp; the same shirt Declan wore nearly two months ago when he last met with

Laurefen. What once stunk of adolescent sweat had matured into something else, but he didn't notice. The room stunk of body odor and self-pity, a combination most the Directive steered clear of. John occasionally stopped by, mostly to drop off food and check he was breathing. Mary-Lou visited whenever she made it back to Kingsbreak, but never stayed long. Declan assumed Laurefen had her busy on Directive business, but she did not talk about it and he no longer cared to ask. Mainly, he stayed wrapped in a blanket, thinking about how useless he was.

You knew it. You've known it since you were six years old-since Dad sat you down and told you about your test. Sure, some things have changed slightly, but not the result. You'll never do magic; you'll never be like your parents. Anyone with an iota of Potential can do whatever they want with you. Lyle nearly broke you in half. Horace had to save you. Then Ava had to save you. Then Mary-Lou had to save you. Then Laurefen. You might as well be a newborn baby with how useless you are...

The same inner monologue repeated for weeks. It varied slightly. Some days, it focused on how Horace should be starting a college of his choice if Declan didn't exist. Other days it was his parents, cold casts being carried into a van that Declan was too weak to stop. Lumps of iron started haunting his dreams. At first, it was Dreyfus, but now the misshapen boulders came with other names, his parents' names.

You can't save them. Laurefen will never teach you anything. You're dangerous, too dangerous. So dangerous that you might as well be nothing.

Declan squeezed his eyes shut. Hot, salty drops carved fresh lines across the grime fixed to his cheeks. He rolled over and buried his head in the tear-stained pillow. The afternoon sun illuminated the squalor where he slept.

What are you doing here?

He tried to think of a satisfactory answer. Or any answer.

There's nothing for you here. You're probably endangering everyone by being here.

Declan pressed the pillow against his head, to drown the voice out like he had so many times before. This time, it wouldn't be silenced. The voice went on, screaming in his mind.

But you can't leave, can you? You have no power! You don't even know how to get off the island!

"Stop it," he whispered.

You really are helpless.

"Stop."

If only Dreyfus could see you now. Do you think he would have let himself be turned into a pile of metal so that you could cry in bed?

Declan grabbed the rails of the bed and pulled his head into the stone wall. The thud of his skull against the stone was just loud enough to muffle the voice. He did it again, and again, harder, louder. The voice in his head gave way to the sweet rhythm of stone. A warm sensation bloomed atop his head. It spread down his face, onto the bed, until everything became sweet, silent and black.

CHAPTER 22
DECLAN

WHITE CURTAINS, white walls, a shining silver trolley, the sharp smell of pine cleaner. Declan blinked under the harsh florescent light and the room came into focus. Katie sat cross-legged, perusing a magazine on her lap with a pen pressed against her lips. She started to write on the page, frowned, then stopped. Amber arrived with a paper bag. She took one look at him and smiled. "Declan. You're awake!"

Katie glanced up. "Oh! I didn't notice." She put the magazine down, Declan glimpsed an incomplete crossword. "How are you feeling?"

A dull ache radiated from the crown of his head. Declan tried to sit up and failed. "Sore," he said. "How did I end up here?"

"What do you remember?" Katie asked.

Amber adjusted her hair as she settled into a seat. She dug a sandwich out of the paper bag and floated it across the room to Katie. The sight of the magic was enough. Memories poured back like dripping treacle. The voice in his head, it had been relentless. He had tried to drown it out. "I don't remember anything," he lied. Katie and Amber exchanged meaningful glances. Declan's cheeks burned. *They know.*

"Declan, we've all lost things to Haberdeen," Amber said, her expression solemn. "We're not going to sit here and tell you we understand how you're feeling. But you're not alone here."

Katie nodded her agreement. "We want you here at King's. More importantly, we want *you* to want to be here." She held his eyes. "We thought we were doing the right thing, giving you time and space to work through your pain." Her gaze dropped to the floor. "That was a mistake. I'm sorry."

"Sorry Declan," Amber added. "We should have been there for you."

Declan shook his head; the movement ignited a wave of pain. "No, no, no." His croaky voice stumbled over the words. "No. You didn't do anything wrong. You don't need to apologize at all!"

Amber put her hand on the edge of the bed. "We do. You lost everything. Your entire life changed overnight. That is huge. And we just *left* you to figure it out."

"You're not alone, Declan." Katie said. The corners of her eyes sparkled.

Declan wasn't sure how to respond. He lay back against the thick pillow and touched his head gingerly. *Tell them the truth*, he thought.

"Well, well, well." John said, beaming as he walked in. "Look who finally decided to join us."

Amber scrunched up the paper bag and threw it at John, who caught it mid-air with a twirl of his fingers and sent it straight back at her. Katie looped it around her head and into the bin. John sat by his bedside. "Feeling better?" he asked.

"Still a bit of an ache," Declan said, patting his head.

"Hold still then." John put a palm on his mop of curls and Declan's skin erupted in goose pimples. When the icy sensation passed, the pain went with it. He sat up in his bed, moving his head from side to side.

"Thank you."

John nodded. "No worries, but what we're all wondering is why it was necessary."

"John!" Katie threw him a glare that he could not intercept.

John shrugged his shoulders. "What? That was a nasty head injury. I want to know how it happened, or why."

Declan's cheeks burned.

"What happened," Amber started, narrowed eyes staring venom at John, "was that we did a poor job of being friends. Declan needs rest now." Her expression softened for a moment, then she glared at John. "If he wants to talk about it, he can do it when he's ready." It was odd to see her so outspoken.

"Fine, fine. Captain sensitivity." John rolled his eyes. After a brief pause, he turned to the door. "Well, he's awake, he's better. Let's go."

Declan blinked. "Go where? Actually..." he looked around the room. "Where am I?"

"This is an Imbusion lab," Katie said.

"A what?"

"An Imbusion lab. People learning to imbue objects with magical powers study here."

Declan frowned, confused. "So, it's not a hospital or medical center?"

Katie shook her head. "Nope."

"So, what am I doing here?"

A smirk formed on John's face; Katie's hands moved in a quick zig-zag. John groaned like he'd been punched in the gut. "What was that for?"

"Be nice," she said. Then she shrugged uncomfortably. "We didn't like the smell of your room."

Heat rose *again* in Declan's cheeks. He wondered if it was possible to run out of blushes.

"Well," John said, eyes on Katie as he straightened. "Correct me if I'm wrong, but I think it's time for an adventure."

Declan eased himself onto the linoleum floor. After months in bed, his legs were weak. He stood, wobbled and found his balance. Amber and Katie watched like protective hens. Declan turned to John. "What did you have in mind?"

"There's an island—north of Kingsbreak."

An enormous map of Euryma had hung in almost every classroom at Arman Moore's. "No, there's not," Declan said. He knew that map like the back of his hand. Kingsbreak was the largest island in the Mediterranean Sea, surrounded on all sides by Euryma.

"Yes, there is." John smiled. "You've never heard of it, though."

Amber and Katie grinned too. Declan looked at them skeptically. "You're telling me there's a mystery island in Euryma that nobody knows about?"

Katie laughed. "No. Some people know about it. Just not many."

"And why is that? What's on it?"

Katie opened her mouth. John cut her off. "An adventure. You'll have to wait and see."

"And Laurefen is okay with this?" Declan asked.

Amber looked sideways at John. "Uh, Laurefen actually isn't on campus right now."

John grinned. "And what Laurefen doesn't know won't hurt him."

"And Mary-Lou? Michael?" Declan was getting the sense that this adventure might not be approved by all members of the Directive.

"They're off on assignments," Katie said. "We're holding down the fort and are all in agreement that you need a little holiday."

"Don't overthink it, kid," John said, his eyes twinkling. "You're gonna love it."

Declan shrugged his shoulders. "Well, in that case... Let's go on an adventure."

Crystal waves lapped against a pebbled beach, splashing ankle-depth waves over the sand and stone. To the east loomed a distant coastline. Ahead of them waited nothing but water. Katie puzzled over her crossword while Declan and Amber stared at the water.

"Why do we need a boat again?" Declan asked.

Katie looked up from her magazine. "It's a secret."

"But can't John create an Opening to get us there?"

"Not here, he can't. You've heard of the Ancellum, right?"

The word was vaguely familiar. "The what?"

Katie gestured to the island. "The ancient spells that keep Kingsbreak safe."

"Oh, yeah." Declan recalled Laurefen's promise of safety. "The unbreakable old magic, right?"

"That's it. The place we're going has similar protection."

"So how was it that Laurefen could make an Opening to get us here?"

Katie gestured back the way they came. "John took us to Cedrus, a special spot earmarked for Openings. There's no such special spot on—"

"Shh!" Amber grinned. "Don't give anything away."

Katie glanced at her palm; the knowing glance Declan had come to learn was an incoming looptap message. "Here he comes." She folded her magazine into a backpack as a whining roar built in the distance. A small boat came around the island's edge, water sprayed over its white and black trim; John pulled in close, and the large outboard motor dulled to a gentle purr.

"That's our ride?" Declan tried to keep his voice level. It was going to be a tight fit for all four of them.

"That's our ride." Katie walked knee-deep into the water and John waved his hands in a series of straight lines. A white rope danced off the back of the boat, it slithered towards Katie like a charmed snake. Once she had it, she pulled it in to shore. "All aboard!"

Amber's fingers danced as the boat came closer. A narrow path of water froze over and sections of ice lifted off the surface to form a neat staircase. Declan followed her up the staircase in awe. He expected the ice to be slippery, but it was surprisingly firm. They squeezed three bodies into a seat made for two, then Amber clicked her fingers. The staircase collapsed with a splash.

John sat at the stern of the boat with a compass in his hands. "It's not far, should only take half an hour." He pulled a large lever. The motor roared to life, and they were off. The boat jumped and bumped across the small waves. Declan cast a nervous glance back at the island.

"It's fine," Amber said, grabbing his hand. "Once we reach deeper water, it will be a smoother ride."

Declan nodded, painfully aware that a very pretty young woman was holding his hand. He tried to act natural, hoping Amber would leave it there.

When they hit the open water, she let go. She smiled as they skimmed north along the Mediterranean Sea. "I'm not a big fan of the boat myself."

"Why not?" he whispered back.

Amber nodded to the water. "I grew up in the northern end of Euryma. We're the only landlocked state in the Dominion. I'd never seen the sea until I came to King's."

"Can you swim?"

Amber looked indignant. "Yes, I can swim," she said. "But water this deep... It's a little freaky."

Declan left his palm upturned within reach, just in case, but Amber failed to notice. The salty air became a powerful breeze; it whipped Declan's hair from side to side and he suddenly felt more alive than he had in weeks. Katie pulled out her magazine, and the wind tore it from her hands. It vanished into the swirling blue and Amber laughed. "That might be the first crossword you never finish!" she shouted over the roar of the motor.

Katie looked back over their shoulders. Declan had a sneaking feeling she wanted to dive into the water after it. "So, you can't tell me where we're going, but can you tell me what it's called?"

Katie bit her lip. "The name depends where you're from," she said. "The island is home to a lot of—" John cleared his throat loudly. Katie rolled her eyes. "—A lot of history." She shrugged. "It goes by a bunch of different names. The people from Gaul would call it Pasici. If you're from Vitulus, you'd call it Nonla. The Iberians call it Noahi."

"Noahi?" Declan blinked.

Katie raised an eyebrow. "You've heard of it?"

Declan laughed. "Only in bedtime stories. Noahi was the safe refuge for the enchanted animals. The wicked people were killing all the magical creatures, so the Wise Old King put them on a mountain in the sky to be safe." John shifted slightly and Declan couldn't help but feel like he was hiding a smile. Amber seemed very interested in her fingernails. Declan met Katie's eye. "But that's just a story, right?"

Katie raised her hands in mock confusion. "Who knows?"

Declan shook his head. *They're messing with me.*

The sea stretched ahead of them like a rolling field of blue glass. Their boat carved the tranquility into a line of whitewash behind them. It was a sight to behold, but Declan's stomach soon became preoccupied with the constant bounce of the waves. He leaned forward and focused on his feet.

"You okay?" Amber asked.

"A bit queasy," Declan muttered. The rocking continued, and just as he thought he would have to lean over the boat to vomit, the motor cut. The engine's roar dissolved into silence.

"We're here," John announced.

An enormous mass of white stone cliffs emerged from vivid blue. Stunted trees dotted the coastline wherever they could take root and a herd of what Declan could only describe as purple-zebra-mountain-goats wandered along the limestone precipices, stripping the gnarled branches clean.

"Wanderbeast," Amber said, pointing up at the creatures. Declan's jaw hung wide open, sore stomach forgotten completely.

"Those things up there are the reason we're still alive," John said.

Declan looked up at the wanderbeast. Their rich purple stripes shone in the sunlight. "What do you mean?"

John pulled the lever, and the boat shuddered in the island's direction. "See that big one on the left?"

Declan followed his outstretched fingers to a particularly large wanderbeast. "Yeah?"

"Watch this." John swung his hands in a pendulumlike motion and the rocks below it began to crumble.

"What are you doing?" Declan said. "You're going to kill it!"

"Watch," Katie said.

Without missing a beat, the purple zebra goat flicked its head. A circular portal appeared in front of it and it hopped through. The limestone edge gave way and crashed into the water.

"Up there!" Katie pointed to a different ledge. Declan watched in amazement as the very same beast walked out of thin air unharmed.

Declan let out a breath he didn't know he was holding. "They can teleport?"

John nodded. "Witches and wizards figured out how to create Openings from studying them."

"You can learn magic from animals?"

"Kind of," Katie said. "You've seen John create an opening before, haven't you?"

Declan nodded.

"It's a pretty intensive piece of magic, quite slow."

"Gee, thanks Kate."

"Well, it is," she countered. "Let's see you escape the ground falling beneath you with no notice! Anyway," she continued. "We can't learn their magic, but we can imitate it, or at least some of us. We call it biomimicry and those who can do it—"

John cleared his throat importantly.

"Like John." Katie rolled her eyes. "Are called mimics."

Declan turned to John. "So, mimics can do anything that magical animals can do?"

John shook his head. "Kind of. I still need to learn how the animal does it. It's harder for me because I am a mimic and a manipulator. You know what that is, right?"

Declan nodded. "I've never heard of mimics, but I've known plenty of manipulators. My dad was—" he stopped abruptly. The thought hurt, and he took a moment to recover. "My dad is a manipulator," he said weakly.

"So, biomimicry has a slightly different approach to it. As a manipulator, I'm limited to the surrounding materials, with biomimicry I can copy animals that use magic in a very different way, but it's not as natural to me as pure mimics, it's slow and takes a long time to master each skill."

"Is one better than the other?" Declan asked. He forced the memories of his father back into the part of his mind he never touched.

"Not really," John said. "You can think of manipulation as the magic power of humans. If animals were smart enough, they could probably study us and mimic it, albeit in a weaker and slower way. Manipulation is what witches and wizards do best. It's fast and it's powerful. Biomimicry gives you some diversity and you can pretty much pick your abilities based on what animals you want to study."

"So, what abilities did you pick?"

Amber and Katie exchanged looks; their faces split into large smiles. "Yeah, John," Katie said. "What did you pick?"

Despite the onslaught of giggles, John remained composed. "Well, obviously I can create Openings, which I learned from our friends up here," he nodded to the wanderbeast chewing idly in the sun. "I also went with healing, which I got from the golden salvamander."

"And…" Amber said as Katie broke into a fit of giggles.

John sighed. "And I can change my appearance like the stone octopus."

Declan raised an eyebrow at Amber and Katie, who were laughing openly. "What's so funny?"

Katie was struggling to breathe, so Amber told the story. "John was just learning how to take on the appearance of others when he started to fancy one of the new students. What was her name again?"

"Bridget," Katie said between breaths.

"I'm not sure he needs to hear this," John said. His cheeks were pink; it was as uncomfortable as Declan had ever seen him.

"Well," Amber continued, ignoring him. "John decided to give himself some extra-high cheekbones and extra-large muscles to introduce himself to her…" she trailed off in a fit of laughter.

Declan was smiling in spite of himself. "And?"

Amber couldn't finish. She was laughing so hard the boat rocked. Katie had to take over. "So, he goes up to her in front of the whole junior cohort and she screams and runs away."

Amber bent over, struggling to breathe. John was beet red; an embarrassed grin plastered his face.

"What happened?" Declan asked.

"He… He…" Katie couldn't even say it. Tears rolled down

her cheeks. Finally, she caught her breath. "He didn't quite do it right, instead of high cheekbones he had the face of—"

"A stone octopus!" Amber shrieked and collapsed into another fit of laughter.

"Not my finest moment," John said with a wink. "She never spoke to me again. Turned green every time I saw her." Katie and Amber continued to laugh, and Declan joined them. He felt like a new person. It was the first time he had laughed in months. "Alright, you maniacs," John said. "Let's find a place to land." John spun the boat around, the motor roared. Katie and Amber giggled as they bounced over the waves.

"So wait," Declan said. "Are you telling me Noahi is real?"

"Well, it's not a mountain," Katie said, wiping her eyes. "But yes, this is the island that the kings of old dedicated it as a sanctuary to the creatures of Euryma. Most of them have since been hunted to extinction everywhere else but here."

"And that's why it's a secret," John said. "If word got out that a treasure trove of magical abilities was hiding just off the coast of Vitulus, it would be madness."

"How does it stay hidden?"

John shrugged. "No idea. Katie?"

Katie shrugged. "No one knows how it works. It's ancient magic, long lost. In a way, that is good. If we don't understand it, we can't undo it. From what I've read, it is theorized that Nonla," she glanced at Declan. "Or Noahi, or whatever you call it, exists in a separate reality that is tethered to our world by knowledge."

Declan scratched his head. "What does that mean?"

"It means that you can only visit this island if you're in the company of someone who has been here before. If some

Vitulian thrill-seekers went joyriding across the Mediterranean, they'd pass straight through it."

"It's cool," Amber said abruptly. "That we can trace our presence here right back to the Kings and Queens of Ancient Euryma."

Declan thought about it. Arman Moore had fought for King Fendragon. He wondered if his greatest-grandfather had ever stepped foot on this island.

John steered them into a shallow cove. The water was so clear that the boat seemed to levitate over the white sand. Amber created another walkway of ice and they exited onto a tiny beach with a steep dirt path cutting into the hills.

John tied a thick rope to a gnarled stump. "Welcome to Noahi!" He tossed a backpack over his shoulder. "Let's get started."

CHAPTER 23
DECLAN

"WHERE ARE WE GOING?"

After weeks in bed, Declan's legs were on fire. Katie must not have heard as she continued to climb the dirt track into the hills. The landscape below was a thick carpet of green smeared across white cliffs. John led the group, with Amber close behind. Katie hung back with Declan, though he hadn't decided whether it was out of pity or because her short stature wasn't quite suited to uphill climbs.

"It's an adventure!" John called from ahead. He waited with Amber at the top of the hill. "You're gonna want to catch this view. C'mon!"

Declan ignored his tired muscles and pushed on. Katie groaned; her face was bright red. *Definitely not protecting me.* When Declan reached the top, he froze. "Wow."

The summit overlooked a deep valley cut by a winding river. The valley itself was unremarkable, but Declan's eyes grew wide at the kaleidoscope of color that filled the grassy slopes. Herds of purple wanderbeast mingled with creatures of every imaginable hue. It was mesmerizing. Animals of a thousand shades and shapes jostled about like a scene from a child's dream.

It wasn't until Amber tapped his shoulder that Declan realized John had been talking all along.

"And that's a beacon gecko, funny little fellas that love the color orange. At night, the pink and blue marks on their skin drift around and glow like a lava-lamp. Keep your distance, though."

"Why's that?" Declan asked. The plump blue lizards appeared harmless.

"Their saliva is a potent depressant. A good nip will leave you as woozy as a teenager who got into his parent's liquor cabinet."

Declan nodded absently. Something incredible had caught his eye. "What are those?" he pointed at an enormous goat with golden horns.

"The gilded ibex? I already told you..." John's eyes narrowed. "Have you been listening?"

"Uh, kind of?"

John rolled his eyes, then chuckled. "Ugh, alright. It's a gilded ibex, strong enough to move a boulder. And those horns—pure gold.

"Pure gold?" Declan shook his head in amazement.

"Yep. No stretch of the imagination to guess why people might hunt that one."

"Do they have any magical abilities?"

"Besides being ridiculously strong? They can heat their horns until they glow white hot, attracts all kinds of bugs that get zapped by the heat." John winked. "Cooked insects make a great protein supplement for herbivores."

"And what about those?" Declan pointed to a flabby four-legged beast that looked like someone had put a jet-black walrus on hooves. The strange herd of creatures inhaled the grass with enthusiasm.

"Onyxelles. Mimics have been trying to figure them out for years."

"Why?" Declan asked.

"Invisibility," John said. "They can vanish at will."

"Those things? Invisibility?" Declan held back a laugh. "You've got to be kidding me?"

"Look closer," Katie said.

Declan concentrated on the onyxelle's matte black fur. "What am I looking for?" he asked.

"Don't worry about the ones you can see. Watch what's around them," she said.

Sure enough, little patches of nearby grass were disappearing in chunks, consumed by an invisible force. "Amazing," he whispered. "And what about—"

"There are hundreds of different animals down there," Amber said. "They are amazing, but that's not the adventure we're here for."

Declan's shoulders dropped. He would be happy to stay there all day. "They're so cool!"

"They are," Katie agreed. "But there are plenty of books about magical fauna at King's. I'm sure John can load you up with some light reading to pass the time."

John gave him a thumbs up as Amber started walking along the edge of the hill. "Believe me," she said. "This is just the beginning."

Declan dragged his eyes away from the valley. "You mean there's something better than this?"

"You have no idea."

The sun settled into a slow afternoon descent. Amber continued to lead while Katie huffed and puffed from behind. Soon, a bubbling chorus joined them. They were walking by the same river that ran through the valley of magical creatures. The trees here were taller. Declan's neck prickled with the eerie sense that something was watching him. He hurried to walk alongside John.

"Are there any dangerous animals on the island?" he asked.

"Not really," John said. "I mean, magical animals have abilities that can be dangerous if you're caught in the cross-fire, but any apex predators would have wiped everything out a long time ago."

"But don't predators keep the number of animals in check?"

"Doesn't seem necessary. The whole place seems perfectly balanced, probably magic involved."

Declan stared up at the trees. "So, what *is* the most dangerous thing here?"

John looked thoughtfully out into the trees. "Well, there are paralysis ants, one bite from them and you're a garden ornament." He stroked his short beard as they walked. "Though they don't tend to bite unless provoked. Hmmm. Probably fire bears."

"Bears?" Declan stammered.

"Fire bears," John corrected. "They're herbivores, live off fruit and honey, *lots* of fruit and honey. But they're quite...well, they're not very good at sharing. Plus, they do have a nasty habit of bursting into flames." He smirked at Declan. "They won't go after you. Stay away from their honey and you'll be fine!"

Declan swallowed. They entered a small clearing.

"Stop here, can you?" Katie called in protest. "My legs aren't as long as yours."

John dug into his backpack. "Roadside snack," he called, tossing each of them an apple. "Got water, Katie?"

Katie shook a silver flask from her own pack in response and gulped it down. Declan suddenly realized he had not drunk a drop all day. Katie finished a monumental drink from the flask, then tossed the bottle in his direction. "Drink up," she said.

The water was icy cold and almost sweet. No matter how much he drank, the flask never emptied.

"Pretty cool, hey?" Katie said. "Bottomless flask. Amber imbued it to refill from a mountain stream in the Clovish goldfields."

Declan stared in amazement, then bit into his apple. It was delicious. He lay back on the soft forest floor while he chewed.

"C'mon guys, we're so close now," Amber said.

"What's the hurry, Amber?" Katie asked, lying back as well. "Bookworms like me aren't used to this much walking. Let me recharge for a few minutes."

Amber sighed and sat; her long hair fell neatly around her. She chewed her apple impatiently.

"Check out the flowerflow," John said, pointing to a patch of orange growing off a fallen trunk.

Declan sat up for a better look. A mass of orange petals rippled and moved along from plant to plant as if suspended in a garden fountain. They flowed across from one stem to the next in an endless loop. "Are they..."

"Magic?" John answered. "Yep, though quite weak. You need to dry them like tea leaves to get any effect, and even then, it never lasts long."

"What do they do?" Declan's eyes were fixed on the floral ballet.

"Plants are Kate's domain." John looked over at Katie sprawled out on the ground. "Hey Kate, what do the orange ones do?"

"Nothing special." Katie spoke without moving. "Orange flowerflow tea will make your hair grow thicker and your nails stronger for a couple of days."

"Pretty boring," John said. "There are some cool ones, though. Purple gives you about ten minutes of super strength. Blue ones let LAMPs use magic for an hour or so."

Declan's eyes snapped to John. "Blue ones give you powers?"

"If you can find them. They don't bloom often."

"Where do you find them?" Declan asked in a rush of excitement.

John laughed. "Slow down, Declan, you don't need flowerflow tea to learn magic. You have Potential, in spades. Spades upon spades and shovels on shovels."

Declan tried to cover his disappointment. "Yeah, okay."

Katie sat up. "Even if we could find it, I would caution against it, Declan. Flowerflow tea has its risks. Addiction is a real possibility. It's banned in most states of Euryma for good reason."

"Are we done talking about flowers?" Amber was back on her feet. "Kate's up and looks capable of walking again. Let's go!"

Katie poked her tongue out. "You try hiking on these tiny little legs."

John helped Declan to his feet. "Not far now," he said. "You'll love it."

They followed Amber through the trees. The river's bubbling symphony grew to a dull roar. John glanced back. "We're here."

He disappeared around a corner, and Declan followed. Around the bend, encircled by trees, was a circular blue pool, misted by a small waterfall.

"Wow," Declan whispered.

It was beautiful. Afternoon sunlight filtered through the trees, casting little rainbows across the clearing. White stone, crisscrossed with emerald moss, bordered the edge of the turquoise water. Declan felt as if he had stepped into an artist's dream.

Amber whooped with delight and ran towards the water.

Declan glanced at John. "No swimsuit required?"

"Just watch."

Amber hit the surface with an almighty splash, yet nothing changed. Her hair and her clothes looked like they simply refused to absorb water. Declan blinked, unable to make sense of the sight. John climbed along the edge of the white rock and dove smoothly into the water, leaving the faintest ripple. When he surfaced, he was also completely dry.

"Your turn!" Katie called from behind him.

Declan walked to the edge of the water. The vivid green-blue was indescribable. He dipped his hand into the pool. It was like a cool spray of mist, completely weightless.

"C'mon! Jump in!" Amber called.

Declan took a deep breath and jumped. What followed was the most peculiar sensation of his life. A body of water that was not wet. Instead, it felt like a dense collection of cold air, as if someone had packed too much winter wind into one room. He dipped below the surface. It was amazing—he could see perfectly. Diagonal lines of sunlight created a striped pattern on a polished surface. The whole floor of the pool was smooth except for one small imprint, a small hole shaped like a crescent moon. Declan swam to the bottom and ran his finger around the imprint's edge. He pushed off the ground and floated to the top. Katie waded into the pool as Declan paddled towards John and Amber. "What is this?"

"Dry water," Amber said.

"Imaginative name, right?" Katie joked.

Declan ran his hand through the liquid. "But how?"

"We assume that it's what happens when a river flows for centuries through an island packed with nothing but magical plants and animals." Amber smiled at him. "Do you like it?"

"I love it!" He pointed to the base of the pool. "There's a little moon carved into the bottom. Does that mean anything?"

"Nothing we understand." Amber grinned, then vanished below the water. Her long hair trailed behind her like a ribbon.

Soon they were joking and splashing around, perfectly dry, yet completely refreshed. The sun dipped lower until the waning light stretched long fingers into the trees. Katie started telling Declan about her first trip to the island while Amber and John tossed pebbles in the water and raced to collect them. Declan watched as they laughed together, then turned back to Katie, who had stopped mid-sentence. "What is it?"

"It's getting dark," she said, staring into the trees. "We should head back. The boat ride can be difficult in the dark. C'mon."

Declan followed her to the water's edge. Amber surfaced, holding a white pebble triumphantly.

"Time to go," Katie said.

"Not a bad idea," John said, emerging with his own pebble. "We still have to hike back to the boat and I don't want to be on the boat after the sun goes down."

"Fair call," Amber agreed.

John smiled at Declan as they climbed out of the pool. "What do you think, kid? Was that a worthwhile adventure?"

Declan looked back at the bubbling water. "That was awesome." He paused for a moment, unsure of himself. "Thank you. I needed this." He hesitated, and his gaze dropped to his feet. "It's been a really rough couple of months. I'm sick of being useless. My family is gone, my friends are gone, and although everyone thinks I'm capable of being some powerful wizard, no one will teach me magic."

When Declan finally looked up, Amber had tears in her eyes. "Your family and friends aren't *gone,* Declan. We're doing everything we can to find them and then save them."

"And you have friends," John added. "You have us."

Declan's ears burned. "Thanks," he managed, blushing a sunset.

Katie looked up at the sky. "As beautiful as this little heart to heart has been. We need to get going."

"Yeah, alright," John said. "You're not going to slow us down, are you?" he teased.

"Well, that's why I want to leave now." She started back up the track.

Amber remained with Declan. "John's right. We're here for you, okay? If you need anything, ask us. No more bloody heads and messy rooms, okay?"

Declan avoided her gaze. "Yeah, okay," he mumbled. Amber touched his elbow, then started up the track. The morning felt like another lifetime ago, one filled with pain and loneliness. He looked up the path. Amber's hair shimmered with each step. *Not so alone anymore.*

The gradual slope down to the pool had been easy going. Now, it was an uphill climb, not steep, but still taxing. Katie and John led the way, with Amber next and Declan following behind. They passed through the clearing where they rested earlier when something blue caught Declan's eye where the orange flowers had been. *Is that flowerflow?* Declan stopped in his tracks. John's words repeated in his ear. *Blue ones let LAMPs use magic for an hour or so...*

A surge of excitement sparked inside him. Declan slid to his knees by the clearing's edge. *I'll fill my pockets and dry it, then I'll...*

A wriggling pile of tiny blue lizards gorged themselves on the orange flowerflow. Beyond them, a larger lizard with a pink tail rose onto its hind legs, startled by the sudden arrival. The lizard moved like a viper. Declan jumped back, tripping over himself in the process, but it was too late. His wrist bore a circular purple bite. The mother gecko settled in front of its babies that wriggled to safety beneath the flowers.

Declan stumbled away. The clearing was empty now and the bite mark itched worse than anything he'd ever experienced. *What did John say about those lizards?* His heart started racing. *And where is Jo... Josh? Joel? Where am I?* His thinking was sluggish. He tried to stand and collapsed, like his legs had been deflated. Trees transformed into long strands of light that jiggled. The movement hurt his eyes. *This way,* Declan thought, stumbling down the path. *They'll be just up ahead.*

Garish gold spilled into the forest, creating a labyrinth of vibrant trees. Declan wandered through the sunset in a haze, unsure if the intense colors were real or in his mind.

There was something off about the path. *It's not supposed to be this easy*, whispered a quiet voice. *It was harder before.* The forest floor hummed beneath him. Sometimes, it would jerk sideways and throw him to the ground. Declan soon ran out of knees to scrape. When the path's movement grew too unpredictable, Declan climbed into the undergrowth of the forest where he could hold on to the trees to keep him steady. The shaking stopped, and the trees became still. When the island finally settled, Declan was lost.

Punctual evening stars peeked down from above. Ahead, a dim light illuminated the thick forest. *Maybe that's them.* Declan labored through the shrubs and vines until he came upon the source of the eerie glow. It was a beehive unlike any beehive he had ever seen. Translucent honey dripped from its edges; it magnified the light like an oil lamp.

That's not them. Declan turned to leave. Turned to find himself face to face with an enormous silver bear.

His stomach dropped.

The bear sniffed at him with a wet nose as big as the palm of his hands. Jealousy shone through its tiny black eyes. It stared at him, then looked over his shoulder at the hive brimming with honey. Declan stood perfectly still, not daring to move, not daring to breathe.

The bear growled a low growl. A long growl. The air grew hot. Declan remained frozen in place. The bear rose to its hind legs.

The forest shook, blazed, and illuminated as the fire bear burst into a roaring inferno.

CHAPTER 24
DECLAN

WELL. *I'm dead.*

Declan cowered before the flaming bear. He stumbled backwards, and the ground vanished. The bear roared—clearly upset by his abrupt disappearance—and Declan careened off every rock and tree stump down the steep side of the hill. He landed on a thick carpet of leaves; the smell of rot filled his nostrils.

Flickering orange flames licked off the fire bear's back as it charged down after him. Declan crawled in the other direction. While he struggled through the thick forest, the bear carved its own trail, swiping trees and bushes aside with paws that glowed like coals.

Declan found his feet under a wave of adrenaline and rode it as far as he could. The bear provided just enough light to see a path below them. He had no idea where it would lead, but it had to lead somewhere. Declan tumbled over a small ledge into darkness. He pressed himself against the rock wall.

Night became day as the bear approached. Dim trees

grew brighter, brighter, until Declan thought they would ignite. He waited, frozen in the sweltering heat.

The bear sniffed at the air. Once. Twice. Then a low growl. Declan refused to move. Hunched against the low outcrop, he waited for what felt like hours. Finally, the fire bear wandered away. As its heavy footsteps grew quieter, the light dimmed, and the night cooled. Declan took a deep breath and stood up. He looked over the rocky wall and saw only blackness.

Far below, a small spherical orb bobbed along a straight line, illuminating a young man beneath it. It could have been the miniature moon above him, but the man looked deathly pale.

"John!" Declan shouted from the trees. The man stopped. Declan waved frantically from above. "Up here!"

"Declan?" John called back. "Where are you? I can't see you!"

Declan opened his mouth when an explosion of heat erupted beside him.

The fire bear's roar drowned John out. The beast was so close it singed the hair on Declan's arm. It raised a gargantuan glowing paw. Declan braced for death. A ball of water whizzed past his ear and splashed into its jaw. The fire bear snarled and stepped back.

"Get out of there Declan!"

Declan pushed off a tree and ran towards the glowing white orb, towards John. The fire bear tore after him. It swiped wildly at the pumpkin-sized balls of water John sent hurtling through the air. Declan's foot caught a stray root. He stumbled forward into a mouthful of dirt, then rolled down into a small clearing. Declan recoiled when he hit the ground. The ground in the clearing felt wrong, like an oily carpet. It stunk of rotting leaves. Declan tried to stand, and the ground came alive, barking, whelping, rushing across the hill, away from the fire bear, away from John. Declan was riding in thin air, propped slightly off the ground by some invisible force.

Onyxelles! I'm being carried away by a bunch of onyxelles!

He bounced helplessly from side to side as the invisible creatures stampeded into the night. John's floating white orb shrunk to a pinprick, but the fire bear continued its chase, herding the onyxelles deeper into the forest.

Declan clambered to his stomach so he could see ahead of him. If he rolled off the onyxelles, he would be trampled. That left only one option. He would have to go up. Declan looked ahead for something to grab onto. The invisible herd rounded a corner and his chance appeared. With no time to doubt, Declan leapt, arms out, in a desperate attempt to catch a low branch. He hit it hard; flesh met wood with an awful crack. Declan hoped it was the tree and not his ribs. He pushed the thought aside. *Just hold on.* The noisy rustle of the onyxelles vanished into darkness.

Declan dropped to the ground as the fire bear crashed through a wall of brambles. The flames coming off its back were now enormous. "Are you serious?" Declan shouted. The bear turned towards him; the bonfire flared white. Declan shook his head. "You suck, you stupid bear."

He turned and ran. The bear lurched after him. The onyxelles had carved a path through the forest for Declan to follow. His legs screamed their exhaustion, but Declan had no time for them. He had to turn around, sneak past the bear and head back to John. At the peak of a hill, the onyxelles' path diverged, cutting into a sheer cliff to the right. *About time something went my way, I'll duck around and let the bear run past.* He turned the corner and froze. It wasn't a path. It was a narrow alcove. A dead end.

He'd barely turned back when the bear rounded the same corner and cut off his exit. Declan tried gripping the wall to climb, but there was nothing to hold.

He was trapped.

The fire bear stood on its hind legs. A triumphant roar pierced the forest. The creature was easily twice Declan's size. A monstrous pillar of heat flame that set the night ablaze.

So, this is how it ends. A whirlpool of guilt swirled in Declan's stomach. *All those people who fought. All those who were captured. All those who died on my account. Wasted.* The bear dropped to four legs. To his surprise, Declan was no longer scared. He was angry. *My parents, captured, and I can't do anything for them because I wanted to take a day off!*

Anger pulsed in his chest, bubbling like a pot of water. The fire bear paused, almost as if it sensed the change. It stepped forward, then hesitated. Bubbles of anger expanded in Declan's chest. *I ruined Ace's life because I wanted dry clothes. How stupid. Ava gave herself up for me. Dreyfus...*

The bubbles grew and combined. Every cell in Declan's body quivered, swirled, frothed. He was boiling inside and he couldn't control it. The night turned cool as the bear's flames were extinguished. It whimpered and turned, fleeing into the night.

Declan leaned against the cliff, fighting to stay upright.

The bubbling anger was out of reach, out of control.

It fed itself, swirling like a powerful hurricane. His spent legs gave way. He collapsed to his knee. The stone beneath him split like thin ice. The surrounding forest vibrated and hummed. Louder. Louder. Deafening. And then everything went white.

"Declan?"

"Is he okay?"

"Declan. Wake up."

"I've never seen anything like this."

"We need to get him back to Kingsbreak."

"Declan." Amber's voice was soft, but there was something else. Fear. Anxiety. Declan couldn't tell.

His eyelids were so heavy. Something lumpy supported his neck; a backpack, or maybe a rolled-up sweater. Declan forced his eyes open. Amber knelt beside him. Stars twinkled behind her. She smiled when their eyes met. "Declan! You scared us so much!"

"We were so worried about you!" Katie echoed. She knelt on his right. John stood over them, face pale. A silver orb floated overhead.

"What... what happened?" Declan asked. The rocky alcove was nowhere to be seen. He now lay on a smooth stone floor. "Where are we?"

John shook his head in disbelief. "You're exactly where I found you. I have no idea how you did it..."

"Did what?"

"You..." John paused, as if lost for words, then gestured to their surrounds. "You levelled about a half mile of forest."

"I... What?"

"Look around you," John said. "You did this Declan."

John's glowing orb illuminated an enormous expanse of nothing. On the edges of the polished surface, the remains of gnarled trees bent outwards like a bomb had gone off.

"What do you remember?" Katie asked. Her voice was level, but her expression betrayed her. She looked afraid.

Declan leaned back against the backpack. Stars glittered overhead, interrupted only by a wisp of passing cloud. "I was following you back from the waterhole and..." *I saw some flowers that made me think I could use magic.* "And I got distracted. Then something bit me... One of those blue geckos!" The events played in his head as he spoke. "And I reacted bad, everything was hazy. Then it was dark. I'm in the forest. I saw a fire bear. It... it chased me. I saw you!" He nodded at John. "But onyxelles carried me off. The bear cornered me here and..." The words died in his mouth. All three waited with wide eyes.

"And what?" Amber prompted.

"And I got angry." Declan took a deep breath. "Really angry about how stupid it would be for me to die after so many people had sacrificed so much for me."

John's lips were a thin line. "And then?"

"And the bear ran away. But... I couldn't turn the anger off. It had this... this *momentum* that I couldn't control. The ground started to break and everything went white."

John and Katie exchanged meaningful glances.

"You're sure it was white?" Katie asked.

Declan nodded.

"I wonder if they could see it over the coast," Amber said quietly. "Or if the protective spells kept it bottled up..."

"Does it matter?" John said. "Declan. I've never seen anything like that." He was smiling now. "That was incredible."

Amber nodded. "Amazing," she whispered.

Declan frowned. "I always thought I'd be happy the first time I used magic. But it wasn't what I expected." He looked from John to Katie, to Amber. "I mean, it didn't feel like it was me. I had no control at all."

"Nothing a bit of training couldn't fix up," John said. Katie looked alarmed.

Declan sat up. "Laurefen won't train me." He climbed gingerly to his feet. John helped. "And after this, who could blame him? I'm closer to being a bomb than a wizard."

"Don't lose hope just yet," John said.

"John," Katie cautioned. "Laurefen isn't holding back from training Declan because he's mean. It's a matter of safety." She gestured to the flattened stone around them. "Can you imagine if this happened at King's?"

"She's right," Declan said.

"Is she though?" John looked from Declan to Katie. "We've been on the back foot against Haberdeen since she showed up." He turned back to Declan. "If we can train you to harness that power, you could turn the tide."

"That's no small 'if'," Katie said.

John raised his hands. "Fine, fine. I'm not going to rebel against Laurefen or anything like that. But we've all lost people, Kate. You know better than most. Good wizards, good witches. Family. We pretend like things are okay, but they're not."

Amber nodded. "And if we don't figure out a way to stop her, they're only going to get worse," she added.

Katie stared at John, then turned to Declan. "What do you think?" she asked. "From what you felt, do you think you could manage it?"

Declan shrugged his shoulders. "I have no idea. Honestly, I had about as much control as a leaf has over a storm-drain. But who knows what might happen with training?"

Katie chewed her bottom lip. "I'm not going to say I think we should train him, but it's definitely worth another conversation with Laurefen." Her face split into an unexpected smile. "And who knows, maybe you'll be the all-powerful answer to our prayers."

"I'll drink to that," John said with a wink.

"Not just yet," Katie said. "We need to go back to the boat. Laurefen's due back tonight. If we're not on campus when he returns..." She let the threat hang in the air.

Declan remained still. His feet rooted to the spot, his head spinning with the promise of possibility.

CHAPTER 25
DECLAN

"You. Did. What?" Laurefen stared daggers at John. "What were you *thinking*? You could have killed yourselves!"

"It's not what you—"

"You could have killed Declan!"

"Laurefen, he was perfectly—"

"No, John. Enough! We warned you about this. You know the stakes!"

After struggling back to the boat in darkness, Declan, John, Katie and Amber had arrived at the northern end of Kingsbreak, only to find Laurefen and Michael waiting for them. Now they stood by the shoreline, bathed in the light of the moon and the anger of the Dean. Declan stared at the ground, cheeks ablaze with guilt.

As mad as Laurefen was, Michael was worse. "Idiots! All of you," he growled. "Taking the boy to Noahi. What were you thinking?"

Amber shook her head. "Michael—"

"Did Drey mean *nothing* to you?"

The words hit her hard. Declan wished he could disappear into the sand.

"We're not idiots," John muttered.

"And you! You arrogant little fool. You think your father—"

"Michael." Laurefen's voice was hard. "That's enough."

"No. Laurefen. It's not. You keep *encouraging* me to give these... these *children* time to figure things out." He looked at Declan with disdain. "They're not King's material. They're not Directive material. This stupid stunt could have killed the boy, the boy my brother sacrificed himself for!"

"Be that as it may—"

"I'm tired of you defending them!" Michael turned from Laurefen and spat at John's feet.

"Careful," John said.

"Or what?" Michael snarled.

John and Michael raised their hands simultaneously.

"Enough!" Laurefen was faster than both. John and Michael's arms snapped against their sides. "Now is not the time for the Directive to implode!" He turned on John. "You had no right to take Declan off the island. It was a foolish decision that could have had irreversible consequences." He turned to Michael. "Dreyfus is gone, Michael. I loved your brother, as we all did. You have my deepest sympathies, but we have had time to mourn. You have had time to mourn. You need to swallow your anger and look to the future. Do not let your rage tarnish his legacy."

After an eternity bottled in a moment, both men nodded. Laurefen released them and they swayed to catch their balance. Michael swept all of them with a piercing glare. "I've had enough, Laurefen. I'm leaving. You'll know where to find me."

"Michael," Katie whispered. They were her first words since they'd climbed off the boat.

Michael turned on his heel and walked away. Laurefen pinched the bridge of his nose. He looked exhausted. "Why?" he asked, staring at Katie.

"He needed it," Katie said. "Depression was more likely to kill him than anything on Noahi. No friends, no family. He needs to be a normal person, to have fun and see that life can still be good."

"He did magic," John said.

Laurefen's hand dropped. "I beg your pardon?"

"He didn't need us to protect him. He saved himself by scaring off an adult fire bear."

"And wiping a chunk of the island off the map," Amber added in a shaky voice.

"What do you mean?"

Amber swallowed. "The area where he did the spell. It was levelled."

"Nothing but a limestone slab," Katie added.

Laurefen turned on Declan, who had done well so far to avoid questions. Now, he trembled under Laurefen's gaze. "What did it feel like? Doing magic?"

Declan looked over Laurefen's shoulder. John shook his head. Declan got the message loud and clear. *Lie to him. Don't tell him you blacked out or you'll never learn magic.*

"Declan?"

"I, uh. Felt fine."

"Fine? How?" Laurefen pressed.

Declan sensed Laurefen's patience failing. "I mean, it was like I had power going through me. It didn't hurt, it just came out... like water from a hose."

Laurefen turned to the others. Amber stared at her fingernails. John wore a mask of indifference. Half of Katie's jaw was in the sand.

"Katie?" Laurefen asked slowly. "Is there something you would like to say?"

She closed her mouth with a snap. "Yes." She took a deep breath. "Declan is lying."

Declan's stomach dropped. John shot Katie a venomous glance. Amber didn't look up.

"Declan got angry. So angry he couldn't control it. He passed out and turned a section of forest to dust." Katie's eyes never left Laurefen. "But it was amazing. That much power in one burst. Laurefen, this might be the key to defeating Haber—"

"Go to bed," Laurefen said. "Do not speak of this again. In fact, you would be better off forgetting it happened altogether."

"But—"

"No, Katie. It was foolish of you to put Declan in this position. Go to bed, take Declan and make sure he gets back to his room. John. We need to talk. You too, Amber."

A pool of disappointment washed over Declan like a wave. He met Laurefen's cold eyes. "Will I ever learn magic?"

Laurefen shook his head. "No, Declan." The finality in his tone cut like a knife. "Go to bed. I will speak to you when I must."

Katie beckoned him towards the path; begrudgingly, Declan followed. They walked in silence towards the eastern side of the college. Every muscle in his body ached, every step hurt, but worst of all was the disappointment that weighed on him like chains. He didn't look at Katie. Her betrayal stung more than he could admit.

"I'm sorry, Declan," she said at last. "I know you want to learn magic. I know how excited you were, but we need to stay united. As soon as we start lying to one another, things will fall apart. The Directive needs to stay strong. If we don't stop Haberdeen, nobody will."

Declan said nothing. *It's her fault. I was so close. Laurefen would have agreed to training and I would finally be able to start.*

"I know you're angry. You probably think I threw away your one chance to learn magic, but you have to understand, if we fail, that's it."

I would be able to control my power. I could help stop Haberdeen. Get my parents back. Get Horace back. Get my life back.

"And we can't fail, Declan. We have to stop her. She killed my father, but my mother... my mother might still be alive. We need to stay together. I *need* to save mom."

For the first time, Declan noticed the sobs interspersed between Katie's words. A small sniff carried in the darkness. In a moment of clarity, his anger melted away. *She's just like you. She's trying to save her family, too.* Declan kicked a rock down the path. "How did it happen?"

Katie didn't answer. They walked until they reached the soft glow of the King's College lamps. Trails of tears lined Katie's cheeks. "My parents were Directive members. They were the first to discover what the Fatesmiths were doing, but they didn't know how fierisation worked. Mom was turned to iron; dad was killed trying to save her."

"I'm sorry," Declan said.

"That's why Laurefen took me. That's why he took all of us."

"What do you mean?"

"Me, Amber, John. All our parents were part of the Directive. Amber's are fierised and John's are dead."

"I... I didn't know." They walked in silence; Declan tried

to absorb the new information. "So, the Directive is a family thing?"

"Oh, no. Nothing like that." Katie sniffed and wiped her eyes. "No, but family members don't need to pass Approval and Laurefen had no time. No time, needed help, you know?"

Declan didn't. "What *is* Approval? I know it's a test, but how does it work?"

"I don't know. I know that it can only happen at a specific time. Laurefen has to set it up." Katie sniffed again. "If you pass, you have the qualities King Fendragon demanded of his closest subjects; nobility, honesty, courage, all that stuff. If you fail, you generally end up insane."

Declan waited for her to laugh or somehow signal that she was joking. She didn't. "What happens in the test?"

"We don't know. None of us had to do it. Our parents passed and somehow that counts for something."

They continued past the grand architecture of King's without a word. *They're all like me. John, Kate, Amber. They're all just trying to do right by their families.* Katie stopped at a door and Declan looked up. They were outside his empty dormitory.

"I'm sorry, Declan. I want you to learn magic. I want you to stop her. But I want you to do it the right way. Not in a way that fractures the Directive. This may be our only chance of fixing the mess that Haberdeen has made."

Declan nodded. "Yeah... I understand." He paused. "I'm sorry I lied."

"I'm sorry you felt you had to. Give Laurefen time, he'll come around." Katie touched his arm. "Good night, Declan."

She walked away, leaving him alone in the dark. Dawn's

first light peeked over the horizon. Declan walked inside, still in a daze. To his surprise, his room was tidy. A pile of clean clothes lay atop a wooden chest. Declan showered and dressed with the intention of puzzling out how he used his power.

Instead, he was asleep before his head hit the pillow.

CHAPTER 26
DECLAN

DECLAN WOKE to someone shaking his shoulders. A dark figure leaned over him. "Get off me," he slurred.

"Shhhh!" John whispered. "We've got to go!"

"Go?" Declan rubbed his eyes and sat up; bright sunlight streamed through the edges of his dorm curtains. "Go where?"

John wore blue jeans with a khaki coat. A brown leather duffel hung over his shoulders. "Laurefen wants me to go meet Mary-Lou in Sabriva. What he really wants is me out of his hair."

"Out of what? Why?"

"Because he's working with Haberdeen. And that's why he doesn't want you learning magic."

The words washed over Declan, but they didn't make sense. He blinked. "What?"

"He's the leak." John glanced out the window. "Laurefen's working with Haberdeen."

"No." Declan pushed his dark curls to the side. "He saved us! All of us. If he was the leak, he would've just let us die."

John shook his head. "Unless you were too powerful to kill. Look at what happened when that fire bear attacked."

"What do you mean?"

"They can't kill you. You're way too strong. Much stronger than either of them."

"But... no... that makes no sense."

"It does," John whispered. "If they can't stop you. They'll imprison you. Except you're too strong for that too, so it has to be in a prison you don't realize you're in."

Declan's eyes expanded. "I'm the opal eagle."

"What?"

He locked eyes with John. "Do you have any proof?"

"You saw Laurefen last night. He just found out he has the means to stop the ironhands and instead he forbids us to mention magic around you, then sends me to Sabriva on a goose chase."

"So, no proof."

"Amber said she'll keep a close eye on him."

"She agrees?"

John paused. "She agrees it is possible."

"And Katie?"

The pause lasted longer this time. "Kate may be compromised. I'm not quite sure what side she's playing for. Amber's going to watch her too."

"So, what's the plan?" Declan eyed John's bag. "Where are we going?"

"Tamhill."

Declan's heart jumped. *We're going home.* "Why?"

John flashed a toothy grin. "To do the opposite of what Haberdeen and Laurefen want. To teach you magic, of course."

The rotating triangle faded away, leaving only the empty street behind it. The Opening was gone and King's College with it. Sweat speckled John's brow. They had passed Michael on their way out. Declan expected they would be stopped before their escape even began, but Michael had wanted nothing to do with them. The feeling was mutual.

Tamhill smelled like home. The familiar fragrance carried memories of the normal life he had left behind. It smelled bittersweet.

"King's College has residences all across Euryma, but Laurefen will check them first," John said. "Do you have anywhere we could stay?"

Declan considered it. "We could try my..." he stopped. It would be painful to go back, if it was even still standing. *Can I even handle it?*

John shook his head. "They know where your house is. We need to lie low until you've had some time to train. Somewhere out of the way."

Declan's heart skipped a beat at the thought of training. *It's finally happening.* "My old school has empty dorms."

"Won't they have boarders?"

"Not anymore. They stopped the boarding program years ago. We'll have to lie low during school hours."

"With the ironhand presence here, I doubt school's even running." John stroked his short beard. "Still, best to be careful. Do you mind if I disguise your appearance?"

Declan shook his head.

John waved his hands in a zig-zag fashion. He grinned. "You make a fantastic old man." The smile transformed as his beard melted away and he shrunk into a hunched old woman.

"An old couple, are we?" Declan smirked.

The old woman winked. "Nobody ever suspects the elderly."

"People might notice our rucksacks."

"Tell them they're full of knitting-needles and dentures."

They hobbled out of an unused park to a crowded bus stop. South Tamhill was LAMP territory. It showed. Citysweeps weren't employed here, the stop's Perspex windows were covered in graffiti.

"What do you make of that?" John whispered. He nodded at the roof.

Declan looked up. Scrawled in red writing were three words. 'Kill the wiz'. He shrugged and kept his voice low. "Witches and wizards take advantage of these people. My friend..." Declan felt a stab of guilt at the mention of Horace. "He grew up here. His parents hate magic."

The surrounding people looked miserable. At school, they called South Tamhill 'Raghill', a population of laborers responsible for everything the magical community considered beneath them. It was the perfect entry point, free from prying eyes.

"The people here don't look right," John whispered.

Declan agreed. A filthy bus lumbered to a halt. The people climbed on in silence. They looked whitewashed, like they had been drained of color. "My friend would always talk about how witches and wizards needed to be brought down a peg, how they needed to stop treating LAMPs like dirt." The man two rows ahead of them coughed, loud, rasping and terminal. "I see what he meant."

John shook his head at the sputtering man. "We don't realize how lucky we are."

Seven stops later, they reached inner Tamhill. Declan

led them to the connecting service for Arman Moore's, as he had hundreds of times before. Now it felt surreal, like revisiting a childhood memory. The feeling intensified when they reached the wrought-iron gates of Arman Moore's Preparatory College. Declan remembered how imposing the sandstone pillars once looked. Compared to King's College, they looked small.

As predicted, the school was empty. John transformed back into his usual self and assured Declan he no longer resembled an old man. They hopped the fence and rushed up the path to the red brick building that once served as a student residence. The plain doors were fitted with iron padlocks, so John created an Opening inside. It wasn't until they entered that they saw the Opening had destroyed an internal wall. John shrugged innocently as a section of plaster shattered on the floor.

Declan picked a room with intact walls and packed his rucksack away. John sat on a mattress that looked firmer than the floor. Declan took a deep breath. "Ready?"

"For bed?" John said. "I don't think I've slept in two days!"

Declan shook his head. "For training."

"What? now?"

Declan nodded.

John raised his hand to cover a yawn. "You're eager."

"I've been waiting my whole life." It was the first time Declan had said it out loud. *I've spent my life pretending that being a LAMP was okay. No more lies.*

John rolled his eyes. "Fine. Give me fifteen minutes to close my eyes and we'll start your first lesson."

Declan tried to play it cool, but he couldn't. A smile crept across his lips and he let it. *I'm going to learn magic.*

Exactly seventeen minutes later, they stood in a large quad with sandstone walls bordered by circular garden beds. Butterflies fluttered in Declan's stomach; his feet tapped on the bricks. John rolled up his sleeves. "The most common form of magic is manipulation," John said. "It's the type of magic that almost all witches and wizards are naturally inclined to do."

Declan nodded. Probably too quickly. Probably too many times.

"Manipulation at its most basic level is simply finding nima and then moving them to accomplish your goal."

"Nima?" Declan asked.

John nodded. "The entire world around us is made up of what we call nima. Nima could be threads of matter, or threads of energy, all connected. The only difference between LAMPs and magical people is that magical people are capable of seeing and feeling these threads."

Declan let the words sink in. "So magic is kind of like knitting?"

"No." John shook his head. "Knitting you use needles and you weave threads together. Manipulating is more akin to playing the guitar. Let me demonstrate."

John ran his hand through the air, his fingers slowly crooked around nothing. "Right now, I've hooked my index finger around a hydronima, or a free-water thread. That's any water not bound to a plant or animal."

Declan leaned closer and stared at his bent fingers. He couldn't see anything.

"Now if I tug it," John clenched the finger into a fist, "I can pull all that free-water, water in the air and soil, towards me."

A small, spherical blob appeared at John's knuckle. It grew to a translucent marble and continued to swell until a wobbling ball hovered over his open palm. Declan gasped. "That's all water from around here?"

"No, but that was enough for my purposes. As soon as I let go of the nima, I'm no longer manipulating the threads," he looked down at the ball. "Now, if I want to throw this, I need to manipulate a different nima."

"Air?" Declan asked.

"No, that will just break it up. Imagine putting this," he nodded to the orb, "in front of a strong fan. It would fall apart."

"So?"

"Think. What did I say earlier about nima?"

"That they're like threads?"

"Yes," John nodded. "But threads connecting what?"

Declan shrugged, confused. "Everything?"

"Exactly. All matter and all energy. So, if I want to throw this, I need to manipulate kinetic energy, and I do that by grasping a kinima in two places with one hand," he looped his hand in an intricate motion, "and then in a third place with the other hand."

Declan watched John's slow and deliberate movements in wonder. He couldn't see any threads, but at this speed, he could see John weave a crude slingshot. When he let go, the ball soared across the courtyard and splashed into the wall. Declan clapped his hands. "That's so cool!"

"Makes sense?"

"It does- and it's *simple*. Growing up, my parents never talked about magic." Declan couldn't wipe the smile off his face. "I've always thought it was something complicated and mysterious."

John flourished his hands, and—to Declan's surprise—

a new ball of water appeared. There was no slow swelling to size this time. It was as if the rippling orb appeared from nowhere. "It's so different when you do it fast," Declan said. The sphere floated above John's open palm. "I could follow it before, but as soon as you move quickly, it's just... dancing fingers."

John sent the ball flying. It soared across the courtyard and hit the wall with a satisfying splash. Declan grinned. "How do I do it?"

"First," John said. "You need to be able to find nima. You can't manipulate what you can't touch."

Declan looked down at his hands. Tiny jewels of sweat glistened along the lines of his palms. "How do I do that?"

With a twist of his fingers, John created yet another watery sphere. "As you manipulate nima, they grow thicker." John continued to loop his hands again and again. The ball grew to a boulder. "The thicker the nima, the easier it is to feel it."

The boulder grew as large as Declan. "Uh... How thick does the nima need to be?"

"Pretty thick," John said.

Soil in the nearby gardens dried and cracked as the boulder grew to the size of a car. It quivered, like a pool in zero gravity.

Declan looked to John. "What do I do?"

"Feel around. It's running straight past you, about as thick as my wrist."

"For what? What does it feel like?"

John frowned. "You know, nobody's ever asked me that." He looked up, thoughtful. "Like a rope made of custard."

Declan put his hands forward and grasped at the empty air. "I feel like an idiot."

"You look like one too." John winked. "Up a bit higher. Higher. Tiny bit more. That's it."

Declan closed his hands around the air, but nothing happened.

"Slow down. Gentle." John cautioned. "You're right there, but this is all brand new. Focus on what you can feel."

Declan closed his eyes and focused on his fingertips. He felt the warm afternoon sun heating his palms, the court-yard's gentle breeze, but no custard rope. "I've got noth-ing," he said.

"Here, try this," John said. "Leave your hand there, you're right on it. I'm going to let the nima go and all this water will rush back through it. As soon as you notice any sort of pressure between your fingers, grab hold tight."

"Wait, what?"

"Ready?"

"No! Wait!"

"Set."

"Wait, wait, wait!"

"Go!"

John let the nima go. Declan squeezed the air. Almost immediately, the orb of water exploded and saturated the entire courtyard. Declan looked like he had been dropped into the ocean. John burst into laughter.

"Not funny!" Declan huffed. "I told you to wait!"

"I thought you'd grab it. Did you feel anything?"

Declan shook his head. "I don't know. It happened so quickly. I just panicked."

John looped his hands once more. Declan watched the water draw out of his clothes as if by some invisible vacuum. A moment later, he was completely dry and a new ball of water wobbled before him. "Shall we go again?"

The afternoon sun meandered low on the horizon, long shadows stretched across the courtyard, Declan grit his teeth and tried again. *I'm literally grasping at straws*, he thought as he reached into the air.

They had been trying for hours. They gave up on hydronima once Declan had grown tired of being soaked from head to toe. John summoned aeronima, which produced small powerful tornados that spun in place like a science experiment. Declan could not feel those either. He couldn't grasp the geonima that pulled stone out of the courtyard walls or the dendronima that let John pull wood chips from nearby trees.

Declan groaned as the makeshift cube fell into splinters. "It's not working! I can't feel anything!"

"You're tired," John replied. "You haven't slept. Give yourself a break."

Declan shook his head. "One more time."

John rubbed his eyes; the bags beneath them had darkened as the afternoon wore on. "Fine. Should we go back to stone and brick? You said you felt something with those, right?"

Declan hadn't, but John had threatened to call it a day. "Yeah, sure. Let's do that."

John flicked his hands and a trail of dust swirled together into an enormous boulder. Declan reached out for something, anything, that felt like magic.

"Down," John said. "You're up too high."

Declan slowly lowered his hands.

"There," John said. "Right there in your left hand. Perfect."

Declan closed his hand slightly and concentrated. His

entire being focused on his fingertips. When he was sure he was ready, he nodded. "Okay. Let it go."

The boulder dropped with a thud, the ground shook, the pavement cracked. Declan's stomach dropped with it. John sighed. With a wave of his hand, the boulder collapsed into a pile of sand that rushed back into the walls on an invisible breeze. "It's your first try, Declan. Stuff like this takes time. Nobody gets it straight away."

Declan wasn't sure he believed him. "Is this the only way you can learn?"

John stared at the cracked brick at his feet. "There is one other way," he said uncertainly. "But you won't exactly like it."

"What is it?"

"Trauma." John looked exhausted. "Extreme trauma sometimes provides the kick needed to get things moving."

Declan frowned. "Trauma... Like what?"

John shrugged. "Like getting chased by a fire bear, or maybe visiting the scene of some painful memories."

"Painful memories like..."

"Declan. Let's get some rest. We can try again tomorrow. Seriously, nobody gets it the first time."

"And if I don't get it tomorrow?"

"Well, then we can talk about other options."

Declan nodded. "Alright. Thanks, John."

They walked back to their rooms in silence. John yawned and rubbed his eyes while Declan thought about his first failed lesson. As John's soft snores echoed down the hall, Declan lay on his hard mattress. Wide awake, mind-running wild. *Painful memories are only a bus ride away.*

CHAPTER 27
MARY-LOU

LAUREFEN AND MICHAEL stood face to face in a circular room, sabers ready. They bowed before settling into starting positions.

Mary-Lou wanted to slap them both. *The boy's a ticking time bomb and they're playing games.*

Michael struck like a viper. Laurefen parried the blow. Compressed aeronima dulled the rattle of their sabers. They traded strikes until Michael lunged too far forward. Red sparks burst from the spot where Laurefen caught his collarbone.

"Three points." The older man smiled. "I take the lead."

Michael grunted. He wiped sweat from his palm and reset. Another short bow and the duel recommenced.

Mary-Lou seethed in silence. She still couldn't believe what had happened. *Declan lost control. Declan used magic.* Katie had shared the details before leaving on Directive business.

"Ha!" Michael stood triumphantly as blue sparks flashed against Laurefen's stomach. "Two points. Tied at fifteen."

"Next blow wins," Laurefen said, bowing low.

Mary-Lou rolled her eyes. She needed to talk to them. They needed to listen and understand before it was too late.

Red sparks announced the end of the duel. Michael threw his saber on the ground.

Laurefen laughed. "Still plenty of life in these legs." He released the bands of aeronima wrapped around him and hung his saber on a wire stand. "Apologies for the delay, Lou. Thank-you for letting us finish."

"Laurefen, we need to talk."

Michael begrudgingly slotted his own weapon on the stand. "News from Sabriva?"

"It's not about Sabriva, it's about Declan."

Laurefen's moustache bristled. He padded his brow with a small towel. "Let's hear the news from Sabriva first. What did Maurice have to say?"

Mary-Lou wanted to scream at them. Instead, she took a slow, composing breath. "Haberdeen owns two-fifths of the Dominion. High Mage Johannasberg grows anxious but refuses to declare any sort of emergency. Maurice thinks the Fatesmiths have leverage over him."

"Johannasberg is a problem," Laurefen said. "Though that would explain why he continues to refuse our requests to meet."

"Is this all from Maurice?" Michael asked. "The man's a rat."

"I never said he wasn't." Mary-Lou struggled to keep her voice level. "But he hasn't lied to us yet. If Haberdeen has leverage, we need to find out what it is." Mary-Lou cautioned a glance at Laurefen. "But we have more important things to discuss. Why didn't you looptap me?"

"Your work is important," Laurefen said. He put a hand

on Michael's shoulder. "We sorted Declan. How is John enjoying his sabbatical?"

"Sabbatical?" Mary-Lou raised her eyebrows. "I saw you sent Katie to Parteno. Where did you send John?"

"Sabriva." Laurefen frowned. "He didn't meet you this morning?"

"This is the first I'm hearing of it," she said. She squeezed her shawl, tired of dancing around the subject. "John can wait. We need to talk about Declan."

A dark realization dawn on Michael's face. "Oh no. Declan."

Laurefen raised an eyebrow. "What about him?"

"It was yesterday." Michael rubbed his temple. "John and Declan passed me across the campus. I didn't think much of it at the time, but they were both carrying rucksacks." He shook his head. "I can't believe I didn't realize."

"That boy is going to be the death of me," Laurefen muttered.

Mary-Lou smiled. "Which one?"

"This is serious, Lou."

"It is perfectly serious." She fixed them with a steely gaze. "And you are refusing to acknowledge your part in it. Katie said you told Declan you wouldn't train him. I'd wager he's run off with someone who will." Laurefen opened his mouth, but Mary-Lou didn't stop. "I have repeatedly told you that the boy is our best hope. You have repeatedly ignored me. You've done it your way and look where it's gotten us."

Michael rolled his eyes. "Lou—"

"No, Michael. I'm sick of hearing it. We've had this argument a hundred times. And *every single time* I have conceded to your 'wait and see' approach. That approach is stupid. It's going to cost us our best chance of stopping the Fatesmiths." She glared at both men.

"But John's so rash," Michael said.

"Can you blame him? He's watched you abandon the boy to himself. Did Katie tell you why they took him to Noahi? Did you even ask?"

Michael shook his head.

"They thought he needed a break because they found him in bed covered in blood. He'd tried to bash his brain in. He's a teenager who watched his parents get turned to iron. You've given him *nothing* but dashed hopes since he arrived."

Laurefen stroked his beard in thoughtful silence. Finally, he sighed. "Okay, Lou, I hear you. What do you suggest we do?"

Mary-Lou fought to hide her surprise. She had never gotten this far before. *Months of trying to convince them and this is where it ends?* She took a deep breath. "Put him through Approval."

"You can't be serious," Michael snapped.

"Why not? If he passes, we will know he has all the qualities to commence his magical tutelage." Mary-Lou locked eyes with Laurefen. "If he fails, then we'll know for sure that he was never going to be our key to victory."

Michael followed her gaze. "Laurefen. You're not actually considering this?"

"I am," Laurefen said. "Lou makes a good point. Perhaps we have gone about this the wrong way..."

"Or he'll go mad in Approval and damage the Well."

Laurefen's faced hardened. "The Well can protect itself." He turned to Mary-Lou. "I will think about it."

"A woman's intuition is rarely wrong." Mary-Lou's smile faded. "Think on it, but don't wait until it's too late."

Michael shook his head. "This woman's intuition has every chance of blowing up Kingsbreak. If he goes mad in there..."

"He won't, Michael." Mary-Lou said. "He can do this."

"How do you know?"

She winked. "Woman's intuition."

CHAPTER 28
DECLAN

"Slow down. You're too tense," John said. He had been saying it all morning. "Picture yourself trying to catch a fish in your hands. You need to ease into it until the moment is right, then take hold."

Red dust caked Declan's face. Sections of the courtyard were marred by magic lessons. John still believed Declan felt a strand of geonima the day prior, so the morning's training had revolved around dropping enormous stone boulders onto the ground.

Declan threw his hands in the air. "It's not working. I can't feel a thing!"

"Relax. Ease into it."

Just tell him you didn't feel anything. Declan ignored the thought and continued to grasp at nothing. Another failed attempt, another spray of dust. His hands fall to his sides. "This is pointless. I'm not getting it."

"You will." John summoned another boulder. "Just slow down."

"We need to try the other way."

John paused. A partially constructed clump of stone

hung in the air. Sweat and dust covered his face. They had been hard at work for most of the morning, with nothing to show for it. "What are you thinking?"

"You said it yourself. Trauma."

John shook his head. "Declan, that's not—"

"I want to go home." He had made the decision before getting out of bed. "If I go back to my house, we can try it there. It might... I mean, seeing it might ignite something."

John sighed. The ill-formed rock crumbled away. "Okay then, but this is *your* choice, Declan."

Declan hesitated long enough for John to raise an eyebrow, which only strengthened his resolve. "It's not working, John. I need to do this. For my parents, for Horace, for Ava." *For me.*

"I understand," John said. "But for the record, I don't like it." His appearance molded into an old woman. "Let's go see your house."

They caught the same city bus from the previous day. Back through town and onto the western side of Tamhill.

"Couldn't we use an Opening?" Declan fiddled with Ava's satchel as he spoke.

"Too many eyes," John said in a low voice. "Laurefen is looking for us, which means the ironhands will be too. We need to stay hidden."

Out the window, familiar street signs sparked a lifetime of memories. John scratched at his palm- he had been doing it all morning. Declan nodded at him. "What's with your hand?"

"It's Mary-Lou." John shook his wrist and scratched again. "She's been looptapping me all morning. Asking where we are."

"Can't you just ignore it?"

"I have been."

"What's it like?" Declan knew what looptap looked like when someone sent a message but had never considered how it felt to receive one. John grabbed Declan's wrist and traced a simple pattern on his palm.

"Like that. Imagine that, over and over, all morning." He let Declan's wrist drop.

"How does it work?"

"Looptap?" John lowered his voice. "It's simple. You have ten fingers. That gives you ten people you can connect with. You take a strand of nima running off your finger and tie it to the strand coming off someone else's finger. Once you're linked, you take that finger, wrap the loose nima around your palm and tap a message."

Declan nodded; he had assumed as much. "Who are your ten?"

"Left hand is for the Directive. I've got Katie, Amber, Mary-Lou and Michael."

"And the fifth finger?"

John's lips twisted. "That was Dreyfus."

"Oh." Declan looked away.

"And my right hand is... Well, at this point, it's nothing. It used to be my dad and some friends..." John stared into the distance.

The bus arrived at Milworth Drive. Declan's stomach clenched and a wave of nausea washed over him. *This is where they were. The last thing they saw.* When he stood, his legs were warm jelly.

John walked him off the bus. "Are you alright?"

What were their last thoughts? Probably worrying about me. They should've just gotten out, gotten away.

"Declan?"

They never made me feel like I was different. They always supported me, tried to build me up. They were my real support-

ers, *the only people in the whole world who had my back. Mom and her enormous breakfasts, her bad singing, her garden pranks. Dad and his jokes, his rants about the system, how he always had time for me. They moved their world out of the spotlight for my sake. I never had a chance to thank—*

"Declan, seriously. Are you okay?" John held his shoulders, his eyes alert. "We don't have to do this."

Tears stained Declan's cheeks. He could taste the salt on his lips. "I miss..." he sniffed, breathed deeply, and wiped his eyes. "I miss my parents."

John's face was somber. "I'm sorry."

Declan took another big breath. "I'm okay. It's down here, on the right."

The houses looked the same as ever. Well-kept, handsome residences. Lawns trimmed with magical precision. John stopped a few steps back. Declan approached number nineteen on his own.

It looked completely normal. Someone had repaired the catastrophic damage caused the night his parents were captured. He had expected worse, expected a crumbled ruin to ignite a fire inside him. He tried to picture it. *The wall was gone. It was in a pile of boards and splinters.*

But now, the grass was perfect, vibrant green. Still, something wasn't right. The road seemed too narrow, trees were missing, some of the neighbors' houses were the wrong color.

John stopped beside him. "Something's off."

The door to Declan's house snapped open.

"Ironhands!" John hissed.

Men and women in black coats flooded across the lawn. John began winding his arms in a wide circle.

"He's creating an Opening," shouted a blonde woman to their left.

223

John's movements changed. A wall of thick air solidified around them. A pillar of water roared like a waterfall. John redirected the torrent. The Fatesmiths backed away and let the surge wash itself out.

"Well, they're not trying to kill us," John said.

"How do you know?"

"They're using water. They must need us alive. Probably because..."

Declan stopped listening. Milworth Drive rippled and the entire street transformed. The manicured lawns became scorched earth. The footpath torn apart as if shredded by giant fingernails. His home was gone, replaced by a splintered pile of jagged ruins. "What happened?"

John shook his head in disbelief. "It's a trap! A trick of the light." He nodded to their shield of air. "I probably tore it down when I made this. We need to leave."

A low rumble echoed down the street as thousands of stone shards levitated ahead of them. With a whoosh, they shot forward. John's protective buffer trembled as a hailstorm of stone slammed into it. "Anything in your bag of tricks?" he asked, brow furrowed. "I can't hold this."

Declan opened Ava's bag. The wall of air shattered with a crack and he was thrown to the ground.

"Run!" John shouted. His hands were a blur. Misshapen stone lumps formed above him. John tossed them down at the Fatesmiths closest to Declan. A moment later, he was thrown through the air into the branches of a nearby tree.

Declan was cornered. Dozens of blackcoats surrounded him. One of them looked familiar. Tall with a red beard. He had been there. He had loaded Declan's parents into the van and driven away. A spark of anger flared in his stomach.

"You know the orders," the man said.

Raul. Declan's eyes narrowed. *His name is Raul.*

"Gentle does it." The man's accent left no question in Declan's. "She wants him alive and well."

The blackcoats advanced, their hands moved in complicated patterns Declan could not follow. A growing wave of water surged towards him. Declan reached into Ava's brown satchel; something warm brushed his hand. *The shield!* He pulled out the clear spike and drove it into the ground. An iridescent dome bloomed around him. The watery wall crashed over it. A second wave. A third. More spells crashed into it. Earth, stone, fire. The shield did not budge.

Declan crouched beneath the shield as the Fatesmiths approached.

"What is it?" A woman asked.

"What type of idiot question is that? It's a shield." Raul stepped up to inspect the dome. "Try to reach through it."

The woman looked at Raul uncertainly.

"On with it," he said.

She eased her hand into the shield. Her fingertips fizzled softly as she touched the wall. The woman pressed harder. The shield crackled with electricity and the woman was suddenly on the ground ten feet back. She did not get up.

Raul ignored her. He stared through the barrier. "Come out, lad. You can't stay in there forever. Surrender now and we'll be gentle."

Declan shook his head. "I'm not going anywhere with you. I know who you are."

"Remember me, do ya?" Raul chewed his upper lip. "Well then, you'll remember I've got your parents. Come with me and you can see them."

Something was building inside Declan's chest. He closed his eyes and tried to control his breathing. The man's voice was tinder, feeding a flame that had begun burning the moment they took John. *Oh no. It's happening again.* He opened his eyes. "Where's my friend?"

"The wizard? We've got him. We could fierise him if you want? Melt him down. He looks like he'd make a great hat rack."

"Leave him alone," Declan wheezed. His insides were scorching hot, a caldera of anger rising like lava. He wasn't sure he could hold it.

"Let's make a deal, lad. You come with us, see your ma and pa, and we'll let the wizard go."

Two blackcoats dragged a blocky figure to the front. It was John. He was frozen upright in a crude block of ice.

"What..." Declan groaned and doubled over. The flames were too hot. White hot, molten stone. He couldn't contain it. He forced himself—trembling—to his feet. His hair brushed the top of the dome. "What have you done with him?"

Raul laughed. "Nothing. He's just cooling..." Declan was shaking. Raul's eyebrows climbed to his hairline. "What are you doing?"

Declan couldn't answer. Raul's confused expression faded; the flames took hold. Declan dropped to all fours. Silver light shone through the veins on the backs of his hands. Instinctively, he gripped the clear spike in the ground and pulled.

The iridescent dome vanished.

"Run. Run. RUN!" Raul's shouts, thick with panic, were the last thing Declan heard as brilliant white light engulfed Tamhill Drive.

CHAPTER 29
MARY-LOU

CEDRUS WAS A SPECIAL TREE—OLDER than the college itself. According to legend, the first Fendragon king planted the cedar sapling a thousand years earlier when the tribes united to form Euryma. A small cobblestone courtyard barely contained its width. For centuries, Cedrus had been the departure point from King's College. The one place on the island unprotected by the Ancellum's power.

Mary-Lou adjusted her skirt as Michael crossed the lawn. He sat beside her, expression grim.

"What's wrong?" she asked.

Michael held out his hand in response. A jade coin rested in his palm. On one side, a portrait of an ancient monarch, on the other, the mythical drevsmok.

The sight of it made Mary-Lou's stomach turn. "Where did you find this?"

"Amber," Michael said. "She said Declan found it in his friend's bag."

"Declan's friend?"

"The Luck."

Mary-Lou stared at the coin. "Is it real?"

227

Michael turned it over, intently studying the coins' edges. "There's no way to know. Vedmark is a whisper of a legend. But it's concerning."

"What is?"

"A coin from our old enemy shows up just as this new magic destroys Euryma from within." Michael nodded to the coin. "You saw the Luck in Tamhill, did she do anything out of the ordinary?"

Mary-Lou thought back to November. It had been a different world. The fight against the Fatesmiths was in its infancy. There had still been hope that they could win. She shook her head. "Nothing you wouldn't see from any other Luck. She used her power openly. Anybody looking would've picked up on it."

"What did she look like?"

"Short hair, dark skin, pretty girl, small but athletic-like a loaded spring."

"No emerald cloak?" Michael grinned.

"No." Mary-Lou smirked. "No green shoes either."

Michael looked down at the coin. His smile faded away. "It is odd. A girl carrying a jade mitka saving the boy... How could she even know he needed saving?"

"Maybe she was in league with the ironhands? They didn't seem to have any trouble finding out. Maybe the Fatesmiths are working for Vedmark?"

"None of it makes sense." Michael clenched his fist. After a moment, his expression softened. "What if the boy *can* use green magic? It would explain why Haberdeen wants him so bad."

Mary-Lou shook her head. "We would have seen it. I spoke to the girls at length today. They told me the whole story. White flash of light- not green."

"Those are stories. What's to say green magic is as much an embellishment as the green shoes?"

"What's to say it's real at all?" Mary-Lou countered. "It's been a thousand years since the Founding. For all we know, green magic is a story made up to scare boisterous children."

Michael looked back at the coin one last time before slipping it into his jacket pocket. "I don't know Lou. Every day, there's more bad news. More witches and wizards fierised, more cover-ups from the High Mage. How is this going to end?"

"I wish I knew."

They sat in silence. For a long time, the only sounds came from the birds in the branches and the wind in the leaves. The silence shattered when an Opening appeared and Laurefen jumped through. Behind him, someone shouted something loud and profane. The window closed as Laurefen dusted off his maroon jacket.

Mary-Lou raised an eyebrow. "Any luck?"

Laurefen shook his head. "No sign of John. I tried all his usual haunts. Checked in with all his contacts. Nobody has seen him in weeks. Any luck on looptap?"

"Nothing. His hand must be on fire with all the messages I've sent." Mary-Lou's lips twitched. "What about his home—in the north?"

"Tried and failed. The house is still the ruin the Fatesmiths left it."

Mary-Lou considered it. *He hasn't taken Declan, Declan's gone with him willingly. Where would Declan go willingly?* "What about Tamhill?"

"John is rash at the best of times, but he's not stupid. It would be idiotic to take him there," Michael said. "It's their whole base of operations in Iberia."

"I agree," Laurefen said. "A return to Tamhill would be most unwise."

Mary-Lou nodded. Still, she couldn't shake the feeling. "Are there any Alumni left in the city?"

"Not many," Laurefen said. "The only one who would know Declan is the headmaster of his preparatory school."

Michael looked at Mary-Lou. "Do you think John is *that* irresponsible?"

"Do you?"

Michael chewed his lower lip, then turned to Laurefen. "I think Lou and I should visit Tamhill."

For a long moment, Mary-Lou thought he would say no. Instead, he nodded. "Okay. I will continue to search our northern holdings. You two check Tamhill. Be careful. Stay out of sight and don't attract attention. I will looptap you if I find anything,"

Mary-Lou looked at Michael. "We'll do the same."

Laurefen tried to smile, but it was a weak attempt. "You'll do the honors, Michael?"

Michael summoned an Opening. Mary-Lou saw the Head City, Sabriva, in the distance. Laurefen waved farewell, and the window shrank away.

"He looks exhausted," Michael said.

"He is. The poor man hasn't stopped in months." Mary-Lou stared at the spot where the Opening had been. An odd idea sparked in her head. "Can I hold on to that coin?"

"Why?" Michael's eyes narrowed. "And don't you say women's intuition."

Mary-Lou pursed her lips. "In that case, I will say nothing."

Michael rolled his eyes and waved his hands. An Opening rotated into existence and sunlight poured through it. On the other side were two sandstone pillars and a lush green lawn.

CHAPTER 30
DECLAN

"Get up. Declan! Wake up!" John blurted. "We need to go! Now!"

Declan lay on his back. John hovered above him. "What happened?

John glanced over his shoulder. There was dry blood in his beard. "They're gone. They ran for cover. They'll be back soon. Especially now they've seen what you can do."

Declan propped himself up on one arm. The entire street had been stripped to nothing. Scorched soil stretched all the way to the bus stop. "Was that..." Declan swallowed painfully. "Was that me?"

"I don't know. Last thing I remember, I'm wrapped in water. Next minute, I'm lying in a puddle and you're on the ground." John pulled him up. "We need to go, like, now."

Ava's satchel lay on the ground. Declan scooped it up and slid it over his shoulder. "What do we do now? Where do we go?"

"Back to your school." John scanned the ruined street. "We need to find cover for an Opening. Can you run?"

Declan pointed ahead. "The tree line there leads to a nature reserve."

John nodded and set off at a steady jog. Declan kept up with ease. Halfway down the road, John stretched his arm to bar Declan's way. "Stop!"

A small Opening appeared ahead, directly between them and the trees.

"Over here." John pulled him to the right. The fingers on his left hand flitted back and forth and Declan tried to imagine threads of magic twisting between them. A shimmering window formed around them, like the air rippling off a hot road. Two figures stepped through the Opening. Michael and Mary-Lou. Declan's heart skipped a beat. "They're going to see us!"

"Only if they're looking closely," John whispered back. "I've made a photonima loop."

"What?"

"I'm bending the surrounding light. Someone did the same for your house earlier."

"We're invisible?"

John nodded. "As long as nobody moves any nima over here."

Mary-Lou's gaze shifted towards them. John held a finger to his lips and Declan held his breath. A long moment lingered. Mary-Lou tossed her braid over her shoulder. Michael knelt to scoop a pile of scorched earth from the ground. "What happened here?"

A dozen Openings interrupted her response. Fatesmiths poured into the street. Declan stepped backwards, but John grabbed his shoulder. "Stay still."

Through a gap in black coats, they could see Michael raise his hands. Mary-Lou nudged him and shook her head.

"Would ya' look at this?" said a familiar voice. Raul's

red hair stood out amongst the crowd. "We came back to catch the mouse and instead found a couple of ghosts instead." He stood face to face with Michael. "We suspected the old lady got away with an iron hand, but you, I'm sure I heard you were melted to scrap."

A vein appeared on the side of Michael's bald head. His jaw looked set in concrete.

"Or was that your brother?" Raul barked a cruel laugh. "We tend to start at the top and work our way down."

Michael moved like a whip, but Raul was just as fast. In a flash of light and sound, half of the blackcoats were on the ground, Raul was on his knees and Michael on his back. They both leapt to their feet.

"That's enough." Mary-Lou snapped in a stern voice.

Raul turned on her. "Listen here—"

"Shut your mouth, you blabbering idiot," Mary-Lou let her shawl drop and raised her hands. There was no iron to be seen. "As you can see, your magic has no hold here." She flicked something green into the air. Declan recognized the coin immediately.

Raul caught it and looked down. His back straightened like he'd touched an electric wire. "What is this?"

"You know exactly what it is. You think the Directive ends with King's? Who do you think is really in charge?"

Raul turned the coin over. "You can't expect me to believe—"

"Try it," Mary-Lou hissed. "Try it and see." She clicked her fingers back and forth and smiled wickedly. "How do you think Haberdeen will react when she discovers it was you who brought ruin upon her little campaign to save the world?"

Raul flinched. "It can't be true," he said.

"Try it." Mary-Lou repeated venomously. "Try it and see what the Knights do to you."

A murmur ran through the crowd of blackcoats. Declan leaned sideways, trying to catch a glimpse of Mary-Lou. After a momentary silence, Raul turned to the Fatesmiths around him. "The boy isn't here. Let's go."

"Mage Raul," someone said from the crowd.

"We're leaving," Raul barked. "That's an order."

The crowd fell silent. A series of Openings appeared. In moments, the blackcoats were gone. Raul held the coin up between his finger and thumb. "Well, this certainly changes things."

"Only for you." Mary-Lou held out her hand. "I'll be having that back now." Raul flicked the coin in her direction. She caught it without taking her eyes off him.

Raul stepped through an Opening and was gone. When the doorway vanished, Mary-Lou seemed to deflate. She breathed an enormous sigh and laughed. "I can't believe that worked!"

"Me neither!" Michael shook his head. "And he bought it. Which is a concern of its own. What do they know that we don't?"

"You know what? I don't want to think about it. This was a win. I'm not ready to spoil it by asking questions about the ironhand's connection to Vedmark." She bit her lip. "Not yet."

"I think you're right." Michael looked straight past them. "And you were right, the boy was here. John too."

Mary-Lou frowned. "Look at this place. Do you think this was all Declan?"

"I'm not convinced of anything until I see it. This part of town was ruined well before the boy left Kingsbreak. Whatever he did today was adding insult to injury."

"We need to find him." She looked down at the green coin. "Our bluff might buy us a little time, but if we can't stop Haberdeen soon, the rest of Euryma is going to look just like this."

Michael summoned an Opening. "Let's head back, see if Damien has any other ideas where the boy might be."

Declan blinked, and they were gone. He turned to John. "What just happened?"

John waved away the shimmering wall of light. He scratched his palm, which had started to scab on top. "They're looking for us."

"Yes, but Vedmark, the coin... that's my friend's coin. They were outnumbered. And the blackcoats, ironhands, whatever. They just... left?" Declan pressed his hands against his eyes. "What is going on?"

"I have no idea," John said. "And by the sounds of it, neither do they. They took a gamble, and it worked." John gestured towards the tree line. "Regardless, we're sitting ducks right now. We need to move."

"Where to?"

John shrugged. "Back to the student quarters. We'll figure out our next move there."

"We could try some more training?"

John's jaw dropped. "Really? We escaped by the skin of our teeth and you still want to train?"

"You saw what happened. We were pinned until I exploded. I need to be able to control it. I can't hope to get angry every time I want to be of use."

John nodded. It was a slow nod, large, exaggerated movements that seemed to accomplish nothing but fill time. "Fine. Let's go back to the school, talk through what happened, and then work out a plan for training."

They walked towards the line of Tamira pines. "That

coin," Declan started. "The one Mary-Lou had. Do you know anything about it?"

"A little." John's face was passive. "A jade mitka from—".

"Vedmark," Declan finished.

John looked at him sideways. "You've heard of it?"

"Amber."

John smirked. "I should've known."

"She said it was a fairy tale, a bedtime story."

"So was magic. Once upon a time."

"Are you saying it's real?"

John didn't answer immediately. When he did, his voice was low, almost as if he worried somebody might overhear them. "The history you learned at school is not *entirely* accurate, Declan. Vedmark played a bigger role in Euryma's beginnings than our institutions care to admit."

"The Founding?" Declan frowned. "That doesn't make sense. Amber said Vedmark formed after Euryma, in response to—"

"I doubt Amber has explored the restricted journals in the King's Library," John said. "Just like you, she learned her history from the victors."

They walked through the forest until Milworth Drive disappeared from view. The normal symphony of birds and bugs was absent, blanketing them in eerie silence. When they were well hidden, John created an Opening back to Arman Moore's. Declan burned with questions. Questions about the jade coin, Vedmark and Euryma's mysterious history, but John seemed reluctant to talk. Declan followed him back to their sleeping quarters in silence.

"I need to go for a walk," John said once they arrived.

"Uh, yeah, sure." The announcement caught him off

guard. Declan shrugged, attempting to remain cool. "Are you okay?"

"Yeah, I'm feeling a little shaken. Today was a close call," he said. John attempted a smile. "If I didn't say it earlier, thanks kid. You saved me."

"Oh, uh, all good," Declan mumbled.

John continued down the path and left him by the entry. Declan stood in a daze. *What have you gotten yourself into?* He shook himself back to reality and tried the door. It was locked. *I guess I'll go for a walk myself then.*

The sky transformed from blue to pink as Declan wandered through his usual haunts. He had been at Arman Moore's for over a decade. He knew the grounds like the back of his hand. Now, he felt drawn to the main quadrangle. It looked exactly the same as it had months ago. He could still picture Mason with a girl on his arm, Lyle unloading her fake apology and Mrs. Winter watching curiously in the corner. So much had changed. Declan wondered how many of his classmates and teachers now resided in iron casts.

He set Ava's bag down and sat by the fountain, shaded by the massive statue of Arman Moore. Even in sculpture form, his great-great-great-great-grandfather never looked happy to see him. Declan had always kept his distance out of respect, or maybe shame. Yet now, with two uncontrolled outbursts of magical power under his belt, Declan felt he'd earned the right to at least share the great Arman Moore's shadow. The bronze-smith had done a marvelous job of capturing the intensity of his eyes. Long robes fell about him, tied with a sash held together by a circular clasp.

Declan frowned. He had never noticed that clasp before. He had never looked so closely. It was a circle divided into two halves. On one half was an axe, carved with straight lines. On the other, a beaked dragon, the very same one carved into the jade—

"Good afternoon, Master Moore."

Declan nearly jumped out of his skin. It was Headmaster Leed. His eyes twinkled above a trim white beard. "Headmaster. Sorry. I..." Declan trailed off, unsure of what to say.

"It's good to see you, Declan. My most sincere condolences for your parents." His shining eyes dimmed for a moment as he bowed his head. "Terrible business being caught up in this Fatesmith racket. I hear you've been staying with some friends." He looked around, as if expecting someone to appear from nearby. Footsteps echoed from the entryway opposite. "Ah, here they are now."

Michael and Mary-Lou entered the quad. Declan's stomach twisted. John was nowhere to be seen.

CHAPTER 31
DECLAN

"WHAT WERE YOU THINKING?" Mary-Lou scowled. "Taking off like that, and to Tamhill, of all places. You could have been killed! Where is John? What a mess he's made."

Michael said nothing, only shook his head.

An avalanche of questions had followed him back to Kingsbreak. Declan remained silent. Now, they waited on a wooden bench outside Laurefen's study.

"You were asked a question," Michael growled. "*What* were you thinking?"

They sat on either side of him like guards, or at least Declan felt like a prisoner. "Laurefen said he'd never train me, so I figured it was time to leave. John tried to talk me out of it, but I wouldn't take no for an answer." The lie rolled off his tongue with surprising ease. "In the end, he agreed that if I had to go, then it wouldn't be alone."

Mary-Lou exhaled through her nose, but her eyes softened. "If you wanted to go, you could have told us. Why just leave?"

Declan didn't need to lie this time. "Because you would have stopped me. I've been under lock and key since I arrived. I went to a deserted island for one afternoon and Laurefen blew his lid."

"You're a fool," Michael said. "Haberdeen owns Tamhill, and she's growing stronger every day. If she gets her hands on you, there's no telling what she'll do."

"Couldn't be worse than being here," Declan muttered.

Michael slammed the bench with his hand and Declan jumped. "My brother died to keep you out of her hands."

Declan remained silent. There was nothing he could say to that.

"We're not keeping you under lock and key," Mary-Lou said. "We're keeping you safe."

"Tamhill is fine," Declan said. "We caught the bus straight through town. Everything looked normal—"

"Of course it does," Mary-Lou said. "The High Mage is using every resource at his disposal to hide the truth. We believe the ironhands have leverage over him. They have the MLEA in their pocket too."

"Why can't the remaining witches and wizards rise up?" Declan asked. "They can't stop all of them."

Michael laughed, as cold as ice. "What remaining wizards? Seventy percent of the magical population are either iron casts or dead. We nearly joined them looking for you."

Declan decided not to mention he had been there. Instead, he pointed at Mary-Lou's hand. "But you've figured it out. Your hand is better."

"Thanks to you and your friend's bag of tricks." A ripple of warmth broke her somber expression. "Amber said it was your idea. Thank you, Declan."

The mention of Ava's satchel made Declan realize he had left it by the fountain at Arman Moore's. "So, if the flareflies worked, let's get more."

"It took your entire box plus twelve others to get the job done." Mary-Lou examined her fingers as she spoke. "That was one hand. We'd need hundreds, maybe more, to free an entire person."

"And flareflies don't grow on trees, boy," Michael added. "We'd need more than are currently in existence to bring back half the people she's taken."

Mary-Lou placed a hand on his shoulder. "We were worried about you, Declan." She glanced at Michael. "We visited your home in Tamhill. We saw what you can do. It's starting to look like you are the one hope we have. But that means nothing if you run willingly into harm's way."

Declan slumped in his chair. He didn't know who to trust. "I'm no hope at all unless I learn to use magic. I can't be of any use unless someone is willing to train me."

Mary-Lou opened her mouth when a gentle click cut her off. The tall door opened. Laurefen looked down at all of them. He looked spent. Long grey hair hung loose and his wrinkled coat had the distinct appearance of a garment recently slept in. "Come in, Declan," he said. Mary-Lou stood. Laurefen held up his palm. "I'd like to talk to the boy privately first."

Declan's insides squirmed. If John was right and Laurefen was working with Haberdeen, he was in trouble. Despite his pleading eyes, Mary-Lou motioned for him to go inside. Declan's heart thundered in his chest. He followed the Dean of King's College into his office.

Laurefen sat behind his driftwood desk. The dark bags below his eyes did nothing to dampen their intensity. Declan shifted on the couch.

"I'm glad you are safe," Laurefen said.

"Thank you, sir."

"Things have deteriorated faster than expected. I am

not sure how much of Tamhill you saw, but we are on the brink of losing this war. And Euryma with it. All under the nose of an incompetent coward of a High Mage."

Declan said nothing.

"As you well know, I have repeatedly refused any offer of training." A knock at the door interrupted them. Laurefen frowned. "You may enter."

The door half-opened and Mary-Lou popped her head inside. She looked deeply worried. "Kate has returned from Odacre. It's not good."

Laurefen rubbed his temples. "It never is. Is it urgent?"

"The ironhands have taken the capital by force. Concordia is theirs, taken in two days."

"What about Amber? Did she return with Katie?"

"Amber remained to help evacuate the Alumni south."

"How many?"

Mary-Lou bit her lip. "Twenty-five. Nine wizards, sixteen witches. It's falling apart Laurefen..."

Declan struggled to keep up.

"Thank you, Lou." Laurefen said.

"We're out of options."

"Thank you," he repeated.

But Mary-Lou refused to leave. "I'm serious. If you keep holding out, it's going to be too late."

"I know." Tension tightened the air. They stood in silence, eyes locked, unyielding. At last, Laurefen fixed Declan with a steely gaze. "Master Moore, I think it's time for you to explore your magical Potential." It took all Declan's self-control to keep his jaw off the floor. "However," Laurefen continued, "I have two conditions you must meet before we proceed, and they are *not* negotiable."

Declan nodded. It was the only response he trusted himself to give.

"First. You need to complete a test of integrity. It is called Approval and is a prerequisite of all Directive members." Mary-Lou nodded at the door. "Second, and this is important..." Laurefen's expression was stone. "You must *not* attempt to train or use magic while you're angry. Do you understand?"

A pin drop would have echoed off the walls. Declan sat still, overwhelmed. He took a breath and let Laurefen's words sink in. John had failed, but Laurefen was the Dean of King's College. If anyone could unlock his magical potential, it would be him. *But what if John's right? What if he's in league with Haberdeen?*

"Declan?" Mary-Lou asked quietly.

"Yes," he whispered. "Yes, okay, I agree."

"Very well." Laurefen sighed. "We will begin immediately. You may be the only chance Euryma has."

It was a sentiment he had heard before. From John, Mary-Lou, even Amber and Katie, but hearing it in Laurefen's voice carried a weight. As the words sunk in, they struck like a hammer. The reality of the situation took hold and Declan suddenly wanted to shrink away. "I'm... I'm not sure I can do this," he managed. He turned to Mary-Lou. "John tried to teach me and nothing happened. I failed. I'm just a kid from Tamhill. I can't stop the Fatesmiths. I can't stop Haberdeen. I can't do it. I'm just a kid."

Mary-Lou placed a warm hand on his back. "We know, Declan. We know. We're not going to make you do this alone. We're all in it together. One step at a time."

"Stay in the present," Laurefen said. He watched them with concern. "Don't worry about Haberdeen. Don't worry about Euryma. Worry about what you can control. Worry about getting some rest tonight. Tomorrow, worry about

Approval. From there, you and I will worry about magic. Together."

"But John couldn't—"

"John is a talented wizard," Laurefen said. "Perhaps too talented for his own good. He struggles to teach what comes so easily to him."

"I couldn't even see the nima."

Laurefen laughed. "Of course you couldn't. Your Potential is little more than a seed. Expecting you to manipulate nima in your current state is paramount to demanding fruit from a sapling."

"But, John—"

"John grew up in a world vastly different to yours, Declan. He has been handling nima in one way or another since before he could walk."

Declan breathed a trembling breath. It all made sense. The difficulty he faced. John's surprise with his failure to perform seemingly simple tasks. Electric excitement ignited inside him. *It's going to work. I'm going to learn magic!*

"Do you accept my conditions, Declan?"

Declan nodded and couldn't help but smile. "I do." He bit his lip. "Now... What is Approval?"

Strong gusts blew outside the dormitory; the trees groaned and shuddered. Declan sat alone in his familiar room. Classes had been postponed indefinitely. According to Mary-Lou, most of their new students were now in hiding. Some of them had vanished entirely. Declan lay in his bed, his mind an engine of ideas.

John was convinced Laurefen wanted me trapped here, never learning anything. But now, Laurefen is going to train me.

What does that say about him? Was John pulling the wool over my eyes? Where did he go when he left me alone? Declan shook his head. It didn't make sense. John had every opportunity to hand him over in Tamhill. He had every opportunity to drop a rock on him or encase him in water, but he hadn't. Declan's thoughts rushed like the wind outside. The more he thought, the less it made sense. Tiredness crept in. His eyelids grew heavy.

"Pssst, Declan!"

Moonlight illuminated a head of long, windswept hair.

"Amber?" Declan blinked as Amber slid open his window. "What are you doing here? I thought you were in Odacre?"

"I was. Katie sent word you came back. Can I come in?"

"Uh, sure."

She climbed inside, pulled him into an awkward hug, and then peppered him with questions. "What happened? Why are you back? Where's John? What did Laurefen say? Did you learn magic?"

"Slow down," Declan said.

"Sorry." Amber put her hands on her lap in attentive silence. "Go ahead."

Declan rolled his eyes, then recounted the events of the last two days. Amber gasped in all the right places. "John's still back there," Declan finished. "He doesn't know Mary-Lou and Michael got me. He went for a walk after we got back from the blackcoats."

"He left you alone?"

"I think he was a bit overwhelmed after we were nearly caught. Twice."

"And Mary-Lou and Michael scared them off?"

"Mary-Lou used the coin." Declan raised his eyebrows. "Did you give it to her?"

"No..." Amber blushed. "I gave it to Michael. He's an expert, has a coin collection the size of this room."

"Well, they used it to scare off the blackcoats. What does it mean? I saw the same dragon from the coin at my old school! It was on a statue of my great-great-great-grandfather."

"No idea."

Declan brushed a curl out of his eyes. "And what about Laurefen? He wants to train me now. Is he good or bad?"

"I don't know." Amber chewed her lip, her face conflicted. "John was so convinced when we got back from Noahi. Laurefen told us that if we made you angry to do magic, he'd remove us from the Directive. It didn't make sense... then..."

"Then?"

"Mary-Lou told us about Ire Tides."

"What?"

Amber stood and paced his dorm. "It's one of the main threats the Directive was created to fight."

"What are they?"

Amber glanced over her shoulder like she expected Mary-Lou to pop out of the shadows. "You said John taught you that manipulation is done using nima."

"Yeah?"

"Well," she stood and began pacing the room. "Sometimes, people get frustrated about how much or how well they can handle nima. So, they push bits of *themselves* into the nima."

"What?"

Amber shuddered. "They hold a nima, then push their own energy into it. This creates a vacuum. A void within their Potential that allows them to absorb the magic itself."

"But why?"

"It allows them to handle more, do more, be more powerful, but at a cost." She stopped and looked down at Declan. "The part of themselves they push into the nima doesn't come back. They slowly lose whatever it is that makes us human."

Declan considered it. "But what does it have to do with me?"

Amber dropped to the bed beside him. "Mary-Lou said people can accidentally create Ire Tides when they're angry. They lose control and do it automatically." For the first time, Declan saw tears in Amber's eyes. "Declan. You're using anger to use magic. If you keep doing it, you might..." she trailed off, but the unspoken threat lingered.

Declan ran his hands through his hair. "So Laurefen was looking out for me all along?"

"It certainly seems that way."

"And John?"

"I've been trying to reach him. I think if he comes clean to Laurefen and explains why he took you, he'll understand."

"I hope so..." Declan failed to stifle a yawn. When it passed, he smiled. "Did I tell you? I'm doing Approval tomorrow."

"You are?"

"Yeah." His head was heavy. "Laurefen has nominated me to do it."

Amber looked surprised. "Does that mean he's going to train you?"

"Uh, pardon?"

"Is Laurefen going to train you?"

Another yawn sabotaged his attempt to reply. Declan nodded awkwardly as he covered his mouth.

Amber laughed. She sat down beside him, her hand

rested on his knee. "I'm really glad you're back." She was close, so close Declan could see the silver flecks in her eyes, the faint freckles that speckled her cheeks.

Without warning, she kissed him. Her lips were soft, her skin smelled like honey, and for some terrible reason, all Declan could think about was Ava. A stinging sense of guilt pricked him and he pulled back.

Amber's cheeks went bright red. "I'm sorry, I just—"

"No, it's fine, it's okay." The words spilled from him like water. "I mean, that was... lovely..." Declan cringed. Inside, he wondered if it would be better to shut up. Without warning, he yawned again, and Amber suddenly laughed.

"Declan, you're exhausted. Get some sleep. Approval won't be easy. Let's just leave tonight as tonight and we can talk more another day."

She stood to leave. Declan's brain seemed composed of molasses. He tried to say something clever, but he was too tired to think. With one final wave to Amber, he sank into his bed and closed his eyes. Outside, the wind raged. Inside, Declan was fast asleep.

CHAPTER 32
DECLAN

"ARE YOU EVEN *LISTENING*?"

Declan looked up from the dark passageway. "Sorry. Can you please repeat that last bit?"

They stood before an ominous stone entry. It punctured an otherwise ordinary hill at the southern end of the island. Gray clouds blanketed the morning sunlight. Laurefen let out a short huff. "Declan, this is important."

"I know, I know. Sorry, I was distracted."

The corners of Mary-Lou's lips twitched upwards. Michael grunted his disapproval. Amber and Katie exchanged glances, then looked away, smirking.

"Okay. Once more," Laurefen said, exasperated. "Please pay attention."

"Yes, I will. I'm sorry."

"At the end of this tunnel is a doorway. You must speak your full name and repeat these words: 'I subject myself for Approval'. Say it for me now, so I know you have it."

Declan repeated the phrase.

"Once more." Mary-Lou smiled sweetly. "To be safe."

Declan did it again. She gave him a thumbs up.

"Good," Laurefen said. "Once you enter the doorway, your memories will be temporarily altered. You will lose all recollection of this place. You will find yourself in... an *uncomfortable* situation. One that will require you to make a difficult choice."

"What do you mean, difficult?" Declan heard the quaver in his voice.

"A choice that demonstrates your character." Laurefen's tone was serious. "One choice will satisfy your selfish desires. Another is fitting of a Directive member." He locked eyes with Declan. "You will have no memory of this conversation. You will not know you are in a test. To pass Approval, you must forsake your vices and make the noble choice of your own volition."

Declan exhaled. He had not held his breath on purpose. "Okay, so I go in, say my name and that I want to do the test. Once I'm in, I make a noble choice... That's it?"

"It is." Laurefen's expression remained grim. "But be warned, Declan Moore. Many have found their choice too difficult to make. Witches and wizards have left their sanity down that passage, driven mad by what they find seeking Approval."

An eerie shiver climbed Declan's spine.

"Are you sure you want to do this, boy?" Michael asked. "It would be easier to walk away."

"Michael!" Mary-Lou snapped. "He's going to be fine."

"You belong to a long line of honorable witches and wizards," Laurefen said. "Nobility is a quality I suspect is in your blood. Once you pass Approval, those who descend from you will always be welcome at King's College." He nodded towards the entry. "Are you ready to begin?"

"No." Declan said. His shirt felt too tight. His neck itched.

Katie laughed. "You'll be fine."

"You are very noble, Declan," Amber added. They had yet to talk about her visit last night. Declan wasn't sure if they would, or what he would say if they did.

"Are you *willing* to begin?" Laurefen's moustache quivered above the smallest of smiles.

Declan sighed. "I guess so."

He stepped into the darkness on trembling legs. The morning light vanished down the winding passageway. Morning air grew stagnant. Soon, the rich smell of decay accompanied every breath. Deeper still, the air grew cold; his plodding footsteps echoed off the narrow walls. A soft orange glow appeared ahead. Declan rounded a corner and came to a stone door inlaid with seven fiery gems that sparkled like embers in a campfire.

Do you really want to do this? You could go mad. Declan ignored the little voice. The glowing orange gems pulsed like a heartbeat. Declan cleared his throat. With a shaky voice, he announced himself. "Declan Walter Moore."

The glowing stones blazed brighter; Declan raised a hand to shield his eyes. "I subject myself for Approval."

The orange gems turned white. A series of metallic clicks echoed down the passage. The door swung outwards to reveal a wall of light that rippled like a vertical pool. Declan looked back at the stone doorway and saw the glowing gems were actually seven small round windows. The light in the entryway looked like liquid sunlight. Declan took a deep breath and stepped into the dazzling luminescence.

Everything faded to black. Declan squeezed his eyelids shut so his pupils would dilate. When he opened them, he was on a second-floor platform surrounded by a crowd of plain looking sculptures. It looked like a storage facility for an art gallery.

Ahead of him, a balcony overlooked a large warehouse floor. Dim exit signs in the corners failed to light the cavernous room, but even so, Declan could tell that the ground floor was filled with more of the same- hundreds, or maybe thousands, of life-sized statues.

A narrow staircase led the way down. The steel handrail was ice cold as Declan descended to the ground floor. When he reached the bottom step, enormous panels of lights flickered to life. *I'm trespassing. I can't be seen here.* The thought had appeared in his head as if by magic. Declan ducked behind a stack of bins.

Footsteps echoed from the far side of the building. The army of metal sculptures blocked his view. Properly illuminated, they looked eerily lifelike, expressions carved with perfect precision, as if the sculptor had simply turned their subject to metal instead of casting it in a mold. Declan stared at a nearby face. It looked familiar.

"Where are they?"

A woman's voice cut through Declan's thread of attention.

"North corner, Madam."

Two figures appeared through the gap. One was a man, tall with a short red beard, dressed in a black coat. A woman in green walked beside him. She was tall too, with pale skin and crimson hair. They vanished from sight. The footsteps stopped.

"So, this is them?"

"Yes, Madam."

"Their names?"

"Angus and Miranda Moore. They were captured in Tamhill, Iberia."

Declan's stomach clenched. *Mom? Dad?* He rose slowly. Over the top of the bin, two figures faced a pair of sculptures positioned alongside the wall.

"Hard to capture, I assume?"

"Yes, Madam. They cost us many men."

"I am not surprised," said the woman. "The Moore's hold a distinguished place in the history of the Dominion."

The man shifted to his right and Declan gasped. Metal faces portraits of fear and anger. *They're not statues, they're my parents!*

"My apologies, Madam, but why are we here?"

"We are here because I will it, Raul."

Raul? Raul! He was there... He took them... He turned them to iron!

"Yes. Of course, Madam." Raul paused. "What would you have me do?"

Declan dropped to his belly. He wriggled like a snake towards his parents.

"I would like your advice, Raul," said the woman.

"Of course, Madam."

"These two individuals were of particular interest to a certain group that wish to undermine our plans."

"The Directive?"

Declan paused. *The Directive.* The name sounded familiar. He searched his memories and found nothing. *Why would a group of people be trying to help my parents? Why do these people even want my parents?*

"Exactly. The Directive sought to save them. Now they have been captured. Ants to honey."

"You are brilliant, Madam."

"Spare me, Raul. My question is simple. Now the ants are mine. What should I do with the honey?"

Declan peeked through one of the statue's legs. Raul did

not answer. Instead, he scratched his chin and surveyed the iron casts of Angus and Miranda Moore.

"Quickly, Raul. The ants are outside and unguarded."

The people who tried to save my parents are outside? Maybe they can help me get them back! It was a golden opportunity. Declan had no idea how he got there, but he knew what he had to do. He shuffled backwards and turned towards the exit.

"Are there any others seeking this witch and wizard? More ants that could be trapped with the same honey?"

Stay low. Stay quiet.

"None that I am aware of, no."

Free the prisoners. Free your parents.

"Well, in that case, best to destroy the honey entirely. We wouldn't want the ants trying to escape for a second helping."

Declan froze.

"You make a good point, Raul," said the woman. A long pause hung in the air. "Melt them down."

Declan's heart lodged in his throat. Surely, the woman didn't mean to *literally* melt them. He turned back around.

"Yes, Madam."

Declan was paralyzed by the moment. *I can't save them by myself. I have to get the others. But if I leave, they'll be melted. Can they be melted? They're solid iron. Iron can't be melted by magic. Unless they melt them in a forge.* Declan's thoughts ran wild. *How long will it take? Do I have time to rescue the others? Who are they?*

He stood slowly and peeked over the mass of iron casts. The man and woman continued to stare at his parents. *What are they waiting for?*

Declan took two steps towards the exit, then stopped.

I can't leave my parents.

Resolute, he turned back to Raul and the mystery woman. He stopped again. *What can I do? If they use magic, I'm done for.* Declan stood rooted to the floor. *I can't leave them, but I can't save them.*

"Begin when ready, Raul."

Raul raised his hands. *No!* Declan needed to stop them, to save his parents, yet help was on the other side of the building. A chance to set them free had dropped, gift-wrapped, into his lap, and all it would cost was his parent's lives. The conflicting pathways tore him apart. *I don't want to make this choice.*

At that thought, a tiny muffled voice echoed in the back of his mind, whispered into the wind from a distance. The voice was quiet. The only phrase he could make out was *a difficult choice.* Declan frowned. The voice was familiar. Very familiar. He'd heard it just recently.

"Faster, Raul, we must return to the prisoners."

Declan tiptoed towards them. He had to save his parents. The whisper grew louder, a stern voice in Declan's mind. *An uncomfortable situation that will require you to make a difficult choice.* It was Laurefen's voice.

"Sorry, Madam, one moment."

"For what? Don't test me, Raul. Do it!"

Declan stopped in his tracks. *Test. Test? Test! This is a test!*

Realization hit like lightning. The conversation on the hill at Kingsbreak flashed like fireworks. Laurefen, serious and frowning. Michael, bitter and cold. Mary-Lou, trying hard not to smile, with Amber and Katie encouraging him. He was in a test. None of it was real. Raul. The woman—she *had* to be Haberdeen. They were figments of his imagination! *A noble choice, to pass the test. I need to save the Directive.* Declan turned around.

"Yes, Madam."

Raul's voice echoed through the warehouse. Declan felt a sharp pang. Real or not, he was leaving his parents behind. He hesitated, then banished the thought and continued, weaving through the fierised witches and wizards and out the exit.

Dirty daylight spilled over the abandoned carpark. The outside world looked like a photo left in the sun. The lot was empty except for a van parked on the far side. It was the same make as the one which carried away his parents the night the Fatesmiths invaded Tamhill, jet-black with small narrow windows running horizontally along the top edge.

"About time you showed up."

Ward spun a set of keys in his hands; they clinked each time they hit his palm. He nodded to the van. "Everyone's already in there. You're the last in the set, kid, so come—"

Declan launched forward and planted his shoulder squarely into Ward's chest. The blond wizard hit the wall with a crunch. Declan leapt to his feet, then drove a fist into his chin. He scooped the keys from Ward's limp hand, then streaked across the parking lot like a comet.

Enormous dirt spikes emerged from the pavement below. Declan weaved around them as a wall of asphalt grew ahead of him. He met it at full tilt, cleared it in a jump. The van lifted off the ground. It floated like a helium balloon. Declan leapt, hands outstretched, and caught the rims of the back tires. Higher it rose. He pulled himself up, wedged his feet against the back wheels, and tried not to look down.

A pair of eyes appeared at the window. "Declan, is that you?"

The van's ascent slowed to a stop. Declan's eyes widened. Gravity kicked in.

Declan threw himself off the passenger step just in time. The van hit the ground with a crunch—the front windows exploded. Shattered glass covered the asphalt. Declan climbed to his feet and was hoisted into the air by an invisible force.

"And here we are." Raul marched towards him with Ward close behind. Both looked furious.

"Put me down," Declan said. "I know you're not real."

Raul squinted at him, then looked sideways at Ward. "What's this? You messed with his mind or somethin'?"

Ward shook his head. He eyed Declan venomously. "I'll take it from here. Hand him over. "

"No chance of that." Raul bunched his fists. "He's mine now."

"The boy belongs to me."

"I don't see your name on him."

Declan stood in disbelief, Ward and Raul went back and forth, distracted over who would receive the credit for his capture. As they did, the invisible bonds relaxed. He could move.

"You were the fool who let him go the night we took his parents."

"And you were the idiot child who left him alive when I told you to take care of it."

Declan wiggled his fingers, twisted his wrists.

"I threw him through a window," Ward snarled. "What are the chances he'd survive that?"

"And the second time? When your boys in maroon picked him up?" Raul thrust a pointed finger at Ward's chest. "You lost him again."

Declan could move his forearm, his elbow, even his shoulder. Raul must have realized something wasn't right, because he turned from Ward in time to see Declan toss the keys towards the van. He flicked his fingers, and the keys froze in the air mere inches from the shattered window.

Declan's arms snapped back to his sides.

"Oh, lad, you're going to pay for—"

A hand reached out of the window. It snatched the keys from the air. Something inside the van clicked, and the door swung open. John climbed out, backed by Katie, Mary-Lou, Amber, and Michael. Laurefen stepped out last. Thick lines of fury cut creases in his cheeks.

Raul and Ward exchanged looks, then fled. Declan dropped to the ground. John and Amber rushed to pull him to his feet. "Are you okay?" Katie asked.

"I am." He looked at the blackcoats across the car park. "Why aren't you going after them?"

"Why bother?" Mary-Lou beamed at him. "They're not important."

Laurefen stepped forward. "You have done well, Declan. You have made a noble choice, and earned our Approval." He put a hand on Declan's shoulder and squeezed. "Michael, take us back."

Michael weaved a large, circular opening, but instead of the usual window, this Opening was a wall of liquid white. Laurefen beckoned him forward. Declan stepped through and emerged on the same green hill where he had started. The clouds were gone. Sunlight warmed his cold skin.

"Welcome back and congratulations." Laurefen had not moved an inch. "Put your mind at ease. Nothing you experienced was real. The tragedies you witnessed were mere lights and shadows. Your memories should return soon, but be assured, you have arrived here by way of Opening, indicating that you *have* made a noble choice and thus, passed Approval."

Declan nodded, unsure of what to say. Mary-Lou

clapped her hands together. Katie and Amber cheered. Michael nodded. "Well done, boy." It was the nicest thing Declan had ever heard him say.

"Oh Declan! You did it!" Amber crooned. "What happened? What did you see?"

"Amber," Laurefen interjected. "We do not ask about what was seen during Approval." Amber went bright red. "Declan, you must be overwhelmed. Mary-Lou will escort you back to your room. Rest up. You have completed the first part of our bargain. Tomorrow, I will meet mine."

Declan fought to keep the grin inside him. "You mean I'm learning magic?"

Laurefen nodded. "You are."

Michael shifted his feet but said nothing.

Declan let the grin out, a smile stretching from ear to ear, but deep inside, his insides squirmed. *I knew. I knew it was a test the whole time. Otherwise, I would have left them to die to save my parents.*

CHAPTER 33

DECLAN

THE ANCIENT LECTURE hall smelled like a library. The wooden floorboards were smooth, faded, no doubt worn away by centuries of students. The whole building seemed to glow in the columns of morning light that poured from the rafters. Laurefen stood at the front. He turned a stick of chalk in his fingers the way an artist might twirl a paintbrush. "There are four broad streams of magic," he said. "Can you name them?"

Declan leaned forward in his chair, eager to show he was a model student, the kind worthy of learning magic. "Manipulation, Imbusion, Mimicry and Luck."

"Tell me about each stream."

"Manipulators use threads of matter or energy to move things around."

"Correct."

"Imbuers charm objects to give them magical qualities."

Laurefen nodded. "And they can also charm places. King's College and Noahi are both imbued with powerful protective charms. Tell me about mimicry?"

Declan recalled his unfortunate adventure on Noahi. "Mimics can learn magical abilities from other magical creatures."

"And Lucks."

"They can..." Declan thought of Ava. "They can make possibilities a reality."

Laurefen's expression was unreadable. "What determines the type of magic a witch or wizards can use?"

Declan opened his mouth to answer, then realized he didn't know. "Uh, I'm not sure, sir. I know John can do manipulation and mimicry."

"That's not the question."

"I don't know, sir."

Laurefen nodded. "That is where we will begin." An antique chalkboard rolled out of the shadows. His fingers moved as if playing an invisible harp, and the stick of chalk began dancing along the board, writing in slanted script. Laurefen paced the front of the hall while the chalk worked. "The vast majority of witches and wizards come to us as highly capable manipulators. Their potential, nourished in a magical environment, has blossomed and they can already see nima around them."

"Uh, sorry sir." Declan pointed at the blackboard. "Am I supposed to be copying this down?"

The chalk stopped mid-sentence. Laurefen almost smiled. "What am I doing?" He flicked his wrist, and the board zoomed away. "I've been teaching this course for thirty-five years, Declan, but never to one student and never in such dire circumstances. My apologies. Let us drop the formality and begin anew."

Declan nodded; glad he wouldn't be required to do any actual coursework. "I just want to learn to use magic."

"It is vital you understand magic first. Magic is a tool.

We use it. It should never use us." Laurefen straightened his jacket. "The type of magic that a witch or a wizard favors is a matter of lineage."

"My mother was an Imbuer," Declan cut in. "And my father a Manipulator."

"And so, it is more likely than not that you will be able to imbue things," Laurefen said. "But these tendencies do not always sit on the surface. Sometimes they will skip a generation. Sometimes three or four."

"So, it's a luck of the draw?"

"A luck of the draw if the game is rigged. Your closest relatives hold the most sway, but the magical population is so intermingled that there is always a chance a new child will be the first mimic or imbuer in his or her family, a talent gifted from a long lost or little-known lineage."

Declan let the words sink in. "Is that the same for Lucks?"

"To a degree," Laurefen said. "But of the four streams, Lucks are the least common."

"Why?"

"Who knows?" Laurefen gestured to an aged map on the wall. "Once upon a time, every Luck in existence came from Hispania, the land now known as Iberia. These days, Lucks tend to gravitate towards the affluent suburbs of Sabriva, but even there they are not vocal about their abilities lest someone fear they are being taken advantage of."

Declan frowned. "You're saying they use their powers to make money?"

"Only implying it." Laurefen shrugged. "Lucks have no ability beyond manipulating chance, and their power comes at a physical cost. We have never had a Luck at King's College."

A cloud crossed the sun's path overhead and the room momentarily dimmed.

"So how do I learn?" Declan asked.

"Patience, Declan." Laurefen's expression turned rigid. "Magic is performed with a sound mind and steady emotions. The chaotic force you've explored while filled with rage is not magic. Or at least not the magic we want you to unleash."

Ire Tides, Declan caught himself before he said it aloud. He wasn't supposed to know those words. "Sorry sir, I understand."

"Good," Laurefen's shoulders relaxed. "You know the streams of magic. Now let's talk about the ethics of it."

Declan groaned, and for the first time that morning, Laurefen smiled. Soon, they had jumped headfirst into a well-rehearsed lecture about when it was appropriate to use magic and when it was forbidden. "Unless absolutely necessary, you must never use magic on a LAMP, Declan. Many LAMPs carry iron pendants as a measure of protection. The rule of thumb is life or death. If you're saving a life or preventing a death, otherwise, leave LAMPs be."

The morning dragged on from there. By the time Laurefen dismissed him for a break, Declan's head hurt. He'd spent the morning in a one-man-lecture and the mental load of the discussion left him exhausted. Katie met him outside with a sandwich.

"A fun morning of ethics?" she asked, chuckling. She had tied her hair in a short braid and now looked like a young version of Mary-Lou.

"You're looking young, Lou," Declan teased as they sat on the wide cobblestone steps.

Katie poked her tongue out. "Seriously though, how's it all going?"

Declan tried to respond with a mouth full of sandwich. Katie rolled her eyes at him. He gave up on words and did his best impression of being asleep.

"Tired, hey?"

Declan nodded.

"Maybe you should spend more time sleeping and less time locking lips with Amber."

Katie's amused tone did nothing to dampen the wave of heat that rushed up Declan's collar. He swallowed with a loud gulp. "You heard about that?"

"Girls talk," Katie said. "Amber's torn though."

"What do you mean?" Declan tried and failed to sound casual.

"Well, on the one hand, you're cute." Declan blushed ever harder; Katie didn't react. "But you're also about three years too young for her. Plus, she's technically staff and you're technically a student. Big no-no."

"Would it help if I told her I wasn't interested?"

Katie raised an eyebrow. "Got a girlfriend back in Tamhill?"

Declan's mind went straight to Ava. "Not quite."

Katie raised the other eyebrow.

"I'm... just... with everything going on, I don't have time for personal stuff. Does that make sense?" He took another bite of his sandwich.

"You're quite sensible for a teenager," Katie said. "Probably for the best too. Laurefen told Mary-Lou he was going to try to deliver a semester's worth of information in a month."

Declan groaned. "Wha?"

"Don't speak with your mouth full."

He swallowed with another comical gulp. "Sorry. A whole semester? Seriously?"

Katie grinned. "You can't complain. You sent in an application for King's College and now you've got it. This is what you wanted, right?"

She was right. He was receiving a personalized class at the world's greatest College Mag-Ed could offer. Taught by the Dean himself. The opportunity of a lifetime and he was complaining. "You make a good point," he admitted. The realization sparked something inside him. "Well, I guess I better head back to class then."

"But you just got out?"

"It's like you said," Declan called over his shoulder as he started up the steps two-at-a-time. "This is what I wanted!"

As the month wore on, the nights grew brisk and the days cool. Declan threw himself into Magical Education and Laurefen seemed happy to oblige. They would start early, sometimes while stars still glittered over the dawning horizon, and work late into the night.

The other members of the Directive popped in and out, staying sometimes only for an evening before heading off on any number of important jobs. Michael and Mary-Lou were particularly busy, sometimes visiting every state in Euryma over the course of a day, while he barely saw Amber at all. She had apparently volunteered to take on extra duties. Though he would never say it, Declan suspected he knew exactly why.

The Directive met every Monday night to discuss the Fatesmiths. Katie hinted at some top-secret headquarters beneath the main administration building, but with nobody to overhear them, Mary-Lou's house in the Village had become the unofficial meeting grounds. Tonight, everybody was on campus, except for John, and Declan sat sandwiched awkwardly between Katie and Amber while the conversation grew tense.

"John should be back by now," Mary-Lou said. "The Headmaster at Arman Moore's said he was long gone before we returned to search the school."

Declan blushed. He had been slow to reveal that they were staying at Arman Moore's. By the time Mary-Lou had gone looking, he was gone.

"Uh..." Amber hesitated. "I may have heard from John." She was too pale to blush red, but her cheeks bloomed pink.

"What?" Michael said. "When?"

"Late last night on looptap. He didn't want me to say anything..." Amber's pause was as long as it was awkward.

"What didn't he want you to tell us?" Laurefen asked.

Amber's gaze dropped to her hands in her lap. "He's sorry. Laurefen, he thought you were working with Haberdeen to keep Declan's power under wraps." She spoke faster with each sentence. "Now he's realized he screwed up. He knows he was wrong, but he's too proud to come back until he's made up for it." She looked at Mary-Lou. "He also said he hated having to cut your looptap strand. He waited as long as he could bear, but his hand started to bleed from the itch."

Mary-Lou's lips were pencil thin. "Well, it serves him right."

Michael rolled his eyes. "The stubborn boy will get himself killed thinking like that. How does he intend to make up for this?"

Amber's shoulders dropped. "I tried to talk him out of it, told him to apologize and move on. He said..." she took a deep breath. "He said he's tracking the ironhands' transport vehicles. He's looking to find where they're putting the fierised wiz—"

"We've been trying that for months," Katie said. "Remember all those watch-but-don't-interfere missions we did early on? How many people did we let fall into the Fatesmith's hands in the hopes we could free them all?"

"I know. I told him. He was there, he should know, but he said he was getting closer."

"To finding out where they're stored?" Laurefen had been silent throughout the exchange.

"I guess so... I don't know..." Amber sunk into the couch. "I tried to talk him out of it. He doesn't listen. I've been trying to looptap him all morning, but no response. I'm worried if I keep trying, he'll cut me off too."

The Directive discussed John further, but nobody could agree on what to do. "He is," Michael started, "the most annoying combination of stubborn and clever. He is too talented to track and too pig-headed to ask for our help. I think all we can do is wait and hope he comes to his senses."

Declan nudged Amber while they spoke. "You did the right thing," he whispered. She smiled, but didn't meet his gaze.

The conversation shifted towards rations for refugee alumnus. Just like every week, Mary-Lou argued to bring the magical refugees to Kingsbreak.

"We can't, Lou. All it takes is one spy and we'll be sitting ducks."

"But the Ancellum? This Island is protected!"

"We cannot risk it," Laurefen said. "You know how important Kingsbreak is."

The meeting dragged on. By now, Fatesmiths controlled every state capital except Sabriva. The cracks were beginning to show. Natural disaster, normally managed through magical influence, were returning to the Dominion. Severe hailstorms had ravaged parts of Habsburg and LAMPs were asking why. The Directive discussed the issue at length, but as usual, no agreement was reached. To Declan, these meetings were an echo chamber for a list of troubles they could not remedy. He wished he was in bed.

When they finished, Declan was so tired he could barely stand. He trudged back towards the campus and wondered if Laurefen would let him take a house in the Village.

"A bit dry, aren't they?"

Declan jumped at the voice in the shadows. "John!"

"Shhhh!" John stepped into the light. He looked like he'd been sleeping in a ditch. Ava's tan satchel hung over his shoulder.

Declan looked behind him. The Village lights were bright, but far enough away that they wouldn't be seen. "Sorry," he whispered. "When did you get back?"

"About forty-five minutes ago." He handed Declan the bag with a grin. "You forgot something. Again."

"Thanks!" Declan took it gratefully. "How did you know where to find me?"

"Amber sent word."

"And why didn't you come back?"

John's easy smile faltered. He kicked at the ground. "Listen, I'm sorry Declan. I jumped to a conclusion that wasn't right."

"You mean Laurefen?"

"Yeah. Amber talked to me about Ire Tides. I can't believe I didn't make the connection. I could've done a lot of damage." He looked genuinely guilty. "I'm really sorry."

Declan shook his head. "Don't worry about it. Laurefen

was acting weird. It made sense. Come back, right now, we'll go see him and straighten everything out."

"I can't." John turned away. "I betrayed the College. The Directive. My family. I betrayed who I am. I need to make things right."

"John, that's ridiculous. You were trying to stop the blackcoats. Laurefen will understand."

Something smoldered behind John's eyes. "Declan... When I was a boy, my mom was killed by some rogue wizards. Those wizards were brought to justice by the Directive. My dad ended up making it his life's work to join them, to help save people, so kids like me didn't have to grow up without a mother."

Declan didn't know what to say.

"Then they showed up at our house on Odacre's border. The Fatesmiths knew who we were and where we lived. Dad held them off long enough for me to get away and I fled, like a coward, to Kingsbreak. It was then that Laurefen told me he would look after me and keep me safe. Like dad would've wanted."

"What?" Declan spat. "But he asked you to join the Directive? That's not safe."

John shook his head. "He didn't ask me. I practically demanded to join. To avenge him and everyone else we've lost. Laurefen didn't want to, but I was relentless. Directive members were dropping like flies. He didn't have time to subject new wizards to Approval—so he gave in."

Declan nodded. *I would've done the same.*

"I have to do this, Declan." John continued. "I have to show Laurefen that he made the right choice in letting me join. If I go to him now, he's going to think I'm too reckless. He'll keep me here and I'll never avenge my father. I can't come back until I've found them, and once I do, we can save them, all of us, together."

Declan understood. *If I had the opportunity to save everyone I'd lost... If Laurefen wanted me to stay here and do nothing...* He met John's gaze. "Okay, okay. I understand."

John grasped his shoulder. "Thanks, Declan. You're a good friend."

Declan frowned. "Only if you don't get yourself killed. Please be safe. Don't do anything stupid, deal?"

John nodded. They talked a little longer, but the conversation felt wrong—like he was betraying the Directive. When John disappeared into the darkness, Declan trudged back to his room, wondering if he'd made the right choice.

CHAPTER 34
DECLAN

A TRANSLUCENT ORB rotated slowly above Laurefen's palm. It was periwinkle blue, no larger than a marble. Laurefen lowered his hand and eased backwards between the classroom desks. With each step, the orb spun faster.

Declan had not slept well. Dreams of Laurefen discovering John's visit and expelling him from King's College had kept him awake most of the night. He was exhausted but fascinated by the tiny sphere that sparked and crackled. "Is it safe, sir?" he tore his gaze from the spectacle long enough to see Laurefen nod.

"Quite safe now. It's self-sustaining."

"How does it work?"

"You should know, Declan. We've covered knots."

"I know how knots work," Declan said. "I want to know how *this* specific knot will unlock my potential." He stared at the orb. It was a product of tying different nima together and leaving them entangled. *Could it really be this easy?*

"I never said that." Laurefen's eyes remained locked to the knot. "I simply said it was one strategy that we will try. One of *many*."

Declan clenched his jaw. "Sorry, sir, I'm just... I'm tired of having my hopes dashed..."

Laurefen's intense focus cracked for a moment. "I understand. Do not fool yourself by thinking you are the first student at this College to have experienced this particular problem."

Declan nodded, determined now. "What do I do?"

"Hold the knot in your dominant hand and squeeze. I doubt you will feel anything, but the entangled nima may unlock a sense you did not know you had."

"What? Now?"

"When you're ready..."

Declan stepped forward. The knot rotated like a tiny planet. He reached out with his right hand, exchanged a hopeful look with Laurefen, then squeezed.

The resulting explosion threw both of them across the room. Laurefen caught himself with a twist of his fingers. He landed on his feet by the wall. Declan felt his back buckle as he crashed into a crowded pile of desks.

"Declan?" Laurefen cleared the desks with a wave of his hand. Declan lay on the floor laughing. "What is so funny?"

"Quite safe, is it?" Declan let Laurefen help him up. "Pardon, sir, but John's training was a lot gentler."

"My sincerest apologies. Are you sure you're alright?"

Declan stretched out; his back popped as something dropped into place. "Yeah, I'm okay. Not the first room I've been thrown across." He twisted with another satisfying crack.

Laurefen ran a long finger through his beard. "That's never happened before. Peculiar indeed." He looked at Declan and his lips twitched into a small smile. "Perhaps we should begin with a *gentler* approach."

While his theoretical education had been confined to

old lecture theaters, Laurefen had elected to use the smaller classrooms for his practical training. Despite Declan being a one-student-class, the Dean was committed to using the facilities as tradition dictated.

Laurefen led them into a small room lined with enormous cushions. "Take a seat somewhere comfortable."

"Yes, sir." Declan fell into a cushion the size of a bed; it was much softer than the pile of desks.

"Now, close your eyes and sit back. Focus on the beat of your heart. When the inevitable distraction enters your mind, acknowledge it and bid it farewell."

Declan lay back.

"Breathe slow, that's it..."

The door clicked shut, and the room became pitch black. Declan concentrated on his lungs, in and out, in and out. The steady thud of his heart reverberated in his ears. His body pulsed like a slow percussion.

"Excellent." Laurefen's voice was a faint whisper. "Now, imagine a pearl. Picture it. Clean, pure, sparkling, a perfect sphere. This pearl represents your potential. Search yourself. Locate the pearl within."

Declan did his best. He pictured the tiny pearls his parents had shown him on visits to the Iberian coast. They were so small, so smooth. *Pearls. Pearls. Focus on the pearls.* Instead, Declan lingered on his parents, memories of playing in the sparkling water, building sandcastles, eating fresh fruit from roadside vendors.

"Concentrate Declan."

He pushed the precious memories away, refocused his breathing, and searched for a pearl within. He imagined a wooden roller working its way from his head to his feet, seeking out a flaw or protrusion. But there was nothing.

"Any luck?"

"Sir, it's been five minutes."

The door clicked; Declan opened his eyes. Golden purple sunlight painted the hallway walls.

"It's late afternoon, Declan," Laurefen said. "You've been in here for nearly five hours."

"What? Why didn't you tell me?"

"I may have fallen asleep."

Declan stared at Laurefen. "Are you serious?"

"It has been a trying couple of months. This room is imbued to act as a mild suppressant. I must admit, it was refreshing to have a break."

Declan extracted himself from the giant cushion. His muscles groaned. The room may have fooled his mind, but his legs seemed acutely aware of how long he had spent on the floor. "I... I couldn't find it, sir. The pearl. I searched. It's not there."

"Fear not, Declan, you will find it. Remember, you are not the first student to experience such difficulty."

Much to Declan's disappointment, Laurefen called it a day. As they exited the building, Laurefen handed him a small cloth bag. "This is powdered bark from a marble spruce. Leave it to sit in boiling water for thirty minutes and then drink it before bed. It may help you locate that pearl, it may not. Regardless, I should warn you that it tastes terrible."

Declan accepted the bag. "Thank you, sir. Same time tomorrow?"

"Perhaps a little later. I may be less inclined to sleep through your lessons if I'm not required to start before dawn."

Declan chuckled and waved goodbye. As soon as he got back to his room, he boiled water and popped the bag inside. Laurefen was right. It tasted terrible. Declan went to bed quickly, pulsing with excitement. If nothing else, the tea made him drowsy. When Declan woke the next morning, he was the same. No pearls. No power.

———

Laurefen waited at the front of the building, draped in a plum tunic. A black frame bag rested at his feet. He picked it up as Declan approached. "Good morning, Declan. Any luck with the marble spruce?"

"No, sir." Declan swallowed his disappointment, then nodded to the bag. "What's this?"

Laurefen picked it up. Something inside jingled like glass bottles. "A few bits and pieces from the Imbusion Lab. Let's see if we can make something happen." He opened the door with a flick of his wrist and led Declan into a large, open room. There were no desks here, and the floor was spongy beneath his feet. "This is where King's teaches students to manipulate kinetic energy."

The sky-blue walls looked like thin mattresses. "Looks comfy."

"I thought—after yesterday—it may be an understandable precaution."

Declan smirked. "Probably."

"Then let us begin." Laurefen flicked his wrist and the frame bag's clasps snapped open. Two narrow rods jumped up into his hands. One looked like glass, and the other was black, blacker than black, like a rod-shaped hole in reality. "These are nimrods."

Declan snorted.

Laurefen raised an eyebrow. "Yes, I've heard all the jokes. Now, nimrods are ordinary rods of wood that have been imbued with nima. This one is aeronima." Laurefen shook the clear nimrod and a gentle breeze materialized in the room. "And this is lumonima." He shook the other, and the room flashed brighter. Their shadows skewed about them, then wobbled back into focus.

"Sir..." Declan hesitated. "Are you telling me I can manipulate nima by holding those sticks?"

"Nimrods have a very small functional range. They only work with one thread and will explode if overloaded with too much power."

"So about as safe as that knot you had me grab yesterday?"

"That is correct."

Declan rolled his eyes, smiling. "Are they easy to make?"

"A well-practiced Imbuer can bind nima to the rod in moments, but the rods must be prepared carefully over the course of weeks. Here." Laurefen tossed the glass rod through the air.

Declan rushed to catch it; afraid it might shatter if he missed. To his surprise, it didn't feel like glass at all, more like polished wood. "It feels warm."

"The warmth is created by friction between wood and nima. If the surrogate rod is not prepared properly, it would quickly burst into flame."

Declan moved the clear rod slowly. The air rushed around him. Laurefen smiled while he conducted a breezy orchestra. Declan stopped mid-swing, and the wind subsided. "It's a lot of fun, but I still don't feel anything."

"Try this." Laurefen handed him the impossibly black rod.

Declan swished it around. The room flashed from dark

to light, flickering like he was playing with a light switch. "The clear one is definitely more fun," he said, looking down at the nimrods.

"Yes, but fun is not what we're after. Did you feel anything?"

Declan tried once more. "No," he said at last. "Nothing."

Laurefen frowned. "Very well." He gathered up the bag. "Then we need to try something else."

Declan handed the nimrods back. He felt a pang of regret, giving up the only conscious control of magic he had yet experienced. Laurefen must have read his mind, or maybe just his face. He placed a hand on Declan's shoulder. "This happens all the time, Declan. Be patient."

From there Declan tried meditating under a glowing red lantern, holding an icy cube of frozen hydronima, and drinking something that burned like apple vinegar. At the end of each failed experiment, Laurefen would ask if he felt something, and when Declan answered no, he would nod and move on to something else.

"Okay, Declan, reach out gently and tell me the moment you notice something different.

The clear gloves on his hands looked ridiculous. Declan concentrated on his fingers, but the only sensation was the sweat on his palms. He remembered his failed attempts at grasping nima with John. It was the same thing all over again. "This isn't working, sir. Can't you just make me really angry?"

He regretted it immediately.

Laurefen's eyes were thunderheads. "Declan, that was a foolish thing to say. Please do not repeat it."

Declan nodded meekly. He went back to grasping at empty air, but his heart wasn't in it and Laurefen must have recognized the reluctance. "Stop, Declan. It's okay. Gloves off."

Declan dropped them on the table. "I'm sorry—"

"No, I'm sorry, Declan. There is no way I can know what you are feeling, but I can see you are frustrated."

Declan nodded at the ground.

"Nevertheless, we made an agreement, and the conditions of that agreement include no magic that is driven by strong emotions, especially anger."

Declan remained silent.

Laurefen considered him. "Let's call it a day." He pulled another small cloth bag from a pocket in his tunic. "Here. Green elm bark. It tastes bitter but not nearly as bad as the marble spruce. Try it tonight and let me know tomorrow."

"Thank you, sir."

Laurefen considered him for a moment. "Just be patient. We'll get there."

Declan had the feeling Laurefen was talking to himself. He trudged outside as the sun set over the sea. Declan wandered back to his dorm to collapse on his bed. Worry paralyzed him, but he was exhausted. When he fell asleep, Laurefen's bag of bark remained untouched in his pocket.

CHAPTER 35
MICHAEL

MICHAEL SAT on a smoothed boulder in the flickering light of the underground cavern. A few feet forward marked a sudden drop into a pit of churning orange light. Inches above it, a scar in the stone marked the magical well's level. Michael stood and stared. Pure, unadulterated magic swirled in its depths. He looked back at Laurefen. "Why are we meeting here?"

"It's the last safe place," Laurefen replied. Seated on his own boulder, he shuffled through a stack of papers. A floating cube of lumonima lit the pages in gentle white light. The papers were Michael's report. It was not an inspiring read. "No free wizards left in Habsburg, Iberia, Gaul or Odacre?"

Mary-Lou scanned the page over his shoulder. "Clovin would be gone too if the High Mage hadn't used it as a bargaining chip."

"So, where does that leave us? Vitulus. How many do we have there?"

"Less than two dozen in Parteno. Most alumni have

vanished, gone into hiding or the non-magical provinces south."

"Can't blame them." Mary-Lou's eyes never left his report. "Haberdeen infiltrated our entire network in Odacre. Who's to say she hasn't done the same in Vitulus?"

"She's had insiders from the start," Laurefen murmured. "They knew who we were before we knew they existed. If we knew who to trust, we could have housed our entire alumnus safely here at Kingsbreak."

Michael now understood why Laurefen had chosen the Well as their meeting place. It was the best kept secret in Euryma, a storage vault for magic itself. *He must suspect one of the others.* Michael turned back to the glowing pit. "It seems we have lost," he said. "I wish that was a shock, but it comes as no surprise. No matter where I go in the Dominion, things are the same. Witches and wizards with nowhere to go, shell-shocked by how quickly their world changed. LAMPs going about their daily lives, knowing something is different, but not certain what. The High Mage doomed us all the moment he decided to sweep the first attacks under the rug." He gestured to the thick scar in the stone. "We could broadcast this very cavern tonight, show the world that the Well is as high as ever, that Remnant Magic continues to refill its reservoirs as it has for a thousand years and it wouldn't matter. Three quarters of the magical population are gone. There aren't enough people left to start an uprising."

"We still have Declan," Mary-Lou said.

Laurefen breathed a long sigh. "I don't know."

"You'll get there. Some students take time."

Laurefen put the report down. "Some do, but they show glimpses, hints, sparks of Potential. Declan... He has nothing. He's clever, and he wants it so bad, but nothing works for him. I have him doing the same exercises that children do, the same exercises even the most basic applicants of the most basic colleges can master within days and he's going nowhere." He looked at Mary-Lou, his eyes dull. "I'm not sure we have the time Declan needs."

They sat in silence. The orange glow flickered gently off the walls. Michael's stomach turned as he entertained an idea he did not agree with in the slightest. "Laurefen. What if the boy dabbled with Ire Tides?"

Mary-Lou shook her head. "Michael! Don't be ridiculous."

"I'm not saying you let him go wild, but once or twice at strategic spots. Direct attacks on Haberdeen's strongholds. The central business district in Biscay, for example."

Laurefen placed his hands in his lap. The light of the well reflected in his sad eyes. For a moment, Michael was sure he was considering it. Then he shook his head. "No, Michael. Right now, we are at risk of losing Euryma. If we give Declan permission and access to that type of power, we might lose the world."

"Is there a plan?" Mary-Lou asked.

Laurefen shook his head sadly. "I wish there was. We have tried everything. *Everything.* For now, the only plan we have is a seventeen-year-old boy who can't unlock his potential."

Michael exchanged a worried look with Mary-Lou. "And if that fails?"

"I will not resort to Ire Tides, Michael. Creating one monster to defeat another is no path to victory."

Michael stared into the Well. "What else can we do?"

Laurefen joined him overlooking the surging magic. Orange light cast deep shadows on his wrinkled cheeks. "We will continue with Declan and hope for the best."

CHAPTER 36
DECLAN

DAYS DRAGGED by with no improvement. Every morning, Laurefen had a new item to hold, a new substance to drink, a new way to fail. Every night he sent Declan home with a new bag of bark that tasted just like bark should.

"Soon, Declan, we're getting close. I know it."

Declan resented the encouragement.

"Be patient. Remember, you're not the first person to have this much trouble picking things up."

Weeks trudged by, hour by painful hour, until one gusty Friday beneath a swirling grey sky. Declan stood waist-deep in a shallow lake with a long silver pole over his shoulders. It was carved with intricate symbols and weighed a ton. Laurefen directed him from the bank. "Slowly now, dip down *slowly*. The pole will catch the hydronima feeding into the lake. Try to *feel* it pulse through the pole."

Declan did what he was told. He felt the cold lake. The cold pole. The cold, never ending disappointment. He could feel so much, but no magic. *Why even try?*

"Good. Just like that. Take a moment, focus."

He concentrated. He willed his fingers to feel something besides the biting chill of the metal.

"What do you feel?"

Nothing. A spark of frustration set him alight. Declan threw the pole off his shoulders and stomped out of the water. His vision blurred behind tears of anger, of guilt, of frustration.

"Declan," Laurefen's tone remained even. "What are you doing?"

"ENOUGH!" Declan shouted; his legs sloshed through the muddy shallows. The rage pulsed in his chest. "Enough of your lessons that don't work! Enough of your disgusting bark! Enough of your fake encouragement!"

"Declan. Steady yourself. You need to calm down."

Declan breathed in staggered bursts. "Or what? Or I'll *use* magic? I'll actually do what we've been trying to do this *entire* time?"

"That's not safe." A faint tremble pierced Laurefen's calm voice.

He's afraid of me. He thinks I'm going to do something. Declan forced the thought into the raging caldera. *Maybe I will.* "I'm sick of it Laurefen! I've had enough! You can't train me! You've had months and I'm still useless!"

Laurefen edged slowly back, palms raised. "Declan, you need *time* to do this. It won't happen overnight. You have to be..."

"Don't you dare say patient!" Declan spat on the muddy ground. "All I've *done* is be patient!"

Declan dropped to his knees. A gale of fury roared inside him. He tried to touch it, to pull it out, to set it free. He reached inside, deep, and tried to take hold, to turn his rage into a magical force.

Nothing happened.

The anger died so fast it was like somebody had pulled a plug. A terrible, overwhelming sense of grief took its place.

Declan fell to his side and began to sob. It was all there. The loss of his parents, of his friends. The constant failure and disappointment, the relentless torrent of dashed promises. Declan let the tears bleed out of him. Through the blurry, salty mess, he watched Laurefen walk away.

You couldn't save them and you still can't. There's nothing left for you here.

Declan didn't know how long he spent in the mud. He didn't know how his anger had failed him or why.

He didn't care.

Night had fallen when he finally stumbled to his feet. On the hill, King's College was a beacon of warm lights. Declan walked in the other direction, through the darkness towards the Village.

Shrouded in darkness, Declan heard voices approaching. Katie and Michael were deep in conversation. So deep they didn't even notice him a few feet off the path.

"I understand your reasoning," Michael said. "I do, but it was never worth the risk. And now this? We're lucky Laurefen survived."

"We can't make assumptions." Katie's voice was an octave higher than usual. "We need to hear the full story."

"Maybe so, but you saw Noahi... Magic like that is dangerous. For all of us, Declan included."

They marched straight past him. Declan meandered after them and tried to rehearse his apology. He had no idea what he would say, but he needed to say sorry. *My failures are my own. Nobody here has done anything but help. I should thank them for that. Dad would expect as much.*

He stepped into the halo of the outermost street lamp. The narrow path widened into a cobblestone road. Declan took it all in one last time. The Village looked abandoned, most of the staff had been caught up in the blackcoats culls, others now worked as informants or protected survivors in safe-houses dotted throughout Euryma.

The Dean's residence was at the top of the road. A tall stone wall bordered a well-lit front entrance. Declan approached cautiously. The windows were wide open and voices carried from within. "He threw a rod of Gaulish Silver in the lake?" Michael's deep baritone sounded insulted. "Does he know how much those things cost?"

"An understandable reaction," Laurefen replied, calm as ever. "Nobody else has ever taken this long."

Declan's shoulders tensed. *I knew it. He was lying the whole time.* He crept towards the open windows.

"You need to stop excusing everything he does." Mary-Lou said. "You're too nice."

"What happened next?" Amber asked.

"He became angry. Very angry. I was concerned he was going to damage the college."

"But.... he didn't?" Mary-Lou said slowly. "Did he control it?"

"I'm not sure. It appeared more as if he tried to no avail. I thought it best to leave him be. The young man has been through ordeal after ordeal. His disappointment must be crushing, and my presence only seems to be intensifying the problem."

"But why? Why didn't the anger feed into magic?" Katie asked.

"The Ancellum, perhaps." Michael suggested.

A long silence hung about the room.

"Perhaps," Laurefen said at last. "Perhaps the lack of inherent danger had something to do with it. Katie, you said he was facing a fire bear previously. Maybe Declan's power is as much a self-defense mechanism as it is an expression of emotion."

The silence returned. Declan considered stepping out of the darkness to make his apology. It would be awkward. He had been listening to their private conversation.

"So, what now?" Mary-Lou asked.

"What do you mean?" Laurefen asked.

"You'll continue to train him?"

"I'm not sure I can."

Declan's heart fell, but not far. He had come to the same conclusion on his own. Still, it hurt to hear confirmation.

"What does that mean?" Katie asked.

"I've tried everything I can think of. I've tried approaches documented in writings from the formation of the Dominion. There is magic in the boy, I have no doubt about that, but as for teaching him to harness it, to control it, I'm not sure I can."

At this moment, Declan realized he had leaned too far forward. He reached out to steady himself, his sweaty hand slid off the smooth stone, and he stumbled forward with a clatter of footsteps. When he caught his balance, he stood right in front of the window.

Michael sighed. Nobody else said a word.

Declan blushed crimson. "I'm sorry." That was enough to start the avalanche of words that tumbled from his mouth. "I'm sorry for getting angry and for leaving and for being a bad friend. I'm sorry for listening just now."

The Directive member's expressions were a mix of shock, embarrassment and disappointment.

Declan continued, not sure where his mouth was taking him. "I'm really glad I got to come here and meet you. I heard what you said... so... I'll just go. Also, Laurefen, I'm really sorry about before. But I..." he paused to breathe. "I, uh, I don't think things are working out. I can't stay here. I'm not some chosen one or super weapon or whatever it was you thought I was. I'm a kid... with no parents... who can't control whatever is inside him. I'm... I'm sorry."

Red faced and dazed, he turned to walk away. A final thought made him turn back. "And Michael, I'm really, really sorry about your brother. I wish the Fatesmiths had taken me instead. It would've saved us all a lot of pain."

And with that, he turned and ran. Tears blew off his cheeks into the night air. He ran down the cobblestone road and into the darkness separating the village from the campus. His chest tightened, but he refused to stop until he reached his room on the campus. He kicked the door open. Someone gray was sitting on his bed.

It was John, his face smeared with gray mud, wearing clothes to match. He looked as if he'd rolled through wet cement. John held a small yellow cube and a winning smile that vanished the moment their eyes met. "Declan! What happened?" He dropped the cube and stood up. "Are you okay?"

Declan tried to put on a brave face. It lasted all of two seconds. "I can't learn magic, John. You tried, Laurefen tried... He tried *everything*." He could feel the tears returning. "There's nothing for me to do here. I need to leave."

He rushed to grab his things, but John grabbed him by the sleeve. "Woah, woah, woah. Hold up, you can't leave."

Declan pulled his arm back. "I have to. I nearly lost it on Laurefen. If it wasn't for the Ancellum, I could've destroyed the whole college."

"Declan. You don't know what it's like out there. Free wizards are gone. The MLEA is Haberdeen's personal army. Kid, if you go out there, you might as well find a garden to stand in because you'll be a statue before sundown."

"Good!" Declan started stuffing clothes into a bag. "At least then I won't have to put up with the constant disappointment of being me."

John rolled his eyes. "Okay, sure. Things aren't going your way. But don't be stupid. Give it a night, sleep on it and decide in the morning. You don't want to miss the party."

Declan continued packing to leave. "Party?"

John smiled. The smile was so big it beamed through his eyes. "I found them."

"Who?" Declan tossed Ava's satchel into his bag.

"The fierised witches and wizards."

Declan stopped. "Which ones?"

John's smile grew bigger. "The ones you'd like to see." He bent down and picked up the small yellow cube. Declan recognized it from Ava's bag. He recalled Amber pressing the top so that it grew in size, a portable storage cube.

"You found my parents?"

"I did, and plenty more. And they're entirely unguarded *tonight*." He pumped a fist in the air. "Do you remember me saying I'd need your help?"

Declan nodded. "Yeah... I can't do magic though, remember?"

"I know. What I need is this." John held up the small yellow cube. "I'll pack them in here and bring them back. By morning, every fierised witch and wizard I found will be safe beneath the Ancellum. Laurefen can get to work using flareflies to bring them back and I will have redeemed myself in the eyes of the Directive!"

A fluttering sensation filled Declan's stomach. *He found my parents.* "Yeah... Yeah, of course. Take it!"

"You're a champion."

Declan looked him up and down. John had left a trail of gray muck all across his floor. "What happened to you?"

"Remind me to tell you later." John winked and slipped the cube in his pocket. "I'll be back soon with the first lot."

He vanished down the hallway. Declan considered the moment, then chased after him. "John!"

John turned at the exit. "Yeah?"

"You're just lifting the iron figures into the cube and bringing them back?"

"Yeah."

"And you're sure it's unguarded?"

"Only for tonight, while they prepare to take Sabriva."

Declan strode down the hall. "I'm coming with you. A second set of hands will make it much faster."

John shook his head. "It's too risky."

"You said it was unguarded."

"Yeah, but you never know, if someone dropped in to check—"

"You're not the only one who needs redemption, John." Declan said flatly.

John sighed. "Alright, but first sign of funny business and we're headed straight back. Got it?"

"Got it!"

"Come on." John strode out the door and Declan followed him into the night.

CHAPTER 37
DECLAN

THEY EXITED the Opening into pitch black. Their footsteps echoed on the hard ground. "Where are we?" Declan whispered.

John stood illuminated by the dwindling light of the shrinking portal "Ursaria," he whispered. The doorway disappeared, leaving them in complete darkness. "Come on, this way."

Declan stumbled forward, following John's footsteps with arms out like a cartoon zombie. Pinpricks of blue light grew in the distance. As they got closer, Declan realized the lights came from behind a large, vertical grate at the end of the path. He looked back, their long circular tunnel stretched far into the darkness.

The grate swung easily on well-oiled hinges. John held a finger to his lips, then gestured for him to follow. Together, they entered a massive dome-shaped building. A curved ceiling stretched high over their heads while enormous blue lights hung from thick steel cables. "Stay close," John said as he led across the floor in a peculiar zig-zag pattern.

"How did you find this place?" Declan whispered.

"A lot of sneaking around," John replied. "I couldn't figure out how their transport vans were simply vanishing. I would follow them to a specific point and they'd be gone."

"They can't just drive through Openings?"

John snorted. He caught Declan's eye and shook his head. "Cars don't do well in Openings." He paused. "Let me rephrase that. Gasoline doesn't do well in Openings. No flammable liquid does. You attempt to drive through one and you'll end up with a fireball on the other end."

Declan frowned. "So, how do they do it?"

John shrugged. "No idea."

"Then how did you find this place?"

John smiled sheepishly. "I painted myself grey, followed them to one of their hits and injected myself with paraviper venom."

"You didn't!"

"I had to. It was the only way to figure out where they were hiding the people."

"But what if they tried to melt you down?"

"Well, I'd be dead, but they didn't. It worked. When the venom wore off, I woke up here," he gestured around. "As soon as I got my bearings, I left for King's." John smiled as they approached a large metal box. "The lights are imbued with some sort of enchantment. Watch this."

He opened the box lid and flipped a switch. The blue lights shut off; a long line of fluorescent panels flickered on. They illuminated the dome and thousands of tall iron casts with them.

Declan's jaw fell open. He now understood why John had moved so carefully across the floor. They had weaved through a chain of fierised witches and wizards. With the lights on, Declan could see a guiding path drawn on the floor.

"Declan?"

A melodious voice struck a chord inside him. Declan spun to see a familiar face behind them. Her eyes shone bright blue. Her messy curls had grown longer. "Ava?"

"Declan, what are you doing here?"

"I'm trying to save you. To save my parents. To save everyone." He gestured sideways. "This is my friend John. We're going to get everyone out of here!"

Ava considered him for a long moment, then shook her head. "Declan, you can't take these people. They need to stay like this."

Declan stared at her. "No, no, no. Ava. Haberdeen, the Fatesmiths, they took these people, remember?"

"Of course, I remember."

"Took them against their will. We need to get them away from here."

"But they're safe here."

"What?" Declan looked at John. He was watching Ava closely, sizing her up, like a lion meeting a tiger for the first time. "Ava, what are you talking about?"

She sighed. "Declan, a third of the planet has been levelled. I didn't believe it at first, but I've seen the proof now. Remnant Magic is destroying entire cities, entire countries. Every time a witch magics up a cup of coffee, every time a wizard summons the morning paper, it adds to the problem. None of these people are going to die. They're just being *stored* here until we figure out how to reduce the build-up."

Declan shook his head. "No, you're confused. It's not Remnant Magic. It's not!"

Ava nodded to John. "Is that what *he* told you?"

"Yes. No. Hear me out. These people are innocent. They're just living their lives, now they can't because they've been imprisoned! We need to let them go!"

Ava shook her head. "Listen to yourself! They are not innocent! Entire countries burn because these people are too lazy to brew a cup of coffee! Someone is pulling the wool over your eyes."

"No. It's not true." Declan's cheeks burned. "Who... who has been telling you these things?"

"Declan. Listen to reason. Remnant Magic is everywhere. Entire cities are nothing but graveyards. This needs to stop!"

"You're lying."

"Why would I? What would I have to gain? Remnant Magic storms are killing millions. Why would I lie about something like that?"

"It's not Remnant Magic! It's the blackcoats! It's Haberdeen!" Declan turned to John to chime in, but he stood in silence.

"You think the Fatesmiths could destroy an entire city?" Ava asked. "An entire country?"

Declan shook his head. He'd had enough. "Ava. My parents are here. I'm taking them, and the rest of them, with me. Come with us, I can show you."

"You can't take them, Declan."

Declan was no longer listening. A pit of rage swirled in his stomach, and he concentrated on making it grow. He forced himself to remember his parents' iron casts, remember them loaded into a van like furniture. He was finally here, finally within reach of them. Fury surged in his chest like a stormy ocean, tossed against the rocks, spraying malice like saltwater.

"It's not going to work, kid," John said.

It was the first time John had spoken since Ava arrived. Declan ignored him and focused his attention on his rage.

"Kid. It's not going to work."

"What are you talking about?" Declan spat.

John shrugged his shoulders. An odd smirk played at the edges of his lips. "There's no explosion coming. That wasn't you, that was me."

Declan blinked. "What do you mean?"

John's smile grew. The edges of his lips curled tighter. It was a cruel smile, one that Declan remembered but could not place. "You're the firefly, kid."

A pit formed in his stomach. John's smile unsettled him. "W-what are you talking about?"

"You're the unremarkable firefly and I'm the flarefly— or at least—the closest a Mimic can get."

Declan shook his head. "You're lying. That can't be!" He backed away from the pair of them. The pieces fell into place. *That's why I would get so angry so quickly, why nothing ever happened around Laurefen, why every explosion was when John was nearby.* Declan continued to shake his head, horrified. "Why?"

John laughed. "You can't break anyone who still has hope. The Directive needed that hope and now, it needs to be broken."

"But why me?" Declan looked around for a way to escape. Ava was smiling now too. *Had she been in on it from the start?*

"You were the first application I pulled off the pile. There's nothing special about you, kid. The fact you're a LAMP just made it so much easier to sell to the rest of them. It could've been anyone. You're nothing, never were, never will be."

John turned and smiled at Ava. Declan saw his chance

and took it. He exploded past the fuse box and along the side wall of the dome. He turned a corner, ignored John's surprised shout, and scanned the room for a door. Footsteps clattered behind him.

A large set of steel shelves leapt off the wall ahead of him. With a grinding screech, they rotated to block his path. Declan skidded to a halt and ducked into the mass of iron casts. He stayed low and weaved through them, right until the lights cut out. Declan was thrown into darkness with nowhere to go.

More footsteps. Declan ducked even lower. Voices echoed across the dome. People were shouting, talking as if they could see in the dark.

"He's in here somewhere," shouted John.

"Find him," Ava called. "Don't let him get away."

Using his hands as a guide, Declan crept forward, pulling himself through the maze of fierised people in the pitch black. Without warning, the blue lights flashed to life. The iron figures vanished and left Declan exposed partway across the dome.

"There he is!"

A burly blackcoat pointed straight at him. Declan turned back and stopped. Blackcoats approached from all sides. Declan tried to run and bounced painfully off an invisible object. *They're still there!* Declan reached forward and began navigating the invisible web of frozen witches and wizards. *I'm going too slow.* He could see John and Ava walking towards him with unsettling ease. More Fatesmiths circled around them. *There's nowhere to go.*

He looked up, hoping for a brilliant idea or a flash of inspiration. None arrived. Declan's arms snapped together as he rose into the air. A sharp-faced woman flashed her teeth. "Got you."

The blue lights turned off; the flickering fluorescents returned. The woman carried him high over the iron prisoners and set him down before John and Ava. Declan glared at her. *She told you she'd come from a family obsessed with saving the world. You should've guessed that she was a blackcoat all along!*

Ava studied him, lips sealed in a tight line. "You need to stop running. We're not trying to hurt you."

"You're lying."

"The world is falling apart. Do you think we want to do this? Do you think we take pleasure in it?" To her left, John grinned. Declan immediately recognized the same heartless smile. *That's not John.* It was a terrible realization. Ava continued. "You've been lied to. Repeatedly. That is no fault of your own. You think we're trying to take over the country? We're not. The High Mage has granted us permission to do this. An unpopular choice, for sure, but a necessary choice." She gestured for the sharp-faced blackcoat to release him and smiled. "We are not your enemy, Declan. The Fatesmiths are not the bad guys."

Declan clenched his fists. "How can I be sure you're telling the truth?"

"There's nothing to hide."

"You're certainly hiding someone," he nodded at John. "That's not his real face."

John's grin grew even sharper. "Smart kid." His eyes remained cold.

Declan turned to Ava. "You said there was nothing to hide?"

Ava closed her eyes, took a breath, and relaxed. "Very well. Show yourself."

John nodded curtly, and his bearded face drifted away like a mask of smoke caught in a breeze. A new face appeared. A boy with blond hair, a cruel smile and ice for eyes.

Ward.

Declan's jaw was clenched tight. "Where's the real John?"

Ward laughed like a hyena. "Dead."

The words cut like a knife. Declan tried to think. "Why? If you wanted me, you could've taken me months ago."

"Typical teenager," Ward sneered. "Only thinks about himself."

The surrounding blackcoats laughed, but Ava didn't join in.

"This was never about *you*. This was about the others. The ones who think they are coming to *save* you."

Declan snorted. "What? They don't even know I'm here. No one's coming for—"

With an unexpected jolt, the whole building shifted. A heavy crack appeared in the wall opposite them, running vertical from roof to floor. Ward stepped forward. The crack expanded like a fork of lightning. A groaning creak and it exploded, blown open by a powerful outward force.

The Fatesmiths turned to face the threat.

Laurefen stood in the settling dust, flanked by Mary-Lou, Amber, Michael and Katie.

Ward exchanged a knowing look with Ava, and his cold smile returned. "Mission accomplished."

CHAPTER 38
DECLAN

"Fierise them all," Ward ordered.

With a flick of his fingers, the room went dark. The blue lights flashed to life, but only for a moment before being torn forcefully from the ceiling and thrown aside. The ground shook as they crashed against the wall. Darkness engulfed them. Declan tried to run and collided with a blackcoat. He drove an elbow forcefully into what felt like a chest, then dashed in the other direction.

Crackling orbs of electricity formed above him, casting a chaotic, flashing light over the scene. Through the shifting shadows, Declan saw Michael toss a pair of Fatesmiths high into the air. A jagged bolt of lightning leapt from the sizzling spheres. The two bodies went rigid. Further ahead, Mary-Lou sent wave after wave of crass cement boulders at Ward.

"Declan! There you are," Katie sidled through the iron maze. "Quick! This way!"

Declan followed. Amber peddled backwards, dodging and diving to avoid a series of shimmering silver squares.

Her long hair streamed behind as she dived between iron casts.

"Stay here," Katie whispered. She circled around the woman bearing down on Amber. With a flick of her hands, she hurled the blackcoat up into one of the balls of lightning. The woman contorted, screaming all the way. As far as Declan could tell, she never came down. "C'mon." Katie grabbed his arm. "Let's go."

"You killed that woman..."

"She would've just as readily killed us. We need to go. We can deal with the fallout once we're back at King's."

Michael had buried a nearby group of blackcoats under a pile of rubble and now pressed down on Ward, who continued to elude Mary-Lou. Amber rushed to help.

Laurefen stood opposite all of them, engaged in a heated battle with Ava. Between them thrashed an upswell of bubbling lava. Ava's dark features were tense as she pushed the searing wave towards him, but Laurefen was equal to the challenge. Under pressure from both sides, the molten rock writhed and convulsed like a tormented fountain. Declan watched, mesmerized.

More Fatesmiths arrived, pouring through Openings like ants protecting their nest. Michael started up the side wall, but a silver square forced him to jump. He landed awkwardly, buckled and fell to the ground, clutching his leg.

"Michael!" Mary-Lou yanked him across the floor towards her. Fatesmiths surrounded them, blocking them from view. One of the electrical orbs fizzled out and died away. The room grew darker.

Laurefen turned back to them as a handful of blackcoats rushed to Ava's side. The molten wall doubled in size. Laurefen threw himself backwards as the wave crashed over the spot where he had stood. A nearby group of iron casts weren't so lucky. They drooped forwards, partially melted. Declan's stomach lurched at the sight.

Ward's cold laugh rang across the dome. "You're outnumbered. It's over."

A ball of fire cut his speech short. Ward retreated back behind the casts. Amber stepped forward, hurling ball after ball of white-hot flames in his direction.

A flash of movement and Ava appeared behind her. Declan was helpless, as Amber was thrown through the air into a mess of iron. A pair of blackcoats ran to finish her off.

"Stand back!" Laurefen boomed. Flares of blue sparks licked up his arms. The room grew brighter, the ball of electricity swelled, a crackling sun of blue light. The blackcoats huddled into a large group at one end of the room with Ava at the front. Laurefen hurled it towards them. A myriad of hands moved in unison to block it. The flashing orb pressed down against them. Jagged tongues of lightning licked off its edge.

"We need to move!" Katie hissed. She led Declan through the labyrinth of frozen witches and wizards. They were headed towards the side of the building, the enormous hole the Directive had torn in the wall. Declan's head swiveled wildly as they walked, hoping to catch sight of his parents. He stopped. Feet suddenly rooted to the ground. Not by magic, but by... *Ava?*

Her iron figure was frozen, reaching out to shield him from Ward exactly the way he remembered. Her short hair and determined expression frozen in place. He looked at the girl pressing against the ball of electricity and then back at the iron cast.

"Declan, come on!"

"That's.... That's not Ava."

"What are you talking about? Come on!"

Declan pointed to the statue. "This is my friend—Ava—the one who saved me." He pointed towards the figures pushing back against the colossal ball of sparking energy. "That's not the real Ava."

Katie's eyes darted from Ava's cast to the impostor holding back Laurefen's spell. Her face paled. "Then who is that?"

The Fatesmiths seized control of Laurefen's spell. They launched the fizzing ball towards him, with a sizzling pop it was extinguished. They were plunged into darkness. When the fluorescent lights flickered to life, Laurefen was bound in long black cords. He struggled to free his hands, but the cords snaked around his fingers, wrapping them tight.

A high-pitched yelp escaped Katie's lips. Declan nudged her. "I think we need to go." She nodded and motioned for him to follow. Declan stayed low behind the iron figures. Behind him, he could hear Ava's voice, but in the grip of panic, he could not understand what she was saying.

Declan ran straight into Katie's back. "Why did you stop?"

"Shhhh!"

Declan looked over her shoulder. A group of blackcoats were systematically working their way through the casts. The tops of their heads were getting closer. Four more closed in from behind. "What do we do?" he mouthed.

Beads of sweat crowned Katie's forehead. Footsteps grew louder. She jerked her head to the left. "I'll go that way. Draw them away. You get to the exit and wait."

"What?"

"No time. I'll meet you outside."

Without a second word, she ran, weaving her way through the figures with loud footfalls.

"Who's that?" A voice called.

"Over there! Get them!"

The entire group rushed away in pursuit. Declan continued forwards. His heart thumped in his ears. He snaked his way through the iron, climbed the concrete rubble, and escaped into the night air. It was freezing. Flurries of white blanketed the ground in snow. Declan circled back to the edge of the building. The fallen wall was the only visible cover. He ducked behind it and hugged himself. *Hurry up Katie!*

The night grew colder, Declan's shivering grew uncontrollable. His fingers went numb. Next, his hands. Soon, he could not feel anything except the biting cold. *You have to go back inside*, he told himself. *What good is being free if you die of exposure?*

He slid through the hole into a small concrete enclave. The whole place must have been enchanted. The moment he passed the threshold of the storehouse, he felt restored, warmed as if sitting by a hot fire. Declan peeked over a massive steel beam and his jaw dropped. The room was filled with blackcoats. They wandered between iron casts, sweeping the entire warehouse, looking for something. Declan grimaced. *Looking for me.*

He ducked back down. A voice carried faintly from the other side of the room. "Find him, melt them all if you have to. He has to be here somewhere!"

He chanced another peek and dropped away immediately. Two men were walking straight toward him. Declan held his breath as they approached. Their footsteps crunched on the debris.

"Anyone check outside?" one of them said.

"Are you kidding?" replied the other. "Five minutes out there, he'd be dead."

"Well, he's not here."

"You're welcome to go outside and check."

Declan lay pressed to the floor, fearing they would hear the thunder of his heartbeat.

"What about the others?"

"The King's College people? Wrapped up at the south entrance."

"What? Why not just turn 'em to iron?"

"Dunno. I guess she wants them awake when she catches the kid."

"Bit sadistic?"

"They've killed a lot of us. Whole lotta thanks for trying to save the planet."

They continued talking as they walked away. Declan considered their words. The Ava-imposter hadn't fierised the Directive, they were captured at the south entrance. There was still a chance. Declan's thoughts were punctuated by a sharp voice. Ward's voice.

"Bring out his parents!"

Declan's heart stopped. His parents *were* here. He rubbed a handful of cement dust it into his hair. He hoped the camouflage was enough as he peeked out from his hiding spot.

"Somewhere easy to see. Up here is good." Ward stood on a low platform with his back turned to Declan. A man approached, dragging a short blue cart with two figures strapped to it. *Mom! Dad!*

Angus and Miranda Moore were propped up on the platform's center. "You have two options, kid," Ward shouted.

Declan looked at his parents. Trapped. Helpless.

"Option one, you come quietly. Surrender and nobody gets hurt."

He blinked back tears as the Ava-imposter climbed up the platform. She inspected his parents, then turned to stand by Ward. "Option two," he shouted. "You watch us turn your parents into an iron glob," she shouted.

Declan squeezed his eyes shut. *I have to surrender.*

"You have sixty seconds to decide."

Declan sank to the ground. He had no choice. The river of adrenaline surging through him died. He started to stand when a little voice in his head fired up. *The entire Directive just came to rescue you, and you're going to surrender?*

I don't have a choice!

Katie sacrificed herself so you could escape? This is how you repay her?

I know!

They came to save you.

They're my parents!

They are. And this is not the choice they would want you to make. It's terrible, but you have to save the others.

The fake Ava was counting down from thirty. A chorus of Fatesmiths joined in.

The voice was right. The Directive were caught but not fierised. He still had time to save them. He just needed to create some sort of distraction. *I need to get angry. Ward was lying! I did that magic, not him! I need to get really, really, really angry.*

"Fifteen. Fourteen. Thirteen."

Okay. Angry about my parents. Declan reached inside, reached for rage, for fury. The counting continued.

"Ten. Nine. Eight."

There was nothing. No anger. Just fear. Fear for his parents. Declan pictured them, his mother, making jokes while making breakfast. His father, drinking coffee and reading the paper. The two of them laughing and smiling in their garden.

"Five. Four. Three."

Declan closed his eyes. *I can't do this.*

"Two."

"I'M HERE!" Declan jumped to his feet and waved his hands in the air. "I'm here! I'm here. Please. Don't hurt my parents."

The little voice inside him fizzled and disappeared.

CHAPTER 39
DECLAN

APPRECIATIVE CHUCKLES ERUPTED from the caucus of blackcoats. Declan's arms snapped to their sides as he was lifted from the rubble by the wall to the platform. Ward dropped his hand. Declan touched down softly on the ground. "Ah, there you are," the fake Ava said sweetly.

Declan fell to his knees in front of his parents. Trapped in iron, they looked just as they had the night Ward and Raul carried them away. For a long moment, he couldn't speak. When he finally tore his eyes away from them, he glared at the woman wearing Ava's face. "Who are you?"

"You know me. I saved you—"

"Don't lie to me!"

"Lie to you? I would never!"

Declan stood up and pointed into the mass of dull gray casts. "Ava is over there! I saw her! You're a fake! Earlier tonight, you said you'd never lie to me. Well, you're *still* doing it!" He blinked the tears from his eyes. "Who are you?"

The woman studied him intently, then sighed. "Well, I guess the ruse is up." She clicked her fingers and changed.

Ava's smooth, dark features faded away. Her lithe, petite figure grew in size and shape. Declan gasped.

Flaming red hair bordered a pale face and vivid green eyes. A deep scar curved from the edge of her lip to her left ear, giving the woman the gruesome appearance of a twisted smile. She was dressed in a long black coat, stitched with the same hammer and anvil that all Fatesmiths bore, only this time in gold thread.

"Haberdeen?"

The woman smiled. "In the flesh."

Declan stepped back. "What... what do you want with me?"

"Nothing, Declan. I wanted your friends. The college professors that parade around Euryma spreading lies about the *necessity* of my cause."

"You're mad!"

Haberdeen shook her head. "Magical power comes at a cost. The people of Euryma have squandered it for centuries, and now, innocent people are paying that price. The Directive, refuse to believe it. They bury their heads in the sand. They hide in the shadows, like snakes, and seek to undo my work." She stopped and looked from Declan to Ward. "Mage Ward here set you up as their one and only savior. A faulty test and the fools bought it. Hook, line and sinker."

Ward grinned. "Almost too easy."

"You've played the part perfectly, Declan. The Directive are mine. With the head removed, the snake will wither and die."

Declan couldn't believe it. "But... my parents? My friends? What did they ever do to you?"

"This is the price that must be paid," Haberdeen said. "I have seen things, things that would make you cower and hide. I have seen what happens to this world if I step aside."

"But, my family..."

"Were a cog in the machine. Unwittingly a part of the problem but still part of the problem- killing hundreds of thousands of men, women and children, because they would rather wave their hands than make their own dinner." Her crooked smile softened. "I am not the villain, Declan. I am doing what has to be done, mercifully. None of these people are in any pain," she said. "Your parents rest in a deep sleep, where they will remain until I solve the problem. Once the world is rid of Remnant Magic, I'll release them all. Why else would I store them here?"

Declan couldn't admit it, but it made sense. "My parents are good people. If they knew, they would stop. I know it!"

"No," Haberdeen said. "Once I make one exception, where does it end?" She shook her head. "Declan, you've been dragged unfairly into this fight. I am sorry I had to use you, but your job is done. Let me fierise you. You can rest peacefully with your parents until we're ready to bring everyone back. You'll be able to come back and live a full life with your family."

"You'll turn me to iron?"

"Only if you want."

Declan looked at his parents. He missed them more than he could describe. He turned to Haberdeen. "Does it hurt?"

Haberdeen shook her head. "The sensation is akin to dipping into a cold bath. After that, it is a deep, dreamless sleep."

Declan sat on the edge of the platform. *What if she's right? What if the Directive was wrong all along?* He thought about his time at Kingsbreak, about Katie and Amber, and how they had welcomed him. And John. *John... What a lie that turned out to be. Haberdeen disguised herself as Ava too. If she was so intent on being honest, why do that?*

"What would you like to do, Declan?"

Declan kept his eyes on the floor. *Maybe it was all part of the plan. Maybe she thought I would listen to Ava...*

"I'm offering you peace and rest until we're ready for you to return." Haberdeen's voice was so gentle, Declan almost believed it.

She's lying. She has to be.

"It wouldn't hurt at all. You wouldn't even be aware. It would be like going into hibernation. A deep sleep that ends with a new dawn for Euryma."

What if she's not?

"You would wake up and your parents would be there. You would be able to go back to your old life in Tamhill. Let me do this for you."

Declan looked at his parents.

Angus Moore's mustache hung over open lips, preserved in a portrait of shock; his eyebrows cemented in a perfect arch. His arms outstretched, with hands curled around an invisible ball. Declan wondered what magic he had summoned when he was fierised. His mother, Miranda, looked fearful. Worried creases decorated the small section of forehead visible beneath her messy curls. She must have seen what was coming. *I hope her last thoughts weren't about me.* Declan wiped a tear from his cheek.

"You can be with them," Haberdeen repeated. "Let me do this for you."

"Why?" Declan tore his eyes from his parents. "Why do you care? I'm a LAMP. I can't do any harm to you or the world. Why can't you let me go?"

Haberdeen's shoulders trembled. For a moment, Declan thought she was angry until a tear traced her cheek. "I'm just trying to do what's best for you."

Declan was stunned. Maybe she *was* telling the truth. He took a deep breath. "How do I know you're not lying?"

Haberdeen didn't respond straight away. She looked at him thoughtfully for a full minute before shaking her head. "I'm not sure you can," she said at last. "All I can give you is my word, but if you don't believe that, what else can I do? You must understand, I'm offering to help you. If you don't want to accept my help, then that's all there is."

"What do you mean?"

"Well," she pursed her lips together. "I don't mean to sound insincere, but you're a LAMP. You have no place in here with us. You have no home to return to. There's nothing in this world for you except pain and loneliness."

Declan hadn't considered she would simply let him go, but if she did, where would he go? Everyone he knew was dead or captured. He could try to save them, though Haberdeen would quickly put a stop to that. "What will happen to the Directive?"

"They will be fierised, like the rest of Euryma's magical population. When the world is safe and they are restored, I imagine they will thank me."

"Why not fierise them now?"

Haberdeen clucked gently and laughed. "Declan. You're avoiding the issue at hand. I am grateful for your help, but my patience is not limitless. You must choose. Fierisation and a future with your parents, or an Opening to Tamhill by yourself?"

Declan considered it. *There's nothing left for me here.* "I want to be with my family." He turned to his parents. "I guess that means I will need to wait until the world is ready for us."

Haberdeen nodded. "I would have made the same choice. You'll be happier this way. Are you ready?"

Declan's eyes never left his parents. "I am."

Haberdeen flicked her wrist. He gasped. A cold sensation ran up his back, as if the discs in his spine were being systematically replaced with ice cubes. His arms grew heavy, their weight pulled at him, but he could not move them. The world grew dark, very dark, like somebody had draped thick curtains over his eyes. Haberdeen faded to a blur and everything went black.

CHAPTER 40
DECLAN

SOMEBODY WAS SPEAKING.

Declan stirred to a faint whisper. He couldn't see a thing. The darkest grey pressed against his eyes like a blindfold. Declan strained to listen. A muffled conversation continued nearby, but the words were too quiet for him to understand. He concentrated, pushed everything away except for the soft voices. Slowly, he began to make sense of the conversation.

"You have done well, Mage Ward."

"All to serve you, Madam. Your powers of persuasion are transcendent. The boy never suspected a thing."

"I was surprised with how quickly he agreed."

"A tribute to you, Madam. I have fierised the prisoners. Where would you like them stored?"

"Oh. Don't bother with storage. Melt them immediately."

"As you wish."

Declan's heart froze. He tried to shout, to shuffle, to move. He tried to do something. Anything. But there was nothing he could do. He was conscious but constricted, completely confined in his own skin, an iron prison. Panic sent his mind spinning. He tried to calm down, to settle himself. Their words were so quiet it was like listening through carpet. The surrounding gloom lightened. A series of blurry outlines appeared ahead.

"Excellent. The Directive have been a thorn in my side for months. They do not deserve the new dawn we bring."

"And the boy's parents?"

Declan's mind jammed abruptly. He froze. Paralyzed. He listened in terror.

"We have the boy. Melt them immediately," Haberdeen said. "They are the key to something far too dangerous to be left alive."

"Yes, Madam."

Declan watched as Ward's outline moved towards two inanimate figures. His parents.

LEAVE THEM ALONE! YOU LYING FILTH! YOU TOLD ME THEY WOULD BE SAFE! YOU LIED! YOU LIED TO ME! I HATE YOU! I HATE YOU! I HATE YOU!

Ward's arms moved in a wide arc. Declan wanted to turn around, to look away, to close his eyes, but he couldn't. Frozen in place, he watched as the blurry outlines of his parents melted away. Shrinking to the ground. Declan pictured their faces, the final faces they would ever make. His blood boiled. An absolute and all-encompassing hatred burned black inside, and he reached for it, hotter than molten stone. He gripped it and tried to wrench it free. To tear it from a festering wound and beat Ward with it until only blood and pulp remained.

But nothing happened.

The figures of his parents shrank away.

Ward returned. "What do you want me to do with the

boy?" His nonchalance made Declan want to shred him to pieces.

Haberdeen didn't respond. Their cloudy outlines grew larger. They stood directly ahead of him. *Kill me.* Declan thought. *You've taken everything else.*

"Leave him for now."

The words cut deep, deeper and more painful than any knife ever could.

"I'm curious, Madam," Ward said. "Why bother with him? He is no threat to us."

"Do you still believe that, Ward?"

The words didn't make sense.

"Your assignment was to infiltrate the Directive and bring them to me. To that end, you have done well. More importantly, you have delivered this boy."

"Apologies, Madam. I don't understand. There are hundreds like him to the north. Why is this one so special?"

"He is not like them. This boy is the most dangerous creature in the world. His power is beyond any scope you can imagine. I could not fierise him if I tried. Not without his permission. Hence the subterfuge. He needed to come willingly."

Caged in his own flesh, Declan's thoughts ran wild. He tried to catch them, to think rationally. One moment, he felt as if he was underwater, inches below the surface, desperate for air. Next, he was being pushed through a hole much too small. His whole body itched. He was a hive of angry bees, an anthill in the desert. The sensations came and went, replaced by something new and uncomfortable, a whirlwind of chaotic anxiety. *It can't be true.*

Haberdeen's voice floated through the madness. "It would be unwise to attempt melting him. It's safer for us to leave him like this. Contained. Controlled."

She's right, said the little voice. *You're trapped. There is nobody left to save you. It's over.*

Reason silenced the wild activity of hope. *It's over. You lost.* His mind went blank. Everything fell away. He felt himself collapse, like his soul was a candle snuffed out by a breeze. He had nothing. He was nothing. He wanted to get angry, so angry that he could burst free, but there was no anger there. There was no hatred, no fury, no pain, no passion. He should have been afraid, but even fear had abandoned him.

He was empty. An abandoned shell, washed up on a beach, bleached in the sun.

Despair.

A wave settled over him. Dragged him from shore into the black. He waited at the bottom of an ocean, so deep and so dark that nothing could ever touch him.

It's over.

You lost.

It's over.

You lost.

Here, in the deepest recesses of his mind, he saw something. A green speck, no larger than a grain of rice. It glimmered in the infinite, inky blackness, drawing his consciousness towards it like a curious moth. Upon closer inspection, Declan saw that it wasn't a speck at all, it was a green coin. Somehow, within his mind, he picked it up. It was hot. Dense. As if it was something much, much bigger, pressed down into something small, trivial, green.

Declan flipped the coin and caught it. Tails. The beaked dragon on its face started to growl.

A surging sensation roared from his head to his toes. It coursed through him, pulsed in his veins, hotter than magma. The power was so absolute, so utterly and unconditionally complete. The despair eroded like dry clay on a hilltop. Declan felt his iron shell ripple and flake around him. He squeezed his eyes tight and tensed.

The world exploded in color.

Declan's vision was restored. Everything clear. A fine mist of iron settled around him. Ward turned in shock. His dark eyes wide. Haberdeen brandished a white dagger. She flicked her arms outwards. A shimmering silver square soared towards him.

Declan clenched his hands. A green flash burst out of him. The square shattered like a mirror. Haberdeen's hands were a whirlwind. More and more squares appeared from nowhere.

As if by some forgotten instinct, Declan clasped his hands together. Electric tension tingled in his fingertips. Declan squeezed. "Enough!"

Haberdeen's spells simply collapsed. Shards of silver fell to the ground and dissolved. Haberdeen stepped backwards, fumbling with her dagger, her twisted mouth agape.

Blackcoats rushed to surround him. The room crackled with magical energy as a myriad of spells were cast in his direction. The Fatesmiths seemed intent on burying him in a concrete sarcophagus.

Declan barely blinked. He crashed his hands together. A wave of vivid green exploded around him, vaporizing everything within reach. Fatesmiths were thrown backwards, some thirty-feet across the room before they hit the walls.

Haberdeen was a picture of panic. Her feet caught something hard, she stumbled.

Declan looked down at it. It was a lump of iron. It was his parents, or what was left of them. Their melted remains bubbled together in a crude pile of dark metal. Ward appeared below and tried to hurl a concrete boulder at him. It dissolved into mist before it left his hands.

Declan tore his eyes from the iron pool and looked at Ward. Ward's smile was gone, replaced by a terrified scowl. He cowered beneath Declan's gaze. Haberdeen saw her opportunity. She tried to make a break for it. With a flick of his fingers, he threw her against the wall. She hit it with a crunch at the far end of the building.

Pure, unbridled energy swirled inside him. Declan turned back to Ward. Green flames licked his arms, running up and down like a dancing wildfire.

Ward turned to run.

Declan let it out. He let it all out. Like a wall of water breaking a dam, like a pyroclastic flow sweeping down a mountain, it surged out of him.

And the world turned green.

CHAPTER 41
DECLAN

AN EMERALD HAZE drifted slowly into the sky, like fog in the morning sun. The dome was gone. Whatever had existed outside the dome was gone. As far as Declan could see, there was nothing beyond the crowd of people who, moments earlier, had been iron casts.

They stood in small circles that formed organically. Occasional shouts of recognition jumped between groups, providing a link to expand a particular circle. All the while, the thrum of conversation filled the air. Declan observed in silence. Nobody noticed him. To them, he was just another face in the crowd.

His parents were dead. Gone. The incredible power within him couldn't save them. *I will never see them again.*

Declan wandered aimlessly between the groups. Fragments of conversation caught his ear, a woman having dinner when a group of men burst through the door. Another settling down in bed. One man described a terrifying ordeal that ended with him cornered in the back carriage of a train. None of the witches or wizards recalled their time as an iron sculpture. Declan wiped a tear from his eye. *At least they felt no pain.* It was a small thing, but it lessened the weight of their loss, if only slightly.

The ground now looked like smoothed quartz. It glinted beneath a rising sun whose appearance made no sense. The time difference between Kingsbreak and Ursaria was only a couple of hours. It should be pitch black, and much warmer. When Declan arrived at the spot where he had started, he scanned the spot where Ward had stood. A thin layer of dark powder was all that remained of the man who killed his parents. *Good riddance.*

"Declan?" Amber pushed through a group of wizards and half hugged, half tackled him. "Declan! You're alive!" She let go and stepped back, her eyes wide with wonder. "What happened?"

Declan opened his mouth, then paused. Mary-Lou's silver braid caught his attention. She walked towards him, beaming like a proud grandmother. Katie and Michael trailed behind her. Katie's jaw hung open. Even Michael looked happy. Mary-Lou pulled him in to a warm, motherly embrace. "Tell us everything," she said. "How did you do it?"

"I... I don't know!" Declan admitted. "John was a Fatesmith, a guy named Ward, all along."

"Mage Ward." Michael grimaced. "Only a teenager, but he is extremely powerful."

"He *was*," Declan corrected. He gestured to the thin pile of dust.

Michael raised an eyebrow. "You mean to tell me?"

Declan nodded.

Amber's eyes grew even wider. "That's Mage Ward? The same Ward who took an entire bus of Alumni by himself?"

"What's left of him." Declan shrugged.

Michael shook his head, then laughed. He clapped Declan on the shoulder. "Well done, Declan. Well done."

"Where's Laurefen?" Katie asked.

"There," Mary-Lou said.

The Dean of King's College was giving instructions to a pair of witches—gesturing from the crowd to an empty patch of glassed earth. Part way through his lecture, he looked up, spotted them, and rushed forward.

"Declan Moore." Laurefen's curled moustache did nothing to hide his smile. "I can only assume this is your doing?"

They all wanted to know his story. Amidst the mass of displaced witches and wizards, Declan found himself describing everything that happened after he left the Village. He told them about the plan to bring everyone back to Kingsbreak, the fake Ava and how he had let Haberdeen fierise him, but when it came time to talk about his parents, the words wouldn't come.

Mary-Lou pulled him into another hug. "Declan. I'm so sorry." She squeezed him tight. "I can't even begin to imagine how you must feel."

Amber hugged him too, and then Katie, reaching up with outstretched arms. Michael shook his head sadly. Declan imagined him picturing his brother's same fate. "I'm sorry," he said.

Declan forced himself to continue. He was just about to describe the green coin when someone touched his shoulder from behind.

"Declan?"

Short hair, sapphire eyes, a mischievous smile.

"Ava!" Declan smiled.

"Declan, what happened? Where are we?" She scanned the mass of people.

"Somewhere in Ursaria."

"Excuse me?" Mary-Lou cut in. "We most definitely are not!"

"We're not?"

"Have you ever heard of snow in Ursaria?" Mary-Lou asked. "Who told you such nonsense?"

"Ward," Declan grimaced. "Of course, he would have lied. Where are we really?"

"Anderma," Amber said. "John—sorry—*Ward* left me a note saying that's where you were headed."

Declan looked at her blankly.

"A stone's throw from the Kara Sea."

Ava raised an eyebrow. "We're in the far north?"

Declan turned to Amber. "What?"

Amber laughed. "Weren't you curious about the midnight sun?"

"I never... I didn't even think about it."

Ava touched Declan's elbow. "So how did I get here? How long was I... captured?"

Declan started from the start. He explained everything he had seen and done since their meeting in Tamhill. He told her about Lyle and her friends, Mary-Lou's timely rescue, King's College and Noahi. He told her about the fire bear—she laughed, a lot—and the return to Tamhill. He told her about training with John—who was really Ward—and Laurefen. Finally, he described the events of that evening. When he got to the end, all five of them stood, gob smacked.

Ava looked around in disbelief. "You're telling me... you did this?"

"I don't know how but...."

"How?" Katie said. "What type of spell did you use? How did you know what to do?"

Declan's cheeks colored. "I don't know. I really don't. I just... did what I needed to do?"

Laurefen exchanged a concerned look with Mary-Lou.

"What you did, was save our lives." Michael said, he looked distracted. "And I think that's enough for now..."

Mary-Lou looked up at the sky. "Is that your enchantment keeping the snow off us, Laurefen?"

"It may be. It's keeping a significant amount of heat in too."

"Perfect. I have a small suggestion, though. May I have a word with you?"

Laurefen gestured for her to lead the way. They walked out of earshot. Michael put his hand on Declan's shoulder. "Declan. I'm sorry about your parents. I didn't know them personally, but from what I have heard, they were great people. They would be proud of you. They would be proud of the lives you've saved today." He looked down at the ground for a moment. "I also need to apologize for my behavior the past few months. Dreyfus and I were very close, but that is no excuse. He sacrificed himself for the greater good, and had he not, all these people here would not be free today. I'm sorry Declan."

Declan didn't know what to say. Thankfully, Amber tugged on his sleeve. "So is Haberdeen gone?"

"I'm... I'm not sure. I don't think anyone could have gotten away fast enough... I guess so."

"I hope so."

Declan glanced at the crowd. "My friend Ace should be here, too. He was taken from Tamhill around the same time as my mom and dad."

"Perhaps," Michael said. He scanned the surrounding crowd. "This is only a small portion of the people

Haberdeen has taken. Who knows where she put the rest of them."

Behind him, people were leaving through Openings in twos and threes. A small group of witches appeared to be organizing the exodus.

Laurefen returned with Mary-Lou by his side. "You've done well, Declan, but the work is far from over. We—"

Shouts rang out from the Openings. They turned to watch a shawled figure push past a man and his wife and leap through a closing doorway. The momentary chaos died with the doorway and order soon returned.

Laurefen shook his head. "Sorry. As I was saying. We still need to locate the rest of the witches and wizards so you can bring them back."

"Tonight?"

Laurefen chuckled. "No. No, not tonight. Tonight, we will return to Kingsbreak. I think some sort of celebration is in order. But our mission is clear. Find the remaining hold houses and free those imprisoned." He nodded at Ava. "Your friend is welcome to join us too."

Ava smiled, but shook her head. "I would love to, but I have my own family to return to."

"I insist," said Laurefen. "If only for the celebration."

"It does sound fun, and I don't mean to be rude, but I've been gone an awfully long time." Ava took a deep breath. "I need to go home."

"And where is home?"

"A long way away," Ava said. "They will have missed me."

Laurefen frowned. "I understand. Do what you must, but you are always welcome at King's College. I will have some of our people organize you an Opening."

"Thank you," Ava said. "Before I do go, would you mind if I say goodbye to Declan in private?"

"Of course," Laurefen said. "Declan is free to do what he pleases."

"Thank you." Ava smiled and gestured for Declan to follow him.

When they stopped, they were a good twenty paces from the Directive. It was a good deal further than Declan thought necessary. "Do you have to go?" he asked.

"I do." Ava nodded. "And you need to come with me."

Declan laughed. "How about you come with me? Come back to King's and I'll show you—"

"No. Declan. We need to leave. Immediately and get far, far away from those people who are acting like your friends."

Declan shook his head, still grinning. "Those people? What? What are you talking about?" He glanced over her shoulder. Mary-Lou, Laurefen and Michael were deep in conversation. Katie spoke to a pair of unfamiliar witches, but Amber watched them. Declan waved to her and she waved back. "They're fine."

"No. They're not." Ava said. After a long pause, she sighed. "Look, I understand that you have absolutely no reason to believe me, but I need you to listen carefully."

"Okay?"

"I am not from Euryma. In fact, I'm from somewhere as far from Euryma as there is. Where I come from, magic isn't plucking nima or studying animals, it's magic. Real magic. The magic you used today."

Declan smiled. "Ah, right. Good joke."

"Shut up and listen. *Those people*," she motioned towards Laurefen and Michael, "know what you are now. I was watching them. The moment you described your power, they went rigid. First chance they get, they are going to *kill* you."

The grin slipped off Declan's face. "What do you mean, they know what I am?"

Ava held his eyes. "Do you know what you are?"

Declan laughed. "Well, obviously, I'm a wizard."

Ava peeked over her shoulder. Mary-Lou and Michael now watched them too. Katie was waving farewell to her acquaintances as they walked towards the Openings. "No. You're not," Ava whispered. "I am happy to tell you more, but first, we need to leave."

"How?"

"Do you trust me?"

For some strange reason, Declan didn't hesitate. "Yes."

Ava smiled. "Then follow my lead. And *don't* look back."

She grabbed his hands and pulled him towards the Directive. It took Declan a moment to find his feet. Once he did, he matched Ava stride for stride across the glass. Declan was fast. Ava was too. Mary-Lou stepped back in shock, while Laurefen moved towards them, his hands raised to halt their escape.

He never had a chance.

Ava slid beneath him while Declan shoved past. They rushed ahead to a shrinking Opening. Ava pulled him through as it shrunk and the window vanished as they hit the ground. The closing doorway had cut the corner of Declan's shoe. *That was lucky!* Declan smiled as Ava brushed herself off. Or *maybe not so lucky after all.*

Two witches stared at them in surprise. It was the witches Katie had been talking to back on the other side.

"Sorry, ladies," Ava said calmly. "Had to make a rush for it. We're in a bit of a hurry. Mind telling me where we are?"

"Uh... Sabriva," one of the witches said faintly.

Ava nodded. "Thank you." She grabbed Declan's hand and pulled him down the footpath. "Perfect." she sounded genuinely relieved. "We can catch the train north. We'll head home from there."

Home?

Declan wanted to ask Ava what she was talking about, but he feared that would create more questions than answers. She led him down the empty streets. He followed without comment.

Twenty minutes later, an escalator delivered them to the most impressive train station he had ever seen. A marble staircase opened on to an elevated walkway lined with bright shops. Even at this hour, the entire place was busy with customers. Sharply dressed men and women perused magazines or sipped on hot drinks from corrugated purple cups. Below them, row upon row of platforms were filled with commuters waiting for sleek silver trains which zoomed to a halt every few minutes.

Ava dragged him to a ticket station, then stopped. "You don't—by chance—have any money, do you?"

Declan raised an eyebrow. "Have I ever had money?"

"I should've known." Ava turned and led him on an excursion through the open-air mall. She walked up and down the various storefronts until she found what she was looking for. A community book shelf, carved in maple, and lined with a collection of worn paperbacks. She chose a book, seemingly at random, and opened it up. A tattered twenty-dollar bill was folded inside. "That'll get us through the ticket-booth, at least," she said with a wink.

Two tickets later, they sat on a sticky metal bench at the

end of an empty platform. Unlike the others, which were so clean they sparkled, this platform was caked in a layer of soot. It appeared unused, but Ava assured him they would be along shortly.

A list of questions had been bubbling in Declan's mind ever since they made their dash to freedom. Having finally caught his breath, he looked sideways at Ava. She must have been waiting for him. "Go ahead."

"You said I'm not a wizard. What am I?"

Ava put her hand on his knee, her expression softened. "You're a Warlock, Declan."

Declan frowned. "What does that mean?"

Ava bit her lip. "Warlocks are... I don't even know how to describe it."

"I've never even heard of them."

"You wouldn't. The leaders of Euryma have worked very hard for centuries to rid the very idea of Warlocks from public knowledge. You might find a rare book here and there in private libraries, but that's all."

"How did they know? Laurefen and Mary-Lou?"

"Because you used green magic. They know the name the Dominion peddles for people who use green magic."

"What name is that?"

"Knights of Despair."

A chill climbed Declan's spine. That name was one he knew. From scary stories to bedtime threats, every child in the Dominion knew to fear the Knights of Despair.

Ava shook her head. "It's a glorified children's story now. Once upon a time, the Knights of Despair and their green magic nearly destroyed the Dominion. The idea is laughable now." Her smile faded. "Okay, you had your question. Now I've got one for you."

"Go for it."

"When you were recounting your adventures tonight, you said Haberdeen had a white knife."

Declan nodded. "Yes, it was more like a dagger. It looked like it was made of bone." He held his hands a short distant apart. "About this long."

Ava chewed on her upper lip. "She shouldn't have that. Not if it is what I think it is..." she stared down the platform.

Declan waited long enough to be polite. A new question burned inside him. When it was clear Ava would not continue, he let it out. "Where *are* you from?"

Ava met his eyes. The corners of her lips twitched. "I think you know."

"Vedmark?"

She nodded.

Declan's mouth dropped open. He had suspected as much, but hearing it in the flesh... "So, it's real?"

Ava grinned. "Legends have an unfortunate habit of embellishing things. I don't live in a city of emeralds and my wardrobe extends beyond the color green, but yes, Vedmark is real."

Declan fought to keep his voice low. "And that's where we're going now?"

"You're going to have to temper these questions when we get there." Ava looked down the train tracks. "But you are correct. We are going to Vedmark."

"Why?"

A loud whistle signaled the train's arrival. Unlike the sleek silver bullets that traveled through Euryma, this was an old locomotive with a large, rectangular front. Declan could see patches of red rust beneath flaking paint.

"Two reasons," Ava replied as the train ground to a halt. "The first is you're not safe here. A Knight of Despair is a fundamental threat to the Dominion. Your friends are going to hunt you. If they don't, others will. That won't stop in a hurry."

The doors opened with a mechanical clank. They climbed aboard and settled into a tattered seat. A portly man with a dirty red beard entered the compartment to punch their tickets. "Interpass?" he asked in a thick accent. Ava dug into her pocket and flipped him a coin. A jade mitka. The man's eyes grew to the size of saucers. "Good. Good." He practically sprinted to the opposite door and left them alone.

Declan turned back to Ava. "And the second reason?"

"You won a battle today, but the war is far from over."

"Haberdeen?"

"No. Don't you see, Declan? Haberdeen is only a symptom. Remnant magic, or whatever it is… Something is destroying this world and somebody needs to stop it."

Declan settled into the threadbare seats and considered it. Outside, the bright lights of Sabriva rushed past. "And that somebody is me?"

"I never thanked you for dumping me in that bin."

"You mean tossing you to the bad guys?" Declan's ears burned.

"Well, you saved me from that too."

Declan blushed brighter and Ava smiled at him. "There's a popular saying in Vedmark, 'We live and we see'. I don't know what the future holds for you. I don't know if you *have* some grand destiny to fulfill. But I was sent to bring you home for a reason."

Declan met her eyes. "What reason?"

"I don't know. We live and we see."

Declan sank into his chair. Soon, the rickety train began to climb, past black lakes, into passes so deep, the surrounding mountains blotted out the starry sky. *What have I gotten myself into?* His parents were gone, his friends very possibly wanted him dead, and now, he was on a train to a fictional country of magical Warlocks.

The train took a sharp turn and plunged into darkness. Declan leaned back and closed his eyes, Ava's words in his ears. *We live and we see.*

THE END

CONTINUE THE ADVENTURE

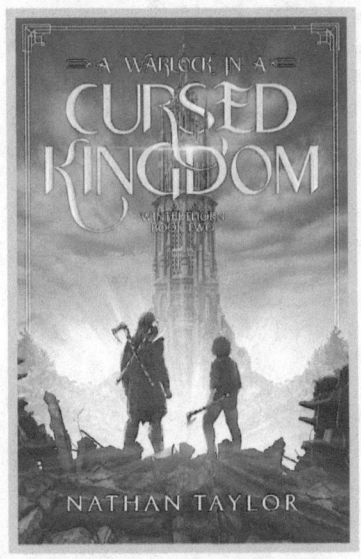

A Warlock in a Cursed Kingdom

About Nathan

Nathan Taylor is an outstandingly distracted author with a penchant for imagining wizarding worlds and magical storms that could knock your socks off.

He gravitates towards ice baths (or rather the dopamine hit that follows), milk chocolate, and issuing stern warnings to his muggle children about the consequences of leaving dirty laundry on the bathroom floor.

Nathan lives in rural Queensland, Australia, which is the perfect place for snake bites, spider bites and picturesque sunsets.

Want More?

Join the Wintersmiths for a free short story collection at www.nathantaylorwrites.com

f facebook.com/ntaylorwrites

a amazon.com/stores/Nathan-Taylor/author/B0CG649CZD